The Spelling Bee of Oz

By
Robin Hess

Illustrated by
Andrew Hess

Ozmapolitan Press/FIRST EDITION, July 10, 2016
All rights reserved under International and Pan-American Copyright Conventions. Published in the United States of America by Ozmapolitan Press. Distributed through Amazon.com.

The following books by Robin Hess are available from Amazon.com: *Christmas in Oz, Toto and the Cats of Oz, L. Frank Baum and the Perfect Murder, Dangerous Accounting*, and *The Zenith Project*.

Cataloging-by-Hess
Hess, Robin 1927-- .
    The Spelling Bee of Oz / Hess, Robin
ISBN - 978-1530968787
Originally published: Vashon, Washington : Ozmapolitan Press.
    I. Fairy Stories. 2. Oz. 3. Somalia. 4. Orphans. 5. Nomes
813.08766 H463s

Printed in United States of America

This book is dedicated to Amira,
the Somali nurse that took care of me at
Virginia Mason Hospital in Seattle in 2008,
and to all the dedicated nurses who give their lives
to helping the injured and the ill.

I want to thank my son, Andrew,
who was then a pre-teen,
for the idea of the Live Wires;
and Fred Meyer, for the idea of
the Invisible Children.

I would also like to thank
my grandson, Elie Hess,
for his excellent photograph
of Arlene and me on the back cover.

By this time, I hope that two features of my books have become expected by my readers. One is the pages identified as "The Oz Books." Not everyone will agree with me, but since it is my book, I feel free to reveal my own opinions about Oz. Beyond the Famous Forty, I have only included those I have read that, due to my training in literary criticism, I find are true to the style and emphasis of the Baum and Thompson books.

Secondly, there have been many times in my reading when I did not quite recognize a character. Or I was mystified about the pronunciation of a character's name. So I include an "Index and Identification" section to identify, locate and give pronunciation for all names, places, magic and some other important things in the book.

I hope you are finding both these sections useful and would be interested in your comments about them.

A Note to My Readers

Dear Reader,   July 10, 2016

Do you know where Somalia is? One of our heroines in this story, Amal, does for she lives in Mogadishu, the capital and largest city of Somalia. It is the furthest eastern point of the central part of Africa. You can get there from the southeastern most city of the United States, Miami, Florida by traveling 8,300 miles slightly south of east to Mogadishu. There you would find yourself in a beautiful land of sun-drenched buildings, golden sands, brown or green grass, tall, thin palm trees and many others of the tropical desert plants.

Amal is a homeless orphan in Mogadishu who returns from Oz to help restore some order to that ravaged city.

When she goes to Oz, Amal will meet Zeebee from America. Although their life experiences have been very different, they become fast friends. It is the good old Spelling Bee that brings them together in a series of adventures that includes Invisible Children and Live Wires and Nomes and Rock Elves and, oh, so much more. I hope you will find all this as interesting as I did. Be sure to write to me about how much you like (or, heaven forbid, dislike) this new adventure. I'll be waiting to hear from you.

Your transcriber of Ozian adventure,
                    Robin Hess
                    27727 94th Ave. SW
                    Vashon WA 98070
                    hesses2go@hotmail.com

Table of Contents

Chapter 1	The Message Tree	1
Chapter 2	The Live Wires	14
Chapter 3	Finding Magic Gates	20
Chapter 4	The Nome King's Throne Room	32
Chapter 5	Mogadishu	46
Chapter 6	Adventure in a Blue Meadow	54
Chapter 7	Metallic People and a Slitherer	63
Chapter 8	The Country of the Invisible Children	74
Chapter 9	Back to the Surface	79
Chapter 10	Negotiations	92
Chapter 11	Deliverance	100
Chapter 12	Welcome	105
Chapter 13	Confusion	116
Chapter 14	The Genesis of a Remarkable Bee	130
Chapter 15	Spellings	141
Chapter 16	In Search of a Spell	148
Chapter 17	The Truth Will Out	159
Chapter 18	Attack!	166
Chapter 19	Insulaville	175
Chapter 20	The Children Meet Ozma	182
Chapter 21	Going Home	198
Chapter 22	Knunk Meets Ozma	212
Chapter 23	Ozma Visits the Nomes	218
Chapter 24	Korph or Kaliko	227
Chapter 25	Upper Stallingham	238
Chapter 26	Amal's Return	249
The Oz Books		260
Index and Identification		265
Who's Who		266
Where's Where		278
What's What		285
Magical Magic		290

Chapter 1

The Message Tree

he big yellow bus was cruising along the rural roads of the Santa Clara Valley. It was filled with princes and princesses, white sheeted ghosts, cowboys and Indians, space adventurers and pirates, a big gray mouse and a roly-poly brown bear. One little girl was dressed in a blue gingham dress with a white pinafore over it and red shoes and she carried a little basket with a toy black dog in it. Halloween would be on Saturday this year, so on this Friday, the day before Halloween, the children had all been allowed to dress up in costumes for the day.

The girl in gingham was eleven year old Elizabeth Warren, and she was the last one left on the bus. As they neared her stop, she pulled her cellphone out of her book bag to check the time – four-fifty-five – right on time. Unusual for a substitute driver who had never been on the route. He had gone through it with not a single missed turn and always stopped exactly where the regular driver did. Now he brought the bus up beside the gigantic lone oak that marked Elizabeth's driveway. She tossed her book bag over her shoulder and started

1

The Spelling Bee of Oz

out the door as the curious little driver chuckled and, with a flip of his wrist, said, "I've brought you to the Message Tree. You'll have an interesting few days."

She turned and waved at him, thinking, That's strange. How would he know that we all leave messages in the crook of this tree? And how does he know anything about my weekend?

But, as she pivoted on her toe toward the old oak, with her blue gingham dress swirling around her, she stopped suddenly, confronted with the inexplicable, for it was not her familiar tree. It wasn't any tree she had ever seen before. It wasn't nearly as big and ancient as her old oak. It wasn't any oak at all. Besides, its leaves were all purple, not a logical color for live oaks. Even its bark was purple. In fact, the grass growing around it had a kind of purplish sheen to it, and the nearby mountains were much higher than those behind her home, and they, too, were purple and covered with trees instead of tan and covered with grass.

"What in the world!" exclaimed Elizabeth. "What's going on here?"

There was a fast clicking sound, a zip, and a piece of light pink paper started coming out of the trunk of the tree. She could see words printed on it. Tentatively, she touched the paper and it came off in her hands. She read, "I can answer the spoken word, but I prefer the keyboard. Your message is to wait right here for King Korph."

"What keyboard?" But before the words were out of her mouth she realized that it was right in front of her, part of a low limb of the tree. Quickly, she typed out,

The Message Tree

"What's going on here? Who's King Korph? Where am I? Where is my home?"

Even quicker, the response came back, "You are typing on my keyboard. King Korph is King of the Nomes. You are in Mordon Acres. Your home is right where it has always been."

This time she typed, "Where is Mordon Acres and what does King Korph want with me?"

The new little pink slip that issued from the tree had printed on it, "Mordon Acres is a large farm in the southeastern part of the Gillikin Country. You'll have to ask King Korph when he arrives."

"Where is the Gillikin Country and what is King Korph king of and when will he arrive?"

By this time, she was getting accustomed to the fact that her questions would be answered by the tree issuing a little pink slip, so she was looking right at the slot when it answered, "The Gillikin Country is the northern part of Oz. He is King of the Nomes. Whenever he arrives."

The exchange continued: "Oz! I can't be in Oz. There is no such place."

"But there is and you are."

"That can't be. But how did I get here?"

"It is, and the bus brought you."

"How could a bus start at Franklin D. Roosevelt Elementary School in the Santa Clara Valley and end up in some Gillikin Country?"

"Not the bus, it's you that ended up in the Gillikin Country."

"But how did I get to the Gillikin Country?"

The Spelling Bee of Oz

"The bus driver said the magic words."

"What magic words?"

"To the Message Tree."

By this time, a small stack of pink slips had built up, but the young girl kept on asking questions, typing, "So, he didn't mean my Message Tree. He meant this tree."

"No. Yes."

So involved was she in trying to find out why she was here, Elizabeth did not notice the small round man approaching her from up the road until he spoke to her. When he said, "My dear," she let out a little shriek and jumped around to the other side of the tree.

"There, there," he continued. "I am so sorry. I did not mean to startle you. I just thought you should know why I had you sent here by my trusty Zort."

As the young girl peered at this stranger, she realized that he was no taller than she, and that he had a beard reaching almost to his knees. His body was covered by some material unknown to her, most of it was gray, but with considerable trimming in various colors. He wore shoes, or something more like slippers, turned up at the toes and made of the same gray material as his other clothing. On his head was a tall six-pointed, golden crown with a mass of his silver colored hair waving out of the top of it.

Elizabeth asked, "Are you King Korph?"

"Of course I am. I'm the new Nome King."

Even as he was talking the tree was spitting out a pink slip that said, "Yes."

Right on its heels, or more precisely, right on the

The Message Tree

tail of the slip, the little girl said, "So what's this about Oz? For cryin' out loud, there is no such place. It's just a fantasy. Even in the movie it turned out to be a dream."

"Ho now, so you think Oz is nothing more than a dream?"

The tree started printing out its answer even as she was speaking: "Apparently she does."

What she was saying was, "At the most. Oz certainly is not a real place. On the other hand, I know I'm not anywhere near my home in the Santa Clara Valley. Nothing looks familiar. The hills are gone and there's all this purple! So, where am I really?"

The tree had started printing an answer, but the Nome led them away from it, saying, "Full of questions, aren't you? But come, let us start on our journey."

She fell in step beside him, starting out along the purple dirt pathway toward the nearby forest. As they did, he continued, "This purpleness shows that you are in the Gillikin Country. That's the predominant color here. And, of course, the Gillikin Country is in Oz. Indeed, my friend, you are in Oz."

"But that's impossible. Tell me something that's possible."

"You may not believe it, but you are in Oz, and we will just have to proceed on that basis whether you believe it or not."

With a small giggle, she responded, "Okay, but that's kind of funny. Since Halloween will be on Saturday, we were allowed to wear costumes to school today and I chose to dress like Dorothy, and here I am in Oz." Again,

The Spelling Bee of Oz

she spun on the toes of her red shoes, making her blue gingham dress swirl around her.

"That's right. I had Potaroo, he's my wizard, I had him look through his magic telescope this morning for a duplicate of Dorothy, and he found you. But, by the way, I have told you my name. Now can you tell me yours?"

Stopping and bowing low, she said, "Of course!" And as she straightened up she said, "I'm sorry. The strangeness of all this made me forget my manners. My name is Elizabeth Warren, but everyone calls me Zeebee."

Starting them walking again, Korph said, "Of course, in public, I will call you 'Dorothy,' but which should a king call you in private, 'Elizabeth' or 'Zeebee?'"

"What should a king call me? Being a king, I suppose you should call me whichever it pleases you to do."

"Humph! So Zeebee, how in Oz did you get a nickname like that?"

"That's because I ran around so much when I was really little. Then my big brother would follow me around with his arms outstretched like this and flapping them," and she stuck her arms out and ran around in circles as she said, "and he would keep calling out, 'Zee bee, zee bee.' Soon people started calling me that. Later, I realized that also 'z' and 'b' were the outstanding sounds of Elizabeth."

"How interesting," said the Nome King.

"You said I'm a duplicate of Dorothy. Do I really look like her?

"Indeed you do."

"But in the movie, well, she looked a little chubbier

The Message Tree

and older than I do."

"Well yes, but remember the movie was not an accurate rendition of the book."

"What book?"

The Nome King heaved a small sigh of relief at that, for he had hoped that this little girl had not read about how Dorothy had helped Ozma rescue the Royal Family of Ev from the old Nome King who had so badly misused the Magic Belt. Now he knew she had not read that book and he answered as though he still assumed she knew the books, "You know, *The Wizard of Oz*."

"You mean there's a book by the same name?"

"Yes, but the movie made a lot of changes. The book was about the real Oz and the real Dorothy is not chubby at all. Just like you. And she has a turned up nose, again, like you. And she has long blonde hair, smoothly combed, just like yours, only a little shorter. The blue gingham dress and ruby red shoes were just the right final touch, although of course, in real life, the shoes were silver."

Zeebee skipped along for a few steps before she asked, "But why do you want someone that looks like Dorothy?"

"Ah, my dear, I have quite a plan and you'll be able to be a big help to me."

"What do you mean by that?"

"Apparently you know a little about Oz?"

"Yes. I've seen the movie several times, but I didn't even know there were any books about Oz."

"That's too bad. There are several good ones, but they tend to get everything wrong. Even the movie

The Spelling Bee of Oz

"Ah, my dear, I have quite a plan..."

didn't get it quite right, because it made it seem like it was only a dream, but Dorothy was actually in Oz and went through many of those experiences."

"You mean the movie's true, then?"

"Much of it is, but not quite all of it." The Nome paused, and then added, "Well, a few things were stretched a bit, but it's generally true, yes."

"Wow! And I'm really right here in Oz!" Then stopping to pull her phone out of her bag, she said, "Just a minute. I have to tweet my friends as to where I am."

"Are you part bird?"

"No. I'm no bir ... Oh. I see. Because I'm going to tweet, you think I'm part bird. Tweeting is something

The Message Tree

we do. Oh. How will I explain it? Do you know about our computers?"

"Do you mean people who add things up?"

"No," she answered as she started punching buttons on her smartphone. "A computer is an electronic device that you can use just to write things out, or use it on the Internet to find almost anything you want or to contact anyone, anywhere."

"I didn't know you had any magic on Earth."

"Oh no, this isn't magic. It just makes use of common, ordinary science. Anyway, a phone has a lot of capabilities. I can talk to people on it. I can take pictures with it. I can go on the Internet with it, and sometimes it doesn't work. Right now, it says 'out of range,' so I can't contact anyone."

"I'm not sure if I understood much of that. Let's see. Talking to people, that I understand, but why do you need a phone to do that? And where are you taking the pictures to, and what is an Internet?"

Holding her phone up in front of him, she said, "This is for talking to people a long, long way away. You don't need it to talk to people that are right where you are, just at a distance.

"Then you're not taking pictures to anyplace. You use your phone to snap a picture. See?" And she aimed it at him, pushed a button and then showed him the result."

The king jumped and said, "That looks like me!"

"It *is* you," said Zeebee.

"But," pointing at the phone, he asked, "how can I be in that little box," then pointing at himself and stamping

9

The Spelling Bee of Oz

his foot, "when I'm standing right here?"

"That isn't you in the phone. It's just a picture of you."

"Like a little picture on the wall?"

"Exactly."

"I don't know how that can possibly be done."

Zeebee scowled and said, "Well, I don't know the science of it either. Somehow, it just works."

"It still seems to me that that is magic that Earth is not supposed to have at all."

"It isn't magic," replied the girl. "This is just plain ordinary science."

"Call it what you will. In fact, it is magic. And so, I suppose that Internet is just some more of your Earth magic?"

Zeebee skipped ahead a little and laughing, said, "Yes. I guess you might say that."

King Korph stopped her by taking hold of her moving hands before he said, "Now, to return to the matter of Oz and the movie you saw. Things have changed since then. Oz isn't the place it used to be, but you're going to help me change it back."

"How can I do that?"

He dropped her hands and continued walking, asking, "Do you remember that in the movie when the Wizard left Oz he placed the Scarecrow in charge of the kingdom?"

"Yes."

"That went along just fine for quite a few years, but awhile back a new wicked witch appeared in Oz. She called herself Ozma and she had stolen the powerful

The Message Tree

Magic Belt from us Nomes. We had had it for a long time, but she managed to steal it from one of my rather thick-headed predecessors. Then she used it to conquer Oz, and proclaimed herself Princess Ozma and Queen of Oz."

"What happened to the Scarecrow?"

"Instead of destroying him, she exiled him to a farm in the Winkie Country."

"And what about the Tin Woodman and the Cowardly Lion?"

"All of them have been tamed by her powers so that they and Dorothy …."

"Dorothy? But she went back to Kansas."

"Yes. But later she returned to stay in Oz. She's here now, and because of Ozma's magical power over them, she and the others will do whatever she tells them to do. And she rules the country with an iron hand. Boy! Anybody do anything she doesn't like and they are in real trouble!" During all of his last few sentences, the Nome King had been growing more and more excited and his voice kept getting louder. But at the end, he was on the verge of tears.

"My, but this sounds very sad," said Zeebee. "Isn't there anything we can do to help the poor Ozians?"

"That's precisely why I brought you here. Imitating Dorothy, you will get the Magic Belt and then we can set things right."

"Really? Sounds exciting. How do we do it?"

"First of all, we have to take you back to the Nome Kingdom and get your hair cut the right length. The rest

The Spelling Bee of Oz

of it depends on a number of details that I'm still working on. But all that will come together before long."

Jumping up and down, Zeebee said, "Oh good, but I don't want to stay away from home too long."

"Of course not. We'll send you home just as soon as we can. After we've straightened out things in Oz, we will have the Magic Belt and I can use it to send you home."

Zeebee turned toward him and said, "Gee, this is kind of exciting."

"Yes, but let us return to your name. As you've said, I can call you 'Elizabeth' or 'Zeebee,' but I sort of prefer 'Zeebee.' It has more of a rhythm to it. But, remember, whenever there is anyone else around, I will call you 'Dorothy'."

"Sure. I think I can remember that okay."

Just then the Nome paused in his walking and said, "Ah, here it is," and pointed at a roadside directional sign.

As they looked at it, it waved its one long arm to point down a side path and said in a loud voice, "Land of the Live Wires."

Turning to go down that wide path, the Nome King said, "On my way here, I had been told to take a very round-a-bout series of roads that used up a lot of time, but I noticed this sign was the same as another one up that way, and it seems that it would cut out a lot of travel time to go through here rather than go clear around."

"Yes," said Zeebee as she followed behind him. "Seems that way to me, too, but I wonder which kind they are?"

The Message Tree

"So, you know what they are. I've never heard of them before."

"There are two kinds of live wires. One is a wire and not really alive. It's just a wire that's connected to electricity at one end and loose and dangerous at the other."

"Hmm. I've heard about your electricity. You use it for giving light and running things."

"Yes. Very useful, but it can also be very dangerous."

The path was wide enough for two, so they were walking side by side and the Nome King turned to Zeebee as he said, "But you said there were two kinds. What about the other?"

"The other kind of live wire is a person who is happy and full of energy, the 'life of the party' kind of person."

"So I suppose they are much safer than the other kind."

"Usually. Yes."

At this point, they were taken aback by the large signboard in front of them:

WARNING
Live Wires Ahead ! !
Proceed at Your Own Risk
You've Been Warned!

Chapter 2

The Live Wires

pon reading the sign, Zeebee said, "So I guess this is the dangerous kind."

Nonetheless, they continued on and she added, "The important thing is to not touch any wire with a loose end lying on the ground and so far I don't see any, but beware."

They had gone about a quarter of a mile when there was the sudden sound of sparks as several quaint creatures catapulted into the road in front of them. They were totally unexpected, and around two feet high. Each was a simple, narrow wire that split in two places. At the bottom it split to provide two legs to stand or walk or run upon. Near the top was a three-way split to provide what looked like arms reaching out from the main body. Each arm was further split at its end to provide tiny fingers – three, four, five or more. At the top was a narrow face with mouth, nose, eyes and ears, although there was no more head above that than what was provided by the top little bit of wire.

One of them did a summersault and landing on his feet said, "We are Live Wires and want to make things lively for you!" As he spoke sparks were emitted from all

The Live Wires

the ends of his wire self.

Another, doing a pirouette and also emitting sparks as he spoke, said, "What has a head and only one foot?"

Quick as a spark, another said, "A cane," while another added, "I thought you meant a war veteran."

The rest of them waved their hands at that last Live Wire and yelled, "Ohhh!"

The Nome King leaned close to Zeebee and whispered with the sound of doubt in his voice, "Are these supposed to be the life of the party?"

She whispered back, "If they're trying, they're failing."

Just then, one of them did a back flip, landing in front

"We are Live Wires..!"

The Spelling Bee of Oz

of Korph, and no sooner did his feet hit the path than he touched the Nome King with his right hand, sending out a spark with a crackle and a pop.

Korph jumped back and said, "Ouch! Leave me alone! That hurts!"

The little Live Wires all laughed and danced around, some calling out, "See the little fat one? See how he jumps away?" And as always when they spoke, additional sparks were bouncing around.

At the same time one of them did a cartwheel, landing beside Zeebee and, with a light touch to her arm, caused her to jerk it away and say, "You're a bad Live Wire! Shocking people is not nice."

This brought more gales of laughter from the little people, still bouncing around and one of them said, standing on his head, "Quite the contrary. Shocking is our nature and it would be bad for us to behave other than the way nature intended." With that, he snapped down to his feet and sprang at Zeebee, giving her another shock.

Another said, "Enough fun. We must now take you to our King to see how he wants to dispose of you."

"King?" asked Korph. "Good. I too, am a King. We can talk to each other as fellow Monarchs."

This brought more laughs and eager jumping on the part of the Live Wires, as the one who had just spoken said, "We'll see about that."

Another said, "He will decide whether to just kill you outright or transform you into something more useful than mere humans."

The Live Wires

Zeebee shuddered at that and even the Nome King seemed to shrink a bit into himself, but he said, "Enough of all this. We'll be on our way," and started off on down the road.

But his way was blocked as more Live Wires sprung from the bushes to block his way. Then, with an occasional prod that made their captives jump, the Live Wires directed them on around the bush they had erupted from. There a side path led off into the woods. Following it for about a half mile, they came to a large clearing full of boxes with hundreds of Live Wires cavorting around and in and out of the boxes. Throughout the village were many statues and other interesting objects. In the very center was a large building, all made of thatch, to which the captives were prodded, jumping all the way.

Inside, they found a large open space with about twenty Live Wires. Here again were interesting statues and various colorful objects hanging on the walls. In the center there was a big, gray metal cylinder, lying on its side and flattened on the upper side of it. Sitting on this level surface was a large black metal box, rectangular, but with a big bulge in front. On top of that was a human looking head with its black eyes looking first at one of the prisoners, then at the other. It had bushy black eye brows above the eyes and above those slicked back black hair. A short but bushy black beard was at the bottom of the rather sallow looking face.

Jabs from their captors made Zeebee and the Nome King jump forward. Then the voices behind them said, "Crawl toward Transformer, our King."

The Spelling Bee of Oz

The two, without pause, dropped to their knees, and began crawling, but again they were jabbed with light electrical current as their captors said, "On your bellies," and the two flattened out and wiggled toward King Transformer.

In a deep voice, Transformer said, "So! Who have we here?"

One of the guards replied, "Oh Divine Sir, despite the warning sign, we found these strangers on the path, daring to enter our country. If you will forgive us, we had a little fun with them as we brought them to you."

"A shocking good time, I hope."

"Of course, your Imperial Majesty, just as you would have us do."

Without further ado, the front of the big black metal box split along its seam and opened down. Inside could be seen a hollow square of metal, wound with wire along two opposing sides. That was nested among a bunch of large, bright colored pieces of plastic which had already started rearranging themselves so that in ten seconds there stood before them a colorful plastic robot with the same head as the former black box and in its center was the square, wire-wound piece of metal. However, it could not move from its position, for its feet were welded in place on the platform on which it stood. Then, looking toward the captives, he said, "So! Who are you?"

Raising to his knees and looking up, the Nome King said, "I am Korph, King of the Nomes."

Transformer laughed a rumbling, ominous laugh and said, "You may be Korph. You may be a Nome, but you

The Live Wires

are no king here."

As he turned his attention to Zeebee, shocks from two of the Live Wires reminded Korph to flatten himself on the ground. For Zeebee it was a reminder to stay flat as she responded, "I am Elizabeth Warren, and I am from Earth."

"Ha-ha-ha!" laughed the Transformer. "The fat one thinks he is a king, so I shall transform him into a crown, one I can wear. And the other is such a gem that I should transform her into a bright yellow diamond."

Chapter 3

Finding Magic Gates

As the mass of Live Wires were driving Zeebee and Korph toward the Transformer Robot, he leaned forward and was just about to touch Korph when the Live Wires outside began screaming and a general tumult erupted. Transformer stopped, looked toward the door and saw a medium-sized, but stockily built black dog run through the entryway. Upon his appearance, all the Live Wires inside let out screams and ran to the far side of the space. As they did, the dog called out, "Come on you two. Follow me. Quickly. It is your only hope."

Zeebee was the first to react and she ran straight to the big dog, followed by the Nome King. By the time they had reached the dog, he had turned and began running through the door, saying, "Stay with me and you'll be safe."

He could easily outrun the other two, so he had to hold back a bit. On the other hand, it was important to get away from the Live Wires as fast as possible, so he kept up a pretty good pace.

However before long, Korph began slowing down

Finding Magic Gates

and soon he had almost stopped as he panted, "I ... can't ... go ... any ... fur...ther."

"You have to. We're not safe yet," said the dog. Then he added, "Okay. Here, climb up on my back," and Zeebee helped him to do so, and off they went again.

At last, the big dog slowed and stopped and said, "It's okay. We can stop now. None of the Live Wires will come this far. They are afraid to get too far from their dynamo, the Transformer. They have to touch him every once in awhile to get more power to stay alive. If they don't, they go dead. We're safe here."

Zeebee helped the Nome King down from the back of the dog and then asked him, "Why did the Live Wires try to stay so far from you. They acted like they were afraid of you.

"They are. I am the Grinderdael because on the outside I look like a Gronendael, but on the inside I am all grinder."

"I'm no better off than I was. A Gronendael? What's that?"

"It's a Belgian sheepdog. But don't ask me what a Belgian is. I don't know."

"Well I do," said Zeebee. "Belgium is a country back on Earth, so that means that's a kind of sheepdog they have in Belgium. But I've never seen one until now."

"I don't know where Earth is, but at least now I know that that is a place where I'd see dogs that look like me, but I'll bet none of them can grind everything up like I do."

"I'm sure you're right," answered the little girl.

21

The Spelling Bee of Oz

"So where are you headed now?" asked the Grinderdael.

The Nome King looked around, almost as though he thought that might give him an answer to the question and then said, "We want to get to the Yellow Brick Road."

Snapping his jaws together and then unsnapping them, the big dog said, "Thunder clouds! I've brought you exactly the wrong way."

"So, which way should we go?" asked the girl.

Sitting on his haunches, the Grinderdael pointed right back the way they had come with one paw as he said, "Right back there!"

"So all we have to do is to go around the Live Wires," said the Nome King.

"'Fraid not," said the Grinderdael. Now he pointed with his right paw and said, "Those are the Gillikin Mountains that come right up to the edge of the Land of the Live Wires, and they are quite impassable." Then pointing off to his left, he said, "And the Great Purple Marsh prevents you from going that way."

"Eggs of lava! What do we do now?" demanded the Nome King.

"What in the world is egg saliva?" asked Zeebee.

The Nome cackled in a way that was meant to be a laugh, and said, "Not 'egg saliva,' but 'eggs - of - lava. And that doesn't make much sense either, but it's something I say when I get really mad." Then he put his hand over his mouth and said, "I'm sorry, I guess I shouldn't use such bad language in front of a little girl."

"What bad language?" she asked.

Finding Magic Gates

"Oh you know, that 'such and such of lava.'"

"You mean 'eggs' is a bad word?"

"U-h-h, a nice little girl like you shouldn't say such things."

Zeebee said, "I don't see what you mean."

"Since those, ah, things are fatal to Nomes. Any reference to them is a swear word. Surely you can understand that."

She laughed a little laugh and said, "It doesn't really make sense, but I'll try to remember to not use that word in front of you," and she giggled again.

"Thank you, my dear. I have to be pretty angry to use it myself." Then looking at the dog, he repeated, "So what do we do now?"

"You just have to continue to the northeast on this road until you come to another road going north and south. Turn right on it and it will take you into the Munchkin Country. By that time, it has turned more to the east and you'll come to ..."

"I know. I know," said the Nome King. "That's the road we were on when we took this short cut. I was trying to avoid that long round about way. Going through the Land of the Live Wires just seemed like a natural way of saving time."

"So now you know why your original directions were so circuitous."

"Indeed. Now we've got to waste all that time going back around again."

The Grinderdael smiled, which wasn't easy to tell from a snarl, and said, "Maybe there's another way. If

The Spelling Bee of Oz

both of you will ride on my back, I think I can get you back through the Live Wires without any trouble. As you saw, they're afraid of me."

Korph looked at Zeebee and she looked at him. Then they both nodded and said, "Okay. We'll do it."

So she helped the Nome King onto the dog's back and then hopped up behind him herself, and off they went, headed south again through Live Wire Country.

At first, everything went well and they saw no Live Wires. Then, all of a sudden, three of them jumped out from each side of the path, giving shocks to Korph and Zeebee. They responded with loud cries and by swatting the Live Wires away. More of them came bouncing out of the next bunch of bushes, but the Grinderdael was ready and he swung his muzzle toward them with a sound of "grrrrnnnccch" emanating from his mouth and all the Live Wires ran away, with none of them to be seen again as long as the grinding sound kept up. And it did until the Grinderdael stopped on the path and said, "All off. We're well beyond the Live Wire territory now."

Both of his passengers did as he said, and as they dismounted, he said, "All you have to do now is follow this path, going south until you reach the Yellow Brick Road, and so I'll say goodbye now."

Zeebee threw her arms around his neck saying, "Oh, thank you, dear Grinderdael! You've rescued us and saved our lives. How can we ever thank you enough?"

He answered, "If I were able to blush, I'd be blushing right now. Your hug is thanks enough."

Then he looked at the Nome King who began looking

Finding Magic Gates

rather uncomfortable. At last the Nome said, "Oh, all right. Thank you, but I'm not going to give you a hug."

"I'd just as soon you didn't anyway, but it's been fun making your acquaintance. So I'll be off to my home and you can be on your way."

He turned and started back through the Live Wire Country as the Nome King and Zeebee continued on the purple path to the south. By this time, the sun was getting close to the horizon and the Nome King said, "It's time we looked for a place to sleep tonight."

"I don't suppose you have hotels here," said Zeebee.

The King's answer was, "What's a hotel?"

"Yes. That's what I was afraid of," replied Zeebee. "A hotel is a place you can stay overnight."

"Oh. We have plenty of those. In Oz, on most occasions, if you can find a farmhouse, the farmer will be willing to put you up for the night, even feed you; but it's been a long time since I've seen a farm, so our hotel may have to be just some sheltered spot – an overhanging rock, a big, spreading tree, even a nice little bush we could cuddle under."

"That's not what I mean by hotel. It's a building, with a lot of rooms and you rent one for the night. It has a bed or two in it and an attached washroom and closets to hang your clothes in and a TV; sometimes, even a refrigerator."

"Umm. How strange, nothing like that here. What is 'rent'?"

"You pay money in order to get the room for a specified length of time."

The Spelling Bee of Oz

"Oh, money we don't have here, either. Even among the Nomes, we just do what we do and share it with others. If you have space or food and someone needs it, you share."

Zeebee cocked her head a bit to the side, thought a moment and said, "That sounds kind of strange. But when you think about it, sharing seems like a good way to go. I like it. And a house: if some farmer wants to share his with us for a night, that's fine. But sleeping under a bush? I hope it doesn't come to that."

Just at that moment they saw a purple farmhouse in a field of purple corn in the distance. This could well satisfy Zeebee's concern, so they hurried toward it.

"You mean we can ask them for food and a night's rest, just like that?"

"Of course. It's the custom around here. Besides, they'll see you as Dorothy and be happy to give food and a bed to you."

With those words, the Nome King stepped up and knocked on the door.

When the farmer answered, he stepped back in amazement, saying, "Why, Princess Dorothy, what an honor! Please do come in and bring your friend."

The two stepped in, Zeebee with a bit of timidity, but the Nome King as it were his right. The farmer called out behind him. "Darling, children, we have visitors. You'll never guess who!"

Four children came running from one direction, and a woman in a kitchen apron and wiping her hands on a towel came from another.

Finding Magic Gates

All, as in one voice, exclaimed, "Princess Dorothy!" And the woman added, "Welcome to our humble home."

The father insisted she sit in the most comfortable chair in the living room. The mother said, "Oh, I'm afraid I don't have anything special enough for your dinner." The children stood in a quiet line and looked at Zeebee in awe, thinking that she was, indeed, Princess Dorothy.

As for Zeebee, she was thinking, *Princess. They are treating me like a princess. I can't wait to get home and tell Kara about this. No way she could believe this.*

However, she did not let such thoughts make her forget her manners and after a proper curtsy, she introduced Korph, the Nome King, to them.

"My goodness, a Princess and a King," said the farmer. Then he added, "And we are the Nornon family," and indicating the children from eldest to youngest, "Fanny, Gerab, Catloo, Verm, my wife Flora, and I am Lomar."

While introductions were being made, Zeebee felt something fuzzy rubbing against her legs. She looked down and saw the red and blue striped cat that had come bounding into the room with the children. She said, "What a remarkable cat."

"Oh, but surely you have seen the stripes of a Quadmunch cat before," said the man.

"Of course," answered Zeebee. She was not quite sure of herself on this, but tried to cover it up in saying, "But I was referring to the way she bounced into the room. I've never known a grown cat to be so energetic."

"Yes," said the man, "that's why we call him 'Bouncy.'"

Boy! thought Zeebee. *I almost gave myself away*

The Spelling Bee of Oz

there. I did mean the red and blue stripes.

Despite the woman's protestations that she had nothing special enough for the dinner of a Princess and a King, the food was excellent and the company was good. The Munchkin family was almost as fascinated by having the King of the Nomes with them as they were at Princess Dorothy being there. By the time they left the table it was quite dark out and the singing of the birds had been replaced by the little croaks of frogs in the night.

For a while they all sat around talking, Zeebee finding one way or another to avoid talking about the life in the palace of which, not being the real Dorothy, she knew nothing.

Since, by now it was quite late, the family showed Zeebee and King Korph where they could sleep in beds. Zeebee had one of the girls' beds, while they doubled up in the other, and the King had the same arrangement with the boys. The next morning they were all up early and breakfast was served consisting of nice fresh plums and purple oatmeal.

After breakfast the two travelers continued on their way, and as they walked, King Korph said, "Before long we will be in my own Kingdom."

"In your own Kingdom? But we're in Oz. Is your own Kingdom so close?"

"Oh, no. If we were going to walk across the country, we'd have to go half way across Oz, then across the Deadly Desert and a part of Ev and then underground."

"You mentioned a Deadly Desert. Is it really as bad as

Finding Magic Gates

the name sounds?"

"Indeed it is. It surrounds the entire Land of Oz and if you so much as touched it, you would be dead in an instant."

"But, you just said that was what we were going to do."

"No. I said, 'If we were going to,' but that's not what we're going to do."

"Is there another way?"

"Of course there is or we couldn't get there, could we?"

"So how do we do it?"

""Ah, yes," said Korph, "you would want to know. It will be quite easy, I assure you. We'll just walk there."

Zeebee paused and slapped her knee, and said with a laugh, "Oh sure, just walk right through those deadly sands."

"Not through them, under them."

"Have your Nomes burrowed a tunnel under the Desert?"

"Yes and no. Over a century ago, the king at that time, Roquat, had his Nomes build such a tunnel to provide a way for people to cross the Desert in safety. But then the wicked Ozma filled it full of dirt because she didn't want the world to know how mean she was to the people of Oz. We will use the same one."

"But how can we if it's been all filled up by Ozma?"

"Ah, but there was something she did not know, nor do you."

Zeebee looked at the old Nome, her suspicions

The Spelling Bee of Oz

aroused. "'Something neither she nor I know?' What is it?"

Looking right at her, Korph said, "Magic Gates."

Hands on hips, Zeebee said, "Okay. Magic Gates. What do you mean?"

"It's a special thing that only the Nomes have. They enable us to do our mining all over the place and still have the ore near our furnaces at home."

Still looking at him with a dubious glare, she said, "So how do you do that?"

Resuming walking and waving his arms first to one side, then to the other, he said, "Magic Gates come in pairs: you put one in one place and its partner in another place, anyplace on the whole planet or on any planet at all. Then, when you step through one Gate, your foot, and you, land on the other side of the second Gate. Say you have a mine under the western Winkie Country, then when you step through the Magic Gate, you are right at the furnace on the eastern coast of the continent."

Zeebee spun on her heel as she exclaimed, "Wow! Some traveling!"

"And old Roquat used a pair of Magic Gates in the tunnel he dug to the Emerald City, a fact Ozma was not aware of, so all she did was fill in the tunnel, leaving the Magic Gates in place. Have you read the book about that event?"

"No. Remember, I didn't even know there were Oz books."

"Oh yes. I'd forgotten. But, as was told in one of the books, Roquat and his friends were going to use

Finding Magic Gates

the tunnel to pay a friendly visit to Oz. They left the Nome King's throne room at midnight and arrived at the Emerald City at sunrise?"

"So?"

"There is a great deal of distance between the two places. He and his friends walked from midnight to dawn of one day and covered what should have taken them fifteen days. That could only be accomplished by using Magic Gates – one just outside the Nome King's throne room and one about half a night's journey from the Emerald City."

"I see. That makes sense, but this does not," and she pointed first at the ground under her feet and then back in the direction from which they had come.

Chapter 4

The Nome King's Throne Room

Zeebee was standing in green gravel and looking back at where they had been walking on purple gravel. And the grass was the same – purple back there, green close at hand. Further away, she could see the same was true for bushes and trees.

Korph saw where she was looking and knew what she was thinking. "Yes," he said, "we have just gone from the Gillikin Country into the area around the Emerald City."

Zeebee blinked her eyes and said, "Goodness, things do change so fast around here."

"Yes," said the Nome King. "You'll have to get use to the colors of Oz: green in the center for the Emerald City area, purple among the Gillikins in the north, blue in the Munchkin Country to the east, red for the Quadlings in the south, and, to the west, yellow for the Winkie Country."

"I should certainly try to remember that," she said as she started in the center and turned in a circle to face each of the compass points as she named the colors, "green, purple, blue, red and yellow."

The Nome King's Throne Room

They walked on in silence for about a minute, and then Zeebee said, "About the original tunnel. Why would they even walk for six hours? Why didn't he put the second Gate right at the Emerald City?"

"That's a good question to which I have no answer, but I suppose that maybe he felt that such a trip should require some effort."

"That's reasonable enough, but it doesn't change the fact that Ozma filled the tunnel with dirt. It still can't be used. Stepping through one Gate just engulfs you in the dirt beyond the next one."

"Ah, but I am smarter than the average Nome. Yes, just stepping through would leave me immobile and useless at the other ate. But since we Nomes are experts not only in digging, but also in the use of explosives to dig holes, I just figured out the amount of explosive necessary and threw a lighted stick of dynamite through the Gate by the throne room.

"Then I picked out a small young Nome named Pak, and I told him, 'Now, Pak, I want you to take one step through that Gate and then step right back through it without a pause.'"

"But, you risked nothing while asking Pak to risk his life! If the explosive had not made a big enough hole for him, he would be trapped in dirt on the other side."

The Nome King, frowned, cleared his throat and said, "Now, now, don't fret yourself, little one. I understand your concern, but, ahem, I knew what I was doing. Yes indeed. Really, there was no chance that the hole was too small for him. Umm, yes. You see, the question was

The Spelling Bee of Oz

whether there was, a-umm, room for a grown Nome to work with his tools." The last words hurtled out of his mouth as though he was afraid they would not get said.

"So, what did happen to him?"

"Oh, of course, he came right back, just as I knew he would, so I asked him, 'Was there barely room for you or was there room for a full grown Nome to stand and work?'

"He answered, 'Plenty of room for a Nome to swing a pick.'

"So I had one of my fastest diggers, Nork, go through with pick and shovel and instructions to dig straight up on the other side of the second Magic Gate. He was to cut a generous stairway into the wall as he went. A second Nome was detailed to shovel the dirt and rocks into a cart, and a third was to wheel it away and dump it where we needed fill."

"Sounds like you had it pretty well planned out," said Zeebee.

"You bet your crown ruby, I did! And when Nork broke through to the surface, we were fortunate that it was in a hill in a small woods twenty miles east of the Emerald City."

A few minutes later the little Nome King said, "Here we are," and led the way off onto the green grass that grew along it, following no path at all, but headed for a stand of green trees in the distance. When they reached the trees, that Nome, a rather thoughtless person, just pushed ahead through the trees and brush, letting the limbs fly behind him. After getting slapped in the face by

The Nome King's Throne Room

the first branch, Zeebee stopped long enough to let him get several paces ahead of her and then followed a safe distance behind.

After about a dozen steps into the woods, they came to a little hill of about five feet in height and the Nome led the way around to the other side, where he stopped. While Zeebee watched, he punched at one particular rock, another and a third until a door opened in the side of the hill, startling Zeebee who said, "My, oh my, you can make some interesting things happen!"

"Just a little more of the special Nome magic," he said, and then, bowing and sweeping his arm toward the door, he added, "After you."

"Not a chance, Blanche," replied Zeebee. "You go first."

"What do you mean 'Blanche?' You know perfectly well that I am Korph."

"Sorry. That's just something we say back home when we want our 'No!' to be real definite."

"That doesn't make much sense to me, but," and he stepped into the short passageway that lay behind the door of dirt, saying as he did so, "you see. It's safe. Come along."

Hesitating only a moment, she followed him and noticed that the door that was dirt on the outside was wooden on the inside. They walked about three feet and there they were standing over a shaft going straight down into the soil. It had a flight of steps cut into its side, circling down and down.

"For us Nomes, going up and down these steps is like

The Spelling Bee of Oz

child's play."

"Not for me!" exclaimed Zeebee, "I'm not sure I want to do this."

"Don't worry," returned the Nome, "Just follow close behind me and also stay close to the solid rock wall. You'll be safe enough."

"Okay, but I'm no Nome and I can't see in the dark going down there. No. I won't go."

"Oh, but of course," and he took a step down the stairs, and said, "See more of Nome magic," as lights came on illuminating the upper stairs. "We could hardly keep all our tunnels lit all the time, so we have a bit of magic that feels the presence of people and turns the lights on as they approach."

"Motion sensors, we call them. Okay, go ahead. I'll be right behind you, but please go slow."

So, the two began the winding trip into the depths, with lights coming on as they were needed. At the foot of the steps was a small room with a metal arch at one side, leading into a space of no more than two feet before coming up against solid dirt and stone. Korph took Zeebee's hand and said, "Here we go through the Magic Gate."

As he stepped through and disappeared, Zeebee tried to hold back, but his hand drew her right along with him and she found herself, still holding his rough hand, standing in a kind of large antechamber. All around the walls were arches with signs over them. The one they had just come through said, "EMERALD CITY." The next said, "NORTH OF RINKITINK." Another said, "WEST

The Nome King's Throne Room

EV." One said, "CENTRAL COLORADO," and there were others with unfamiliar names on them all around the large room. She did not count, but she thought there must be at least a couple dozen Gates here to take people all over the world and to others as well.

The Nome King led her through the one big wooden door there was in the room and Zeebee found herself in a large and magnificent cavern, shining with the reflected light from thousands of gems set in walls, ceiling and floor.

In the center of the room stood a large throne which had been carved out of solid rock with great care. Scattered all over it were many colorful gem stones – diamonds the size of cantaloupes, emeralds, rubies, and all kinds she had no way of identifying. Likewise, the floor, the walls and the ceiling of the room had many other such gems imbedded in them – all sizes from minute to massive. Although none of the surfaces were covered in their entirety, there was a myriad of jewels in place, many of them larger than anything ever seen on Earth.

About a score of other Nomes were gathered in the room. It was unsettling to her that many of them looked at her with a look of something like fear in their eyes.

King Korph, walked right up to the throne, climbed the steps carved into it and sat down. As he did so, a scraggly looking Nome with a broad, black, gold embroidered sash that was angled across the front of his gray suit handed him a heavy and highly decorated scepter. Up to this time, there had been an undercurrent

The Spelling Bee of Oz

of mumbling among the gathered Nomes, but as soon as he pounded the scepter upon the rock throne, there was complete silence.

"Allow me to introduce to you this little girl who will bring our Magic Belt back to our Kingdom where it belongs."

With that, the crowd broke into loud cheers. Allowing it for a while, the King finally raised his scepter which brought immediate quiet. He then reached out his other hand, and patting her on the head, said, "This is Elizabeth Warren. You may have noticed how much she looks like Dorothy Gale. From now on, we will call her 'Dorothy.' This is all part of my plan, for she will bring our Magic Belt back to us."

Again there were loud cheers. This time, as his subjects ceased their noise, King Korph said, "I sent Zort to California to send this 'Dorothy' to me in Oz. He used the magic words to send her to the Message Tree and after a little confusion, I led her through the Magic Gate in the old tunnel near the Emerald City back to our Kingdom and here she is."

There was more cheering and again, as they quieted, Korph said, "That is all. Except for one thing. Schaumkar, come here. Now, the rest of you, be gone. We have things to do."

As all the others filed out, Korph said to Schaumkar, "These red shoes will never do. Dorothy needs a plain ordinary pair of shoes, black patent leather, with a strap across here to hold them on," and he indicated where he wanted the strap.

The Nome King's Throne Room

Schaumkar took measurements and backed out of the throne room. After he had left, Zeebee asked the Nome King, "Why didn't you tell them about the Live Wires?"

"They were not pertinent to our purpose which is the defeat of the wicked Ozma." Then, resting his right elbow on his knee and his head on that hand, he paused a bit before continuing, "On the other hand, maybe they were."

"What do you mean? The Live Wires might help you defeat Ozma?"

"Exactly. One of the main problems I have not been able to lick is the Magic Picture."

"Magic Picture? What is that?"

"Ozma has a picture in her apartment that will show her any place or person she asks it to, and it will show just what is going on at that moment. So, when I send a message to her saying that some part of her kingdom is under attack from another wicked magician, she will just look in that Magic Picture and see that there is no problem."

"You mean the Live Wires could interfere with her picture?"

"No, it's not that. It's just that if we convince the Live Wires to go pester a particular people, then when Ozma looks at them, she will actually see that they are under attack."

"Pretty clever! But how do you expect them to listen to you long enough for you to explain what you want?"

The Nome King hopped out of his throne and said,

The Spelling Bee of Oz

"Never fear. I have a plan. Now, let's have our lunch!"

He rang a big gong standing near his throne and it took only a few seconds for that same scraggly looking Nome to come running through the door behind the throne. He kept bowing as he ran until he stopped in front of the King and said, "What is the pleasure of your majesty?"

"Lunch for me and Dorothy. And, Steward, you know she doesn't eat our food. Get her something suitable for a surface dweller. And make it snappy! We're hungry!"

And it was pretty snappy. In a trice, five men came into the room. Two of them had a table that would fit in front of the Nome King while he sat on his throne. Two of them carried a smaller table for Zeebee and one brought in a chair for her. Even before she could be seated, two more came in, bearing a napkin and silverware for each of them. Then, as Zeebee sat down, another man came in, bringing a mug of something that looked like lava for Korph and a glass of water for Zeebee. She had just said to her host that things seemed to move pretty fast around here when the food started coming in. The King had a big plate of steaming gravel, with a side dish of mushrooms. She received a fine green salad of romaine lettuce, slices of radish and fresh green peas in a creamy sauce. Her main dish was a fine tomato beef soup and a roast beef sandwich. She also had a glass of chocolate milk. For a few minutes both of them were too busy eating to say anything, but soon they began talking about their day's adventure and after a while their empty plates were taken away.

The Nome King's Throne Room

Now Korph said, "Zeeb . . . Dorothy, that is, when you get to Oz you will already be familiar with some of the main characters, the Cowardly Lion, the Scarecrow, the Tin Woodman, Tik-Tok, the Patchwork Girl, the Hungry Tiger . . ."

At this point, Zeebee interrupted, "Tik-Tok, Patchwork Girl, Hungry Tiger . . . who are they?"

"That's right. All you know about Oz is the movie. Each of them and many more are talked about in the books. So I'd better describe the people that you are most likely to run into," and he began to do so.

It took some time to describe and discuss each of the more important personalities she might find in the Emerald City. Once that was completed the King said, "But then there will be all kinds of just ordinary people that I know nothing about, but people that Dorothy will know very well. So when someone seems to know you and you have no idea who they are, you might want to say something like, 'Oh, I'm sorry, but I have such terrible news for Ozma, I'm afraid I just wasn't paying attention.' Something like that. Be prepared."

Next Korph rang a bell and requested that Gralf, his Director of Manufacturing, be sent in. Then, speaking to Zeebee, he said, "I thought you might be interested in seeing how we Nomes spend our days, so I'm having Gralf show you around while I take care of some matters of State."

As he started to leave, he turned to the director again and said, "Lastly, you should show her the public rooms of my palace."

The Spelling Bee of Oz

Then off he went through one of the doorways while the Director led Zeebee through another. It took a few minutes, but soon they came to a massive cavern which was filled by the Nome army doing precision drills. After watching for a while they travelled down some other tunnels to where they could see the Nome miners at work, digging out jewels and metals. Then they came to smithies melting and working the various metals and jewelers putting rare stones in beautiful settings. Finally, he said, "And now you will have the rare privilege of seeing the King's own palace!"

After going through a few more tunnels, they entered a magnificent series of rooms. The ceilings were high and arched. The walls were composed of variously colored polished marble. The floors, of the same substances as the walls, were thickly carpeted with velvet carpets. Heavy silk drapes hung from the arches between rooms. The furniture was of many types, but all made from rich looking tropical woods, highly carved and covered in silks and satins. The rooms were suffused with a strange, indirect, rose-toned light.

Mantels and shelves, brackets and tables were covered with many kinds of beautiful ornaments. They were made of almost anything you might imagine and were of all kinds of things – birds, animals, buildings, leaves, abstract objects, whatever the mind could imagine. Upon the walls were art works of all kinds, many had the appearance of greatness.

It took some little time to complete the tour of the palace, and, by the time the tour was over, it was time

The Nome King's Throne Room

for dinner and Gralf brought Zeebee back to the throne room. Korph was already there and seated in his throne to await the servers.

He asked her how she liked the tour and was pleased that she seemed impressed with all the activity and especially with his palace. Then the food was brought in. The Nome King had his usual hot coals and steaming lava, but for Zeebee there was a fine fillet of salmon with hot corn cut fresh off the cob. She had not realized how hungry she was until she caught a whiff of that.

Throughout dinner they talked, but the King's main interest was in conquering Oz, something he could hardly talk about with Zeebee. Instead, they discussed the food they were eating. Zeebee wasn't able to understand how he could eat red hot coals and he couldn't understand how she could eat things that grew on bushes and that had been alive and wiggling.

For dessert, both of them had rocky road ice cream. However, whereas Zeebee's was the usual delicious mix of chocolate ice cream and bits of chocolate and marshmallow, Korph's was boiling tar with ground up asphalt in it. That last might not sound appetizing to you, but Korph was just as well satisfied with his dessert as was Zeebee.

The conversation had been of only a little interest to Zeebee, because she was looking forward to bed and to sleep. But when the Nome King said, "Off to bed now. We have to get up early in the morning to go see the Live Wires." Her response was immediate: "Not a chance Blanche. I'm not going to go anywhere near them again."

The Spelling Bee of Oz

"That again. I see. But don't worry," said the Nome. "We'll have that dog with us."

"You mean Grinderdael."

"That's him."

"I might consider going in that case."

"Oh yes. You will consider it all right," replied the Nome King, sounding a bit sterner than usual. Then he rang the gong again and his scraggly steward came running back into the room. Korph told him, "Alklank, I want you to take Dorothy to her room and see that she is comfortable and that she gets up in time for a six o'clock breakfast."

Winding through hallways until Zeebee had lost all sense of where she was, they finally stopped before a door that looked no different from a hundred others they had passed. The steward opened it and said, "This is your room while you are here. I will wake you up at five in the morning."

"No need," said Zeebee as she reached into her back pack and pulled out her smartphone. "See I just touch this button and then this icon and ..."

As music started playing the scraggly Nome jumped and said, "How does it do that?"

Laughing, Zeebee said, "Magic!"

Bowing, he left the room and closed the door behind himself.

Zeebee hurried herself, washing, undressing, setting her tablet to wake her up at four-fifty-five in the morning, climbing into her bed and off to sleep in half a moment.

Very soon after she had left Korph in the throne

The Nome King's Throne Room

room, he was joined by Gralf. It only took about half an hour to describe what he wanted and then the Director of Manufacturing left to get his Nomes busy building what King Korph wanted.

Chapter 5

Mogadishu

Amal was asleep in her usual place, a depressed area of ground in an inner corner of a house, most of which had been destroyed in the continuous warfare. It made no difference to her that her comfortable little hole had resulted from one of the explosions that had wrecked this house. It was just that this particular corner had become home to her after the death of her parents when her own nearby home was obliterated.

She was dreaming of the time before, back when Abeh had been a Somalian government minister in a big fancy building downtown. Then they lived in a fine home in one of the most prestigious parts of the capitol city, Mogadishu. Abeh would drive her to school in the mornings and Ma would take her shopping and she had pretty clothes and both her parents and her sisters and brothers were still alive and they had a happy family. That was before the day she came home to find her house destroyed and the bodies of her Ma and brothers and sisters lying out in front of where the house had been. Despairing of any hope at home, she had gone to the

Mogadishu

complex of government offices where her Abeh worked. Unlike some of the buildings, his was pretty much intact, although its façade was pock-marked by bullets and canon shells. Hopefully, she went to his office, only to find him dead at his desk in the ransacked building. The dream of those good times was so beautiful, but very suddenly someone was calling her name, "Amal, Amal."

The dream was over and she was awake. As she jumped up, she realized it was the voice of Mona that had intruded on her dreams, "C'mon, sleepyhead! Did you forget that we're heading for the waterfront a little earlier this morning?"

Amal shook the dust of her bed from her clothes as she said, "Yeah, that's right. Boats'll be unloading this morning."

Another head popped around what was left of the doorway. Like all the children of Mogadishu, he was dark-skinned with black curly hair. But unlike the others, most of whose growth had been stunted, he was tall for his age, tall and rangy. This was their leader, Jamal. He added to Mona's words, "And we should be able to pick up some fruit and grains."

The three skinny youngsters, in their patched, stained and scraggly clothing, ran on down the street. When they picked up Abdul, the only chubby one in the group, he said, "Are we going by Ahmed's this early in the morning?"

Ahmed was a scarf merchant whose little stand was crowded into the principle marketplace of Mogadishu, the Suuqa Bakaaraha. Here there was about every kind of

The Spelling Bee of Oz

merchandise imaginable — foods of all kinds, whatever type of clothing you might want, guns, medicines, trinkets, furniture, scooters, even an occasional automobile. He was a special friend of these children, often providing them with a little extra food and helping them with any problems that arose.

Most of their problems had to do with arguments with other groups of children regarding who had the right to beg or hunt for food in certain places. These were not easy disputes to settle. But the word of a stern adult could go a long way toward doing so, and even though Ahmed usually favored Jamal's little group, his word was obeyed by all the children of the area.

He was only of average height, but he was a hefty person around whom there was a certain authoritative presence. Even as most of the children that frequented the market obeyed his dictums, so too, did most of the other merchants. Yet, despite his imposing presence, he was a gentle and loving person whose love was returned by all.

His wife, Mumino, was just as kindhearted as he, and this little group of children had won a special place in the hearts of both of them. So it should be no surprise that these children often began their day with a visit to the scarf merchant.

But today Jamal responded to Abdul's question with, "Not this morning. Don't you remember? We're going to the waterfront to pick up scraps from the new boat that's due in."

"Uh, yeah."

Mogadishu

Next they stopped for the youngest and smallest of their group, Anab. Her clothes were always a little more ragged than those of any of the others and she was always a little slower than them, but they never left her behind. Everyone saw to it that their youngest "sister" was well taken care of.

Finally, they reached the deserted tumbled down shed where Hawa stayed. She was already up and standing beside it and welcomed them with the news that, "We can take the new shortcut this time."

It was a new shortcut because, until two days before, the area across the alley from Hawa's little shed had been six occupied homes, and they had had to go clear around a very long block on their way to the waterfront. However, a woman from one of those houses had been carrying a burden on her head, walking down the street, when, in passing a group of al-Shabab soldiers, she tripped over the foot that one of them had extended for that purpose. The soldiers laughed as she fell, a sound cut short as she stood with her veil so misplaced that all could see her face. Before they killed her with stones, they exacted from her where she lived. Then they went to that block and destroyed all the houses in it. They were not particular about killing the people, so some escaped, but as they ran, the soldiers called out to them, "Let this be a warning to any whose daughters allow their faces to be seen in the streets."

Government troops tracked those soldiers down and killed every one of them. Proper retaliation? Maybe, but mostly just an excuse for more killing. Such happenings

The Spelling Bee of Oz

were everyday events for these children. It made little difference to them who did the killing: al-Shabab, the government, foreign troops or some warlord. Death and destruction was commonplace.

With the voice of authority, Jamal, said as they cut through the ruins, "'The safest way is the shortest way,' so I hope this really is safe now."

As the irrepressible Amal gave Hawa a friendly shove, she said, "Of course it is, so let's get going," and she followed their leader through a crack between broken boards.

They had gone maybe half way through when they came to a wall which, though half its length still stood, the other half was only about three feet high. They

She gasped and started running away...

Mogadishu

headed toward the lower portion and had just reached it when a fighter from one group or another stepped around the corner and began firing across the empty space, then ducked back out of sight. The children, fearing being hit by return fire, turned and ran along the higher portion of the wall. Amal was the last and the timed hand grenade, tossed toward the place where the firing had come from, landed right at her feet. She gasped and started running away from it as fast as she could, but she had only run a few steps when the grenade's time was up and it exploded.

When the dust from the explosion settled, the only sound was the retreating feet of the grenade thrower. Looking back, the children could see no sign of Amal.

Pearing cautiously around corners the children fanned out to check all adjacent doorways and behind all the remaining walls of the ruins. It only took a few minutes and as they gathered again at the site of the explosion, Abdul said, "That grenade must have hit her directly. There's not a shred of her clothing left."

Anab started crying and sobbing, "She's been blown to bits! What'll we do now?"

As he put a comforting arm around the little girl's shoulders, Jamal said, "We've got to go talk with Ahmed. He'll know what to do."

So off the children went toward the bazaar, all thought of fruit and grain gone; hungry though they were, one of their number was dead and they felt the loss too much to be occupied with anything else.

The area in which these children lived had been so

The Spelling Bee of Oz

blasted by bombs, grenades, fire and gunfire that there was little left alive in it. The children were there and rats were there and various kinds of soldiers made their way through all too frequently, but of other life there was little. Stubs of what had once been trees stuck up in many places. A few ground-hugging bushes and grasses remained, brown, not green. That was all.

But as they moved toward the bazaar, more life was seen. Not all the buildings were wrecked. Ordinary people began to show up. Birds were singing. Cats and dogs were more prevalent than rats. Flowers grew in small gardens and trees spread here and there.

By the time they reached the bazaar, life was everywhere and the streets were crowded. At the scarf dealer's stall, they found only Mumino. She was always fun to talk to, a pleasant little woman. Standing just over five feet tall, no one would call her imposing, nor was she particularly a classic beauty. But she had a simple attractiveness that drew people to her.

Since she did not have her husband's ability to deal with every kind of unexpected problem, she told them, "Ahmed will be back any moment now," and handed them a plate of fruit — dates, figs, cherries, apricots — to chew on until he arrived. They tried to politely nibble, but hunger was more powerful than manners and they practically wolfed the food down, as with tears, they told her of what had happened, but had hardly finished when Ahmed arrived.

In order not to outshine the colorful scarves he sold, Ahmed always dressed in quiet tones. Today he had on

Mogadishu

robes of medium brown and said as he approached, "Here, here. What's going on?"

Explanations began again and when they had finished, he turned to his wife and said, "You won't mind taking care of things for a little longer, will you, my sweet raisin? I'll go with the children to see what's happened."

Still sobbing a bit, they lead him back to the spot of the tragedy. Here he looked around very carefully, and asked them to show him where each of them had been when the explosion occurred and exactly where the grenade had landed, then he said, "No, I don't believe that blast killed Amal at all. There is no sign of her here. If it had been big enough to destroy her without a trace, it would have left a very large crater and would have gotten all of you. No. She just got so badly scared that she ran away, hard and fast. She'll be around again before long. Come on back to the shop and we'll have a little tea and some cookies."

Chapter 6

Adventure in a Blue Meadow

As Ahmed was reassuring Amal's friends, she herself was going through a most extraordinary experience. She found herself on a blue path in a luxuriant blue forest that stretched as far as she could see in all directions. Moments before, when she had realized a hand grenade was coming her way, she had started running away as fast as her little legs could carry her along a familiar brown sand alleyway of her neighborhood, her heavy, wavy black hair fanning out behind her. But she had only taken five steps before the explosion came and on the sixth step she found herself running in this blue dirt. The explosion was over and she was alive. Two more steps, and she stopped to look around. There was no sign that there had been any explosion. There was also no sign of any of her friends or anything at all that was familiar to her. Where could she be? In all her eleven years she had never seen more than eight or ten trees together at one time and none of them had been blue. Here they were innumerable and all of them were blue.

She strolled on, looking here and there, wondering

Adventure in a Blue Meadow

what she was seeing, but soon she thought, *Maybe I should go back the way I came. That would be more likely to take me back to where I live.*

So she turned around, and as she did so she thought, *Or maybe that blast killed me and I've gone to Jannah,* Heaven. A few more steps and she thought, *Or maybe I've gone to Jahannam,* Hell, *and it is just an endless blue road going through an endless blue forest to no where.*

Her next thought was, *These blue trees aren't really all that oppressive. They're rather pleasant, and give protection from the hot sun. The smells are rich. I keep seeing cute little animals running through the trees, and birds, too. I don't think this is Jahannam.*

She pinched herself and it hurt. She walked over to a tree and kicked it with her bare foot, not too forcefully, but that hurt, too. Out loud, she said, "So, I guess I'm not dead and I'm not dreaming. This is real. But where am I?"

Leaving the tree she had kicked, she continued back the way she had come, a bedraggled looking young lady, her knee-length dress spotted with dirt, blood, food and grime, and its edges tattered. Her hair was matted and dirty. Not a very good comparison to the beauty all around her.

Continuing until she was out of the woods, she came to a large blue meadow. Bright and beautiful flowers bloomed throughout it. Most of them were some shade of blue, but there were also reds and white and yellows and oranges and lavenders mixed in, a whole spectrum

The Spelling Bee of Oz

of color. Blue bees were busy buzzing from flower to flower and blue butterflies, as well. There were some very little birds, too, unknown to her that zipped from flower to flower. Their feathers were iridescent and they made a whirring sound as they moved, or most dramatically and, unexpected by Amal, would hover in front of a long tubular flower.

She strolled slowly along the road as she watched the activity on the meadow. Her attention was drawn by a group of birds that came swooping across the center of the field, diving and turning this way and that, one moment near her, the next at the far side of the field. She watched them flash back along her path, then they turned, came by her, flying high into the air, then circling and headed again in the direction she had come from.

But what was this? As recognition crept into her consciousness, she suddenly let out a scream and turned back, heading across the meadow tor the closest woods as fast as her little legs could take her. A giant bee, as big as a huge pillow, was flying toward her, coming along the very road she had been on. In mid-stride, she stopped running. She could no longer move, but all fear of the bee had disappeared.

She heard the soft hum of its voice as it said, "Oh, oh, oh! So sorry about stopping you, little lady, and so suddenly! Sorry to scare you so! Oh my, I didn't mean to. This really hasn't started out right at all, at all."

It hovered down near her and settled upon the ground beside her. "It's been an hour or more since I've seen anyone else and when you ran, I decided I needed

Adventure in a Blue Meadow

to put a stop spell on you and threw in an anti-fear spell for good measure."

"I still don't know that I understand, but how can you talk and how come you speak Somali, and how did you get to be so big?"

"Ah, my dear child, that is easy to explain, but come, let us continue to walk as we talk."

As she hopped up and started walking, Amal was surprised that the big bee settled down on his two hind feet and walked alongside her, but she said, "Where am I?" and looking around, she said, "I know this is not Mogadishu, probably not even any place in Somalia. I've never seen so much grass and so many flowers and trees and so much blue."

"Now, my dear, you have just mentioned two places that, ahem, I am not acquainted with, and I know my geography of Ozeria quite well. Yes I do. So it seems to me, yes it does, that you must be from some other planet."

Stopping in mid-stride, Amal exclaimed, "Other planet? You mean we are not any place on Earth?"

"Earth? Indeed not. No, indeed. No, if that is where those places are located, then you come from a place where magic does not work at all, not at all. No wonder you are surprised at my talking and my size. Goodness me!"

Amal said, "So. Do you mean that I am not on Earth anymore?"

"That's right."

"But how can I ever get back?"

The Spelling Bee of Oz

"Oh, have no fear of that. It is not so hard. Ozma can take care of that for you."

"Who's Ozma?"

"Princess Ozma is the Queen of Oz."

"This Amran Ozma, does she live far from here?"

Because of the nature of language in Oz, the Spelling Bee did not realize that what Amal called Ozma was actually a different sounding word from the word "Princess." Nonetheless, he was hesitant in replying for he was not at first certain that he wanted to change his route. Finally, he said, "Umm. Why ye-e-s-s," and after another pause, "It will take us several days to get there."

"So," said Amal, "We're in Oz or Ozeria or something like that, but what world are we on?"

Fluttering his wings a bit as he walked, the Bee said, "Oh, dear me. I have not been very clear. Let me explain about Oz. Our beloved planet is named Ozeria. We know little enough, yes, not much at all about the other side from our own. But on our side, the northern part of this hemisphere is dominated by our very own continent, Ozia. And in the center, the center I say of Ozia is this fair Land of Oz. Breathe the air," and then he drew in deep breaths. "Ah, smell that, the very sweet air of Oz, scented with all the flowers, the trees, the grass, the soil. Ah, Oz."

"So, we're in Oz on the continent of Ozia on the planet Ozeria?"

"Oh, indeed, you have that right, just right," said the Bee.

"Okay. How do you spell Awz? Is it A-w-z?"

Adventure in a Blue Meadow

"Good try. You might have tried A-h-z or A-h-s or A-h-w-z or A-u-z, even A-w-z, but no, it is simply O-z."

"Hmm. O-z. Okay. Oz. I knew I was not in Mogadishu or even Somalia any longer."

With a warbling laugh, the Bee, responded, "Aha. So what are these Mogadishu and Somalia? Spell them for me, please, dear little one."

So Amal spelled each of them, and the Bee flapped his wings rapidly and hovered in front of her as he repeated the spelling after her.

Once done, he said, "Ah yes, now I've spelled it, now I'll remember it. Oh alas, though, where are my manners? Tch, tch, tch. Here I've gone and given you no proper introduction at all." Then stopping to stand full up on his back legs again, he bowed and said, "Allow me to introduce myself. I am the one and only Spelling Bee. I can spell anything. A-n-y-t-h-i-n-g. Anything." After giggling a little, he said, "Or how about poecilonym, p-o-e-c-i-l-o-n-y-m, poecilonym, which is a synonym for synonym," and he puffed out his abdomen a bit as he said, "Yes, I can spell anything."

"You can? How about 'activities'?"

"Activities. A-c-t-i-v-i-t-i-e-s. Activities."

Amal said, "I thought a Somali word would fool you."

"Ah, dear little one, you also asked about my being able to talk your language. You must realize that all beings have their own language."

"All people do. But I didn't know bees did."

"If we couldn't talk to each other, how do you think one bee can find some good flowers and then go back to

The Spelling Bee of Oz

a hive and tell all the others where to find them?"

"I didn't know they did that."

"In bee language, it's a little dance we do. You probably don't notice the different motions I do, but that is me speaking, and it comes out to you as actual spoken words."

Amal stopped with a frown on her pretty little face. "Hunh? I don't exactly get what you mean."

"See. Now, notice my motions. As I move, you are hearing my voice. It comes out as kind of a sing-songy hum. But the motions are what I would be talking with for any bees that might be around."

As the frown slid from her face, it was replaced by a look of amazement as she said, "Is that so?"

Moving on, the Bee said, "Yes. That is how it works on Ozeria. You speak in your language, I hear in mine. I speak in my language, you hear in yours."

Running her right hand through her dark hair, Amal said, "What a wonderful place! Everybody understands everybody else and you, you can spell anything!"

The Bee buzzed a bit and then said, "We understand each other's words, but I still don't catch on to where you come from. Apparently, it is some place on Earth."

Stopping just long enough to bow, she said, "I am Amal and, as I say, I come from Mogadishu in Somalia, and apparently they have nothing to do with Ozeria, since, as you say, they are on Earth."

"Pleased. Pleased to meet you, dear little Amal," but, fluttering his wings in bewilderment, he added, "I'm no more enlightened about where you originated than I

Adventure in a Blue Meadow

was before. Mogadishu is in Somalia on Earth but whereabout on Earth? Are they anyplace near Kansas?"

"Kansas? Not at all. I think that is in America. We are near Ethiopia."

The Bee shook his head.

"Djibouti, Kenya, Yemen?" As the Bee showed no signs of knowing where any of those were, she finally added, "They are all in Africa."

"Ah, yes," he said. "Yes, Africa on Earth I've heard of. But where are all those places in Africa?"

"They're all in eastern Africa, right about the center and Somalia is as far east as you can get and still be in Africa."

"Yah ha. At least I have a faint idea now. But, have you ever seen a bee as large as I am on Earth, or one that can talk?"

"No. Neither of those is actually possible. I'm probably dreaming ... or dead."

"No, neither dreaming nor dead. You're in Oz. Earth is in quite a separate universe."

Amal's face dropped into a long and startled expression. "What do you mean a 'separate universe?' That would make it impossible for me to get back home. I thought maybe Ozeria was on Mars or something reasonable."

"Oh no. Not really. It's an interdimensional thing. Rarely can you move from one to another. Magic can do it, or a catastrophic event, like a storm, an earthquake or an explosion."

A brightness illuminated Amal's features as she

The Spelling Bee of Oz

stopped and exclaimed "Explosion! That hand grenade. I should have been killed, but instead I was exploded to Oz!"

"Hand grenade. Yes. H-a-n-d g-r-e-n-a-d-e, hand grenade. That is a very dangerous explosive device. Can't recommend fooling around with one of those."

The girl responded, "I know. When it hurtled toward me, I ran. I just hope none of my friends were hurt any more than I was." Unconsciously, she rubbed a bit at the scratches on her left arm as she said, "It's all a bit confusing, but I think I'm beginning to see how it all works, and it is a beautiful land, so I suppose I should just enjoy these days, however long."

"A very fine philosophy," answered the Bee. "What a marvelous opportunity that brought me along at just the right time to be able to guide you to the Emerald City to see Ozma who can use her Magic Belt to send you back home."

Chapter 7

Metallic People and a Slitherer

They continued on their way for a while, talking of this and that until Amal said, "You know, when you first showed up it was quite a scare for me. You seemed like a monster. I didn't know a bee could be so big."

"Oh dear child, I'm so sorry about that. I wouldn't have scared you for the world. I just wanted to ask you if you'd seen my friend, the Tin Woodman."

"The what?"

"You don't know, of course. The Tin Woodman, Nick Chopper, Emperor of the Winkies."

"I'm sorry, uh, sir, but I've never heard of a Tin Woodman. What a place: a woodman that chops tin and is Emperor of the Winkies and a powerful woman who is Queen of Oz."

"Ah yes. But, ah, he doesn't chop tin. He is made of tin."

"What? That's not possible. A man made of tin can't be alive."

"Ah, my dear, that sounds most reasonable to you, but this is Oz."

63

The Spelling Bee of Oz

"Hmm." Amal stopped and scratched her head a bit and then said, "I guess I shouldn't be too surprised. After all, a talking bee as big as you would also be quite impossible in Mogadishu."

"You have it quite right. That is the way it is. But we have a problem."

Hesitantly, Amal asked, "What is that?"

"You are a delightful young lady. Yes. But I need to go on to meet with the Tin Woodman," and as they started walking again, he said, "So, how big a hurry are you in to get back to this, ah... Let me see ... M-o-g-a-d-i-s-h-u, Mogadishu? Took me a moment, but by spelling it I could remember it."

"My goodness, can you spell every word there is?"

"Once I know how to spell it, I never forget and I do know every word in the dictionary, the biggest dictionary there is."

Amal's shoulders slumped as she said, "Back when I was in school, you sure would have been handy to have around. Imagine that! Spelling every word in the dictionary!"

"Ah, little one, that is not even the half of it. Not half of my spelling powers. Not only do I spell words, but I cast spells as well. Any spell that's ever been invented, I probably have it in my repertoire. That's why I could make you stand still and at the same time, make you be unafraid." Then rubbing all four of his hands together, he quickly said, "But now, my question: how big a hurry is it for you to get back home?"

Hesitantly, she answered, "Of course, I'd like to get

Metallic People and a Slitherer

there sometime soon, but do you know how I can?"

"Yes. Yes. Most certainly. Let me see now. Yes. My need to see the Tin Woodman is not all that important. We will continue to the first branching toward the Emerald City. Yes. We will continue with all speed. Once we are there, we will have Ozma send you to Mogadishu."

"Ozma? She can do that?"

"Most certainly. Most certainly. Ozma has a Magic Belt with which she can do almost anything. Yes, almost anything."

"Then we'd better get going again and go as fast as we can, so I can get home all the sooner." Then she added, "Although I would like to see a man made of tin, just not right now."

"Of course. Of course. Right you are," said the Bee as he started fluttering his wings and, taking off, moving faster than Amal could go.

Then he looked back and said, "Oh, dear me. I guess we can't go that fast. You don't fly."

Amal laughed and said, "No, I don't fly, but you know, we really don't have to be in such a big hurry, anyway. Mogadishu will still be there whenever I get home."

The big Bee settled down on the ground, just walking along at the side of Amal and at her own pace. They continued walking in what she eventually found out was a westerly direction, until they came to a small path heading more to the southwest.

The Bee said, "Ah, now, we turn here. This path will take us toward the Emerald City." As they walked along it, single file, Amal asked, "Is most everything in Oz blue

The Spelling Bee of Oz

like it is here?"

"Oh, my oh my, no. Not at all. Only here in the Munchkin Country. Oz has many colors. In the south, that is in the Quadling country, red is the dominant color." Then pointing, he said, "In the west, that is in my own dear home country of the Winkies, the preferred color is yellow, ah beautiful yellow. And in the northern country of the Gillikins you find purple almost everyplace you look. Now guess what the dominant color in the area of the capitol city is, the Emerald City? Yes. Guess that one."

"I don't know, but since emeralds are green, I'd say it might be green."

"Right you are, my lass. Right, indeed. Ozma's favorite color is green."

"But there are other colors, aren't there? Right here amongst all this blue, I see some flowers that are red and violet and yellow."

"Of course. Of course. You're quite right, young lady. Whatever the predominant color, there are always touches of other colors. Oh dear me, how dull it would be if all the world around were just one color!"

"So, the Queen in the Emerald City has a belt that will send me home, but she is subject to this tin emperor in the Winkie Country who rules all of Oz?"

"Oh, my, oh my! I have not done a very good job of explaining. You're right. It sounds like an emperor should be more powerful than a queen, but indeed, our queen is usually simply called 'Princess;' but, still, she is the supreme ruler of all of Oz. The Tin Woodman is Emperor only of the Winkies. I don't really know why he is called

Metallic People and a Slitherer

an Emperor. The rulers of each of the other countries are only called kings, but he is no more powerful than they."

Walking steadily, she replied, "All right. Now, I think I understand. Maybe." Then she laughed.

The Bee said, "You're doing very well and I'm sorry I disturbed you with my sudden appearance. Just wanted to ask you a question. You see I had stopped by the tin castle this morning for a visit with my friend. His staff said he had left during the night, to go see the Tin Soldier."

"Tin Soldier? Is everyone in this country either made of tin or bees your size?"

"No, no," he said, and as he continued, "I am the only bee in all the world bigger than that," and he put his two top hands less than an inch apart. "And those are the only two tin men I have ever heard of. There is a man of copper, but actually, he is not a man. Tik-Tok is really a robot."

"My goodness! What a place this is!"

"Oh, yes. Oz is, it really is, a land of wonder."

"Ah, that solves it. That man of copper, you said he was a robot. We learned about them back when I was in school. So those two tin men aren't really men. They're robots, too."

"No. They are real people."

"But how can a real person be made of tin?'"

"In Oz anything at all can happen and usually does. This is a magical land and in each case, those men were jinxed by a powerful witch, attempting to break up their love for her servant, so that they gradually cut themselves

The Spelling Bee of Oz

to pieces. But a kindly tinsmith kept making spare parts for them so that they remained alive through it all."

Amal paused and tilted her head a bit and said, "That doesn't make very good sense to me. That could never happen in Somalia. Oz is just so wonderful and unexpected!"

"Deedy, deed," said the Bee, and he continued leading them along the path to the southwest.

They continued walking all day. About noon they came to the edge of a flower-filled meadow with several fruit trees on its edge, so the Bee set about drinking nectar from many of the flowers while Amal ate her fill of fruits.

After lunch they continued going to the southwest along the blue dirt road. They had only walked for about half an hour when, suddenly and startlingly, the diamond-shaped head of a large snake poked out from the roadside bushes. Its long, forked tongue flicked out and in several times. Then noiselessly and rapidly, its full length came out – a good five feet of snake stretching across the dusty path in front of Amal and the Spelling Bee!

"That's the deadly Sapphireback Rattercobra!" whispered the Spelling Bee.

At the sound, the snake's head turned toward them and it quickly curled its full length into round coils, one on top of the other. The snake then raised a straight length of itself about two feet above the coil. As it was doing so the large gray spots on his back began turning into bright blue and he opened his mouth very wide,

Metallic People and a Slitherer

"That's the deadly Sapphireback Rattercobra!"

revealing two long fangs.

"See that," said the Spelling Bee," the blue and the fangs mean he's building up his poison."

"Hadn't we better be getting out of here?" asked Amal.

Ignoring her, the Bee picked up a long stick and started moving slowly closer to the coiled snake.

Amal backed further away.

By this time, the part of the snake just below its head had spread out into a large hood. His tail stuck up through the coils and out where it could shake freely, making an ominous rattling sound. Suddenly, the Spelling Bee swung the stick in the general direction of the dangerous snake, but without hitting it.

At the same moment, the snake struck. It flung

The Spelling Bee of Oz

its whole body at the Bee, extending its hooded head toward the Spelling Bee, but he missed and then hissed, "Foiled again by my coilsss."

He lay there, stretched out on the ground, with two knots in his long body.

Immediately, his body began to undulate in an attempt to pull itself out of the knots. He had no success. Finally he said, "Sssombody help me. Untie my knotsss."

In a soothing voice, the Spelling Bee said, "Now my dear friend, just you lie still and I'll have you untied in a thrice or two."

"It'sss all your fault. I wouldn't have ssstruck if I'd known it wasss you, Ssspeller."

By this time, the fangs were no longer showing and the Spelling Bee said, "That's better. Now, don't wiggle so much or I'll never get you out of this."

"I can't help it," answered the snake. "You're tickling me."

"I'll try not to," replied the Bee, as he worked a little slower and more carefully and as he did so, he said, "But see here, Sapphire, why did you threaten us?"

"I didn't know it wasss you. I have bad eyesssight."

As he undid the last knot, the Spelling Bee said, "Yes, but your sense of smell makes up for it, and you had your tongue flipping out quite enough that you should have smelled me."

"I thought I did, but there wasss alsso thisss other sssmell that I never sssmelled before – a ssstranger that might be dangerousss."

The Bee put all four arms akimbo, hands on hips,

Metallic People and a Slitherer

and said, "Come now! You could tell it was just a little girl."

"But little girlsss can be very mean to sssnakesss. They don't like usss."

The Bee laughed and said, "To make a long story short, you enjoy showing off and scaring people. And you did that. She was quite scared. In fact I ought to punish you for scaring her so badly."

"Oh pleassse, Ssspeller, don't punisssh me. … Did I really ssscare her?"

The Bee tapped Amal on the shoulder to get her attention and nodded his head at her. She got the message and said, "I was awfully afraid until the Spelling Bee saved me. I would have been too scared to run. Oh dear me I'm going to faint," and she tumbled over, carefully, so as to not hurt herself.

"Oh! Oh! Oh!" cried the snake. "I really did ssscare her, ssso bad that ssshe fainted. Can I give her one little bite, Ssspeller?"

"You should know better than to ask. Of course you cannot. I should cast a spell on you for even thinking of it," and he started waving his arms around.

Quickly, as he tried to slither away, the snake said, "Oh no. No. No! I was jussst joking. I wouldn't bite a cute little girl like that. You know me, Ssspeller."

"Okay. Just be sure to behave yourself."

"Really. I'll keep my fangsss out of sssight. Jussst let me travel with you for a little way." Then he turned toward Amal and said, "Little girl, pleassse forgive me for being ssso cruel. I wouldn't hurt a friend of Ssspellersss.

The Spelling Bee of Oz

Besssidesss, you are much too cute for me to threaten, in any cassse. Pleassse wake up and be niccce."

Slowly, Amal opened her eyes and got up. Then she looked sternly at the Rattercobra and said, "All right, but don't you ever threaten me again!" and she stamped her foot.

"Yesss. Yesss. I will behave myssself. I will, I will, I will."

So it was that the snake wiggled along beside the Spelling Bee and Amal through many miles of the Munchkin Country.

Right away, the Spelling Bee explained, "I call my friend 'deadly,' but of course, here in Oz, he cannot really kill anyone. But his bite hurts aplenty."

"Then I still would not want to be bitten by him."

"Not much chance," replied the Spelling Bee. "Being both a cobra and a rattler, when his rattle-end coils, his rattle sticks up out of the coils like it should. But then those coils always go around the cobra part that sticks up from the middle."

"Sounds complicated," commented Amal.

"It is," said the Spelling Bee. "As a matter of fact, it's too complicated for the Rattercobra. When his upper part levers like a cobra and tries to strike, he gets tangled in his coils and can't go where he intended. Really quite safe."

"Ah, now you've ssspoiled my sssecret," complained the snake. Then he quickly changed the subject by asking Amal, "Are you an old friend of the Ssspelling Bee?"

"Oh no. We just met a few hours ago. I was just as

Metallic People and a Slitherer

scared of such a giant bee as I was of you." Then she added, "Well, almost anyway. But then he reassured me that he was not dangerous. And then you came along and scared me even more!"

"Do forgive me, my dear child. The fact isss I am so ssscared of everything and everybody that I tend to try to ssstrike firssst."

"I guess I understand," said the girl.

Chapter 8

Country of the Invisible Children

The three of them continued for some time, walking, fluttering or slithering, each according to its own way, and talking as they went. After a bit, Amal said to the Spelling Bee, "I've been with you since this morning and I have no idea how you came to be such a very big bee."

"But my sweet little dear," replied the Spelling Bee, "you don't really want to hear that long dreary story do you?"

"I would think it would be quite interesting. Go ahead, tell me."

"My, oh my, it is a quite a long story. Yes, indeedy deed, it is. Let me see, where should I start . . ?"

But before he could continue his legs suddenly flew out from under him. Before he could hit the ground, his wings started buzzing and in an instant, he was nine feet above the path. All around them, voices were laughing.

At the same moment that the Bee's legs were knocked from under him, Sapphire was hit with several sticks, and Amal's hair was tugged at. Startled more than hurt, Sapphire was quick to disappear into the nearby bushes.

Country of the Invisible Children

Life on the streets of Mogadishu had taught Amal how to move fast. At the moment of the tug, she spun round and grabbed. She could see no one, but her arms closed around a young human body.

"Let me go," the boy's voice yelled.

"I will when you make yourself visible."

"I can't," was the answer.

"You'd better find out how real quick, now," insisted Amal as she moved her grip so as to twist his arm a bit.

"That hurts," complained the boy.

"No more than your pulling on my hair," returned Amal. "Now make yourself visible."

"I can't," he said.

Another voice said, "None of us know how to be visible. We're the Invisible Children."

Yet another voice chimed in, "Do you think we'd stay invisible if we knew how to be visible?"

The Spelling Bee, from up above said, "Most assuredly, it is handy for waylaying strangers."

Another voice said, "Yeah? Well that's about all we can do."

Yet another said, "When no one can see you and you can't see each other, life is pretty dull."

The boy whose arm Amal was twisting said, "That's why we like to pester anyone who happens along."

Amal relaxed her grip on him and said, "Here, take my hand. Then, at least I will know you are there."

"Thanks," he mumbled.

"What's your name?" she asked.

"Binji," was the short answer.

The Spelling Bee of Oz

"By my whiskers," said the Bee, "who made you invisible?"

His answer of, "I have no idea," was echoed by several other voices.

Binji then added, "So far as I know I have always been invisible."

One voice said, "I can remember long ago when I was visible, but one day I was not."

Several others agreed with that but most could remember no time when they were visible.

"Most unusual. Most unusual," declared the Spelling Bee.

Again, the boy spoke up, "We can only barely even see each other. We see each other as kind of a dim outline. We can't really tell who is who."

"But someone's taught you proper grammar," said the Bee.

"No problem attending school when we want to," said the boy. "The teachers don't even know we're there."

Hovering and looking around, not knowing for sure where any of the Invisible Children were, the Spelling Bee said, "'Peers to me that you're kind of lost."

Several voices recited, "Invisible Children. Lost Children. That's us."

The Bee cleared his throat and fluttered his wings a bit before mumbling, "Always invisible, hmm?" So he tried again, "You don't know if anyone put a spell on you?"

There were only a few weak voices that said, "No."

"Let me see, then." And he was quiet for a time. Then

Country of the Invisible Children

he suddenly said, "Ah, it just might work. Yes, indeed. Let's try it." Then swinging his arms to indicate just where he meant, he said, "All of you line up right in front of me here."

There was the scraping of feet, grunting, and not a few remarks like, "Easy there," "I'm sorry," "Don't be so pushy," "It's hard to tell who's where."

Finally, things quieted down and the Bee said, "Goodness me. I don't know if this will work. No, I don't. But I'll try." And, waving four arms and his two antennae, he began a chant:

"Away and gone, the spell is wrong.
Let what's been done be now undone."

There was silence for a while, and then he said, "Are all of you Invisible Children still here?"

All along an invisible line in front of him voices called out, "I am."

Then, flapping his wings slowly, he said, "Sorry about that. Yes indeed, I am sorry, but I thought that if it were a spell, I could undo it for you. Apparently it is not a spell."

"Don't worry," said the boy, "No new loss. We were invisible, and we still are."

The great Bee responded, "Still, I wish … Oh my goodness! Where did Amal go?"

"I'm right here," came her quick reply.

"Where? I don't see you. You've become invisible. It must not be a matter of spells, but of place. This is the Country of the Invisible Children. We just may have, I

The Spelling Bee of Oz

say, we may have solved their problem. It may be that any children that come here soon become invisible."

"Yes," said Amal. "Can any of you see me?"

"Just a faint outline," was heard from several voices near Amal's voice.

"All right then," said the Spelling Bee, "Amal grab one of my hands. Yes. Yes. That's it. Now, let's see how far we have to go before we're out of this most unusual, yes, unusual place."

Amal dragged back on his hand and said, "Let's take Binji along, too. Then we'll know if children who've been here for awhile can be made visible by moving out of this area."

"Good idea," said the Bee, "but we'll have to hurry. The afternoon is running on and we want to complete this before it gets dark. Yes. Dark."

About an hour later, with the two children still holding onto his hands and quite invisible, he said, "The time has come. We'll have to look for food now. Yes, food, and then for a place to sleep for the night."

By the time they bedded down, it was quite dark and soon all three were fast asleep.

Chapter 9

Back to the Surface

In her room, it seemed to Zeebee that she had just gone to sleep when music woke her up. She looked at her smartphone and saw that it was, indeed four-fifty-five. As she hopped out of bed, she said, "Ick, I have to put on the same clothes I wore yesterday, and I'll have to wear them every day until I get back home. But, I wonder if there are any girls in this Nome Country. I haven't seen any. Maybe there are, though. So maybe I can buy some changes of clothing."

As she was washing in the corner basin, there was a knock on her door, and she called out, "I'm already up and dressing. I'll be out in about ten minutes."

The voice of the steward said, "That's fine. I have your new shoes that Schaumkar made last night."

She finished washing, dressed and brushed her hair with a brush on the dresser, then reached out the door for her new shoes and put them on. Just ten minutes had gone by.

When they reached the throne room, King Korph was just coming in through another door. As he climbed into the throne, the scraggly one said, "I will bring

The Spelling Bee of Oz

your breakfasts immediately," and left. In moments he was back, followed by three Nomes carrying the tables and chair and as they went back out, two more Nomes brought in their trays of food.

Looking at the King's tray, Zeebee wondered if the Nomes ate anything other than lava, tar, asphalt and gravel, for there was a glass of lava on his tray and a mixture of the other three on a plate. Luckily, her breakfast was again quite appetizing to her – scrambled eggs, bacon and toast and jam.

During breakfast Zeebee asked the King if there were any women among the Nomes.

"Of course there are," was his answer.

"Then you probably have women's clothing that would fit me. What I have on is getting pretty stinky and bedraggled."

"Oh, of course, you would need some change of clothes. We are going to have to get moving pretty fast after breakfast, but I will have my Steward take you down to stores as soon as you finish, but do hurry, both now and then."

Zeebee did hurry and when she and Alklank reached the supply room, she found that women's garb was, like the men's, all very gray. There was nothing of color, but she guessed she could stand a gray outfit for a few days.

When she rejoined King Korph they hurried into the room with all the Magic Gates and entered the one that said, "Emerald City." In one step they found themselves back in the pit that led up to the Emerald City countryside.

They climbed up the steps cut into the ground,

Back to the Surface

and this time Zeebee was not quite as bothered by the possibility of falling as she had been the first time. Still, she stayed as close to the wall as possible.

When they came out at the top, the Nome King pushed open the doorway, looked around to be sure no one had seen him do so, and then led the way out into the green grass and bushes. After Zeebee had joined him beyond the door, he closed it and worked around at the surrounding dirt and bushes so that no one would even notice it had been in use.

From there, they went back onto the road they had used to reach the door in the first place and headed north where they were soon, once again, in the purple lands of the Gillikin Country. They proceeded along the path until they reached the place where the Grinderdael had left them. Then, they headed up into the mountains where they had last seen him.

When the Nome King felt they had gone far enough, he encouraged Zeebee to join him in calling for Grinderdael. They had been calling continuously for about five minutes, when a high pitched and cross-sounding voice behind them said, "Would you people please shut up? You're disturbing our sleep."

Turning, the two saw a little man, not as much as two feet tall, standing on a rock that they had just passed. He was skinny, had pointed ears, a pointed red cap on his head, curly-toed brown shoes on his feet, and green leggings and shirt with a brown jerkin.

"Oh, my goodness, you scared us! We didn't even know you were here," said the Nome King.

The Spelling Bee of Oz

"Oh, my goodness, you scared us!" said the Nome King.

"Well we are and you are making too much noise." He disappeared, and then from behind them, they heard him say, "You are disturbing my sleep, all my neighbors sleep, and what's worse, all our children's sleep."

Bowing low to him, Zeebee said, "We are truly sorry. We did not know anyone at all was around, let alone someone sleeping. Please forgive us. We will go on our way more quietly."

"We accept your apology." Then pointing at Korph he asked, "Do you speak for that big fat man, too?"

"I'm not so big and fat. You think so just because you are so little and skinny. And I speak for myself. And what I say is, 'It is important for me to keep on calling for the

Back to the Surface

Grinderdael.'"

At that, the elf disappeared, and then from behind them again, they heard him say, "I am Organi of the Rock Elves and you are impinging upon our home territory."

Zeebee bowed and said, "I am Elizabeth Warren of Earth and I am sorry to be impinging on your home territory. But you are so little."

"And you are so big," replied the Elf.

"If you are Rock Elves" said Korph, "then, since I'm a Nome, we are somewhat related."

The Elf disappeared again and then reappeared on a rock off to the side, saying, "Not hardly! We are not untrustworthy, miserly and intolerant."

"If you're implying that that is true of Nomes, I beg to differ," said the Nome King.

"We know your people Mr. Nome. You have hoards of jewels stored up in your great storerooms. And you do not use them for anything. You do not share them with anyone else. They just sit there uselessly. You could at least take them all out of storage and use them to decorate your endless miles of tunnels."

He disappeared again, but this time, he did not return quite so fast and the two had just taken a couple steps on up the hill when he showed up on a rock two feet ahead of them.

"I just made a trip to a large room where I stood on a big rock in the middle of the room, a rock that had a throne carved into it and jewels all over it."

"What were you doing in my throne room, you invader."

The Spelling Bee of Oz

"Look who's talking about invading. Whose rocks are you standing on?"

The Nome sputtered and then said, "These rocks are out in the open and don't belong to anyone."

"Just like gems lying randomly in the ground don't belong to anyone in particular. So what makes you Nomes think you can claim all the jewels, gems and minerals wherever they might be?"

There was more sputtering from the Nome. Then the Elf said, "Look at all these rocks around here. Go ahead, take some of them if you want. We won't stop you." Then looking down, he said, "You can even take this very rock I'm standing on and I'll just bounce over to another one. Take all the rocks on this hill and all of us will just bounce to some other rocks someplace else. We're not selfish or miserly about them."

While he was talking, he kept disappearing and instantly reappearing on another rock, not even interrupting his rapid flow of patter. When he had said, "all of us," hundreds more of the little Rock Elves appeared on rocks all around Korph and Zeebee.

"My," said Zeebee, "you folks do appear and disappear fast."

"Of course. That's our nature," said Organi. "Rock Elves jump from rock to rock whenever and wherever they want to. We do it in an instant when we're staying in the neighborhood. But it takes a couple minutes to get clear to the other side of Ozeria."

Another of the Elves said, "We could claim all the rocks in the world as ours, but we share them."

Back to the Surface

"Okay, okay," said the Nome King. "I get it. You think we Nomes are selfish. Lay off it, please. I'm sorry we disturbed you with our yelling, but we have to find the Grinderdael as soon as possible."

Now a chubbier elf spoke up. His cap had a thin metal rim and points along the rim. He said, "I am Raimen, King of the Rock Elves," and he nodded toward Korph and Zeebee.

Zeebee bowed and said, "I am Elizabeth Warren from the Santa Clara Valley on Earth."

Then the Nome King said, "And I am the renowned King of the Nomes!"

At that revelation, there was a good bit of murmuring from the Rock Elves, but their king just stood there looking at Korph. At last, he said, "So, you claim to be the King of the Nomes. Does that mean that you are Kaliko?"

"Kaliko! No! He is a slave. I, Korph, am King of the Nomes."

"All right then, as one king to another, I ask you what is so important about getting hold of the Grinderdael?"

"We need to do some negotiating with the Live Wires."

At the mention of Live Wires, all the Rock Elves shuddered and blinked out of sight. After a couple seconds, the King appeared again on a high rock near Korph. He said, "What in the world are you going to try to negotiate with the Live Wires? Do you have any idea what they are like?"

"Indeed we do," answered the Nome King. "Their

The Spelling Bee of Oz

Transformer almost transformed us day before yesterday. And that was after his subjects had shocked the daylights out of us. That's why we want to save others from the same fate."

"Good for you, but how do you propose to do that?"

One by one, the other Rock Elves began blinking into existence on various rocks around them as the Nome King was saying, "The Grinderdael will protect us from an attack by them, and we will negotiate to have them attack a neighboring town and we will send word to Ozma that they are doing so and she will come and neutralize them and restore everyone who has been transformed."

"A noble purpose," said the Elfin King. "So, that is why you have been kicking up such a ruckus calling for Grinderdael?"

"Yes," said the Nome King.

"If we find him for you, will you promise not to do any more shouting?"

Again, the Nome King said, "Yes."

The Elfin King pondered a while, then he said, "You Nomes are not very trustworthy, but this young girl has not denied what you're saying, so we'll go look for Grinderdael. We should find him within a few minutes. Wait here."

With that all the Rock Elves disappeared. In about five minutes one of them dressed all in green popped up in front of King Korph, saying, "I've found him! Follow me."

It was a bit disconcerting doing so, for he did not

Back to the Surface

just walk along in front of them. He would disappear from the rock he was standing on, and then reappear on another about twenty feet in front of them, where he would stand until they caught up with him, and then the process would repeat itself.

At last, when they caught up with him at the top of a ridge, he stayed put and pointed down the slope. There stood the Grinderdael. He looked up at them and, in a sarcastic tone, said, "So, you are the friends this Rock Elf asked me to wait for."

"Indeed we are, sir," replied the Nome King. "We need you in order for us to negotiate with the Live Wires."

"Are you crazy?" asked the Grinderdael. "You know what they almost did to you the last time you met them! Without my help you would now be a crown and a yellow diamond."

"Exactly so, but it was your help that prevented that. The thing is, now we need that same help so we can make a deal with them."

Looking a bit askance at the Nome, the dog asked, "What kind of a deal are you trying to make?"

"We feel that if they were to move beyond their own territory to attack another community, we could warn Ozma and she would use her magic to neutralize them so they could no longer prey on passersby."

"And you want me to go with you to protect you while you try to convince them to attack some particular community? Don't you know that they cannot get very far away from the immovable Transformer?"

"Yes, that's part of the negotiating. My Nomes could

The Spelling Bee of Oz

put a wheeled platform under him to get him to the nearest community."

The Grinderdael objected, "Then they would be able to take him anywhere at all and be more threat than ever."

"Not if Ozma has made it impossible for them to shock anyone anymore."

During this conversation Zeebee had been acting a bit nervous, but she did not say anything.

"Let me think about that," said the Grinderdael. "You go eat your lunch and in about an hour I'll be ready to answer you."

"Come," said the King of the Rock Elves, speaking to King Korph and Zeebee, "You can have lunch with us."

"But we don't eat rocks," said Zeebee.

The Rock Elves laughed as their King said, "Neither do we. We pretty much eat the same things you do."

"Not I," said the Nome King, "I'll go where you lead, but when it comes to eating, I do eat rocks. I would enjoy a good bowl of gravel, if that was possible."

King Raimen said, "All right. You can have gravel." Then turning to Zeebee, he said, "We have a variety of juices we can serve. What would you prefer?"

Korph scowled, but Zeebee said, "I like all kinds of juices, but cranberry is my favorite. Do you have any?"

"Indeed we do said the King," and turning to Korph he said, "What about you?"

"A bit of lava would do fine for me."

Again the Rock Elves tittered, but their King said, "Do any of you know where to find some lava?"

Back to the Surface

Several said they did, and the King picked one of them and, with a wink that Korph could not see, he said, "Ranalph, can you fetch some for the Nome King?"

"Of course," said the elderly Rock Elf the King had addressed. And taking the Nome King's hand in his own, the two of them disappeared before Korph could object.

As soon as they had, Raimen turned to Zeebee, and with Organi standing next to him, said, "Being from Earth, you may not know about Nomes. They cannot be trusted. Since you are with him, I am going to cooperate with finding the Grinderdael, but I do not believe what he says and you should be careful about him."

This thought made Zeebee uncomfortable, but since he immediately blinked out of sight, leaving Organi and Zeebee standing in the midst of Elves, she had no opportunity to ask any questions. Besides, she was surrounded by Rock Elves eager to know more about her and Earth. They asked her all kinds of questions: what kind of house she lived in, did they have thunder storms and snow, were there any cities as magnificent as the Emerald City, what kinds of magic workers did they have, and had she ever met her queen? The questions went on and on.

Finally Raimen and the Nome king returned with a very large and boiling cup of lava for Korph. Then the two visitors were led off to a comfortable, grassy glen with a big flat rock in the middle of it. While several of them talked with Zeebee and Korph, a couple disappeared from sight and after several minutes, reappeared, along with several more of the little Rock Elves. Between them

The Spelling Bee of Oz

all, they were carrying a stove with the fire already going in it, plus several bags of food, a food preparation center, dishes, and a number of pans and utensils. These they put upon the big flat rock and began preparing the meal.

No sooner had they begun, than several more of the small people popped into sight carrying tables and chairs which they set around here and there, making enough for all the Rock Elves that were there.

While they were busy setting things up and preparing the meal, Zeebee had whispered to the Nome King, "You weren't exactly honest back there. You made it seem like the only thing you had in mind was getting Ozma to neutralize the Live Wires, when the real purpose of all this is to overthrow Ozma. You didn't even mention that or the Magic Belt."

Squirming a bit, the King answered, "Of course not. You never know whose side they might be on. They could be agents of Ozma's, so we dare not let them or anyone else know what we have in mind. So now, lets' just settle down and enjoy our repast."

Zeebee was not satisfied, but Organi still stood near her and, shaking his head, he put his finger to his lips, so she said nothing. Besides, by this time Zeebee's nose was almost twitching with the smells of fresh cheese being sliced and the heat of the toasting bread. Before long their food was set before them on their little tables. If Zeebee and the Nome King had sat on chairs, they would have been too elevated for the tables, so the Elves put one each of their little tables in front of where each of them sat on the grass. It worked out just right.

Back to the Surface

Sure enough, there was a large bowl of gravel for the Nome King, but he got no salad; whereas Zeebee had a delicious green salad with onions, tomatoes and cucumbers to go with her toasted cheese sandwich. She had a nice big glass full of cranberry juice, while the Nome King seemed as happy as could be with his boiling cup of lava.

For half an hour or so they ate their lunch, enjoying both the food and the company. When most had finished, a number of the elves began cleaning up, gathering dirty dishes and serving plates (empty or not) into their arms and then stepping on a rock, only to blink out to wherever they went, soon returning to gather up more. By the time the Nome King and Zeebee were done, everything else had been cleared away.

For a while longer, they talked with the Rock Elves until they decided the hour was up and they could return to see what the Grinderdael's decision would be.

When they got to where they had left him, he was not there.

"I guess that makes his decision pretty clear," said one of the Rock Elves. "He has left you to your own resources."

Chapter 10

Negotiations

Just then, they could all hear a nearby grinding sound, and above the rocks at the edge of the depression they were in, they could see the head of the Grinderdael. After a few more bites of that rock, he stepped into full view, saying, "I got hungry waiting," and he came bounding down the slope.

Hands on hips, Zeebee said, "So, what's your decision?"

"I've thought about it and I have a few questions."

"Go ahead," said she.

Looking at the Nome King, the big dog said, "First: Your idea is that you want me to take you into the Live Wire territory and be a protection against their shocking you or changing you. Is that right?"

"Yes," said the Nome.

"And the reason you want me to do this is so that you can convince them to attack one of their neighbors. Is that right?"

"Yes."

"At the time I take you there, you will want to negotiate with them to have your Nomes take the Transformer

Negotiations

to somewhere near a neighbor, so they can make the attack. Is that right?"

"Right as dirt."

"But, in order to protect that town, you will already have warned Ozma and she will stop them. Is that right?"

"You've got it."

"So, what's the point? No one gets hurt, but the Transformer and the Live Wires have been moved out of their home territory. There must be more to it than that."

"Of course. If Ozma is going to stop them from attacking that community, she will have to neutralize them. Once that's done, then they will never be able to hurt anyone again. Pretty smart, hunh?"

"Not particularly," growled the Grinderdael. "Why don't you just go to Ozma and tell her about what they are doing, and then she'll take care of it?"

"We have a history, you know. Ozma does not trust Nomes, so she just did not believe me when I told her."

Zeebee's eyes widened at that blatant lie, and she started to say something, but Organi had stayed close to her and he gave her a little punch in the side that made her give that a second thought and she said nothing, again.

In the meantime, the Nome King had said to the Grinderdael, "Now that's the plain and simple truth of it."

Zeebee realized she should not contradict him yet, and the Grinderdael, all unaware of how badly the Nome King was lying, said, "So you mean to make a demonstration case where she can use her Magic Picture

The Spelling Bee of Oz

to see them shocking people? Is that the case?"

"Exactly," replied the Nome King.

"So what if she still doesn't believe you and won't even look in her Magic Picture?"

"We'll deal with that when it happens... if it happens."

"Okay, let me think about it awhile, just a few minutes this time," and he turned his back on them, sat down and thought.

In about two minutes, he said, "Okay. It's a deal. But have you decided what community to have them attack?"

"No. I have no idea of what communities are around here or of where any of them might be."

"Their closest neighbor by quite a way is Insulaville, a couple miles to their west. I think that would be a good choice."

"So that will be our suggestion."

"Are you ready right now?" asked Grinderdael.

The Nome King responded, "No time like the present," and he started to climb onto the big dog's back.

But the dog reared back and said, "No need yet. Time enough when we are close to the Live Wires," and he began to lead the way.

Zeebee said "Goodbye, and thank you!" to the Rock Elves, and the King of the Elves whispered to her, "Don't forget my warning about the Nomes."

Then dog, Nome and girl were off.

Before long the Grinderdael said, "All right. We are getting close now and it is time for both of you to get on my back."

They did and away he went. Before long two Live

Negotiations

Wires sprang from the right side of the path, one giving a quick shock to Zeebee, the other to the Nome King. Both the girl and the Nome gave out brief startled cries which made the Live Wires laugh with glee, but the Grinderdael said, "Unless you want me to grind you into shavings, settle down. We have a proposal to take to the Transformer."

They both scuttled back into the bushes. Then one poked his head out, saying, "What kind of a proposition?"

The Nome King said, "It is one that will be good for you Live Wires and for us as well."

The other Live Wire said, "I don't know of anything that would be good both directions."

"No, you wouldn't. This is my idea and I believe the Transformer would be happy to hear it. So would all of you Live Wires as a matter of fact. So take us to your King!"

The two Live Wires consulted in whispers and then one of them said, "Okay, but you have to leave the Grinderdael behind."

"Don't be silly," replied the Nome King. "If we did that, we would be defenseless."

More whispering among the Live Wires and then one of them declared, "All right. But don't let him get very close to any of us."

And so one of the Live Wires, staying well ahead of the Grinderdael, led them up the hill and into the big building where the Transformer sat. The other had already run ahead to warn other Live Wires to stay out of the way and to alert the Transformer to the return of the

The Spelling Bee of Oz

two victims the Grinderdael had spirited away.

When they arrived, the Transformer laughed a long deep laugh, and said, "So, you want to come back for more of our exciting treatment! But get that hound out of here!"

As the Live Wires started moving a little closer, the dog swung his head from left to right and began a grinding sound. That was enough to make all the Live Wires flee to the wall and even out the doors. Then Grinderdael took two steps toward the imposing Transformer with his teeth still grinding. At that, the King Transformer's self-confidence faded, as did his color, and he opened his mouth a little, but no sound came out.

King Korph whispered to the Grinderdael to stay put and then aloud, said, "I think we have your attention now. We have an offer to make to you."

Seeing that Grinderdael was not advancing further, the Transformer Robot said, "What can you possibly offer me?"

"Freedom," replied the Nome.

"I have all the freedom I need."

"That may be, but your Live Wires don't," said King Korph. "If I put wheels under your platform, then you can move and so can your Live Wires."

"They can move now."

"Yes, but they can't go very far from you or they'll lose their power and go dead. They like to shock people, but very few people come by here, knowing what will happen if they do. I'll bet no one has been by since we came by yesterday."

Negotiations

The Transformer, nodded as he said, "You're right. Not many do come by."

"Okay. We'll give you wheels and then your Live Wires can take you to the nearest town and they can shock those inhabitants to their hearts delight."

"But, you're not just doing this out of the goodness of your heart. What do you get out of it?"

Standing as straight as he could, the little Nome said, "It's very simple. Just that I and my friend Dorothy," and here he bowed to Zeebee, then continued, "and my Nomes have free passage whenever we want to come by here. And your Live Wires will promise not to shock us."

With somewhat of a smirk on his face, the Transformer replied, "That sounds fair. Give me a minute to think about it."

Then everything was silent for almost a minute until the Transformer spoke again, saying, "All right. It seems like a good idea, but we need to put it in writing," and he called out, "Bent Wire, bring some paper and a pen. I have something I want you to write down."

One of the little Live Wires standing along the wall broke from the group, and sure enough, he was a bent wire. He went over to a corner of the room and pulled some paper and a pen from a drawer and then came down to where the Transformer was. In all his movements, he stayed as far from the Grinderdael as possible. He sat down behind the Transformer and started taking down the dictation.

It provided that only a limited number of Nomes could come by and only on certain days. Korph read it

The Spelling Bee of Oz

over, suggested a few changes, the Transformer agreed and after that, both the kings signed it.

Then Korph bowed and said, "By the terms of this agreement, the two of us have the freedom to leave here without worry of being shocked, but how do your Live Wires out there," and he swept his arm around in a great circle, "know that?"

The Transformer raised his voice so all in the room could hear, "All of you inside my palace know that the Nomes and this girl shall never again be shocked by any of you. Now run out and see to it that all the other Live Wires know this. Korph and Zeebee are ready to leave."

"Thank you," said both the Nome and Zeebee as they bowed and turned to go. But as he did so, the Nome King said, "We will be back tomorrow with the new wheeling platform and we will put you on it. Then your Live Wires can push it and move you to a neighboring town where you can all do as much shocking as you want to." With that, all three left, but this time Korph and Zeebee walked freely and safely alongside Grinderdael.

Beyond the Live Wire territory, they said goodbye to their friendly dog and continued down the mountainside, returning to the tunnel and the Magic Gates and thence back to the Nome King's palace. The King gave orders for the making of the special wheeled platform for the moving of the Transformer, and then they had dinner and went to bed.

However, after Zeebee had gone to her room and before he, himself, retired the King called for Knunk to come to the throne room. He was a little smaller than

Negotiations

most of the Nomes, a thin and wiry little man and Korph said to him, "Knunk, you are my most reliable messenger, so I have a message I want you to take to Queen Ozma of Oz."

On hearing those words, the little Nome started shaking, and the King said, "What under Ozeria is the matter with you?"

"But sir, won't she throw an egg at me?"

"Of course not," answered the King. "We haven't done anything to make her angry with us ... yet. She will accept you as a messenger from a fellow monarch." He reached in his pocket and pulled out an envelope with a big patch of gray wax sealing it tight. "Now just take this and deliver it to her. I do not want you to put it in her hands until four P. M. tomorrow. You know the way to go through the Magic Gate to the Emerald City."

"Yes," said Knunk, "I can find it with ease."

"All right. You will have to travel all night tonight and all day tomorrow, and go with all speed so you will make it by four tomorrow night."

"I understand sir. I will be there at four tomorrow night."

"Fine, but before you leave, I need to give you instructions as to what you are to say when you get there," and for the next hour, he drilled Knunk on what he should say.

Chapter 11

Deliverance

On the same morning that Zeebee had asked for fresh clothing, the Spelling Bee, Amal and Binji were up with the sun to continue their journey. For over an hour of walking the two children had remained quite invisible. Then, as they approached a particularly large field of corn shocks, Binji said, "I guess this is where I have to say goodbye to you."

"What do you mean by that?" asked the Spelling Bee.

"There is a definite limit to our land. No matter how hard we try, there seems to be a line all around this area that we cannot pass, and the corn field you see ahead is on the other side of that line."

"You mean I can't go past there either?" wailed Amal. "I'll never get home."

"That's probably right," said Binji.

"Ah now. Let's not give up so fast. No, not at all," said the Bee. "Keep on holding hands, very tightly, and we'll see if I can drag you through. Yes, right on through."

So all three of them gripped their hands as tight as possible and strode ahead. Sure enough, when they reached the edge of the cornfield, without a pause or even

Deliverance

a jerk, they kept right on going and almost immediately, the two children reappeared.

"Hurray!" shouted Binji. "I can see myself, now! And you too, Amal."

"Oh my," said the girl, "I thought all was lost."

"Oh good, goodness!" exclaimed the Bee. "I can admit it now. I was afraid, afraid I'd never see you again. Yes, indeed, I only hoped that the problem might be one of location. Oh, I'm so glad to see you again." And he hugged them both close.

The boy was scraggly looking, dirty and unkempt. His hair was long and tangled. He was wearing several layers of clothing, all full of holes, but, for the most part, the holes at one layer matched up with full cloth on another layer.

He began to cry as he looked at himself. Amal thought he was ashamed to see how dirty and ragged he looked, but he said, "Excuse my tears! I don't remember ever having seen myself before! What a wonder it is!"

The young girl put an arm around his shoulders and said, "There now, it's all okay."

"Oh, yes!" he exclaimed, with a big smile creasing his tear-streaked face. "It really is quite all right."

"So," said the Spelling Bee, "you like the idea of being visible, really being visible?"

"Oh, yes," was the boys quick reply as he turned to face the big Bee who went on, "Then do you think the others would like to be visible, too?"

"I'm sure of it. That is one of our greatest topics of conversation."

The Spelling Bee of Oz

"So it is a good thing that I have done, but I hate to admit to my own personal pride. I know, oh I do know, that all my excitement should be about all of you being able to be seen again." Then, shaking his head, he continued, "But the truth is, I'm also happy to be vindicated. I was upset, yes, upset to say the least, when my Dis-Spell did not work. I feared I was losing my ability. But this just shows that you were not under a spell at all. It was simply a matter of the nature of the place."

As he flapped his wings in preparation for leaving, he said, "Within the borders of the Country of the Invisible Children, all children become invisible." Then he began laughing (Have you ever heard a bee laugh?) and said, "It's as simple as that and I found the solution."

"Hey," said Binji, "you've got a right to be proud of your feat. No one else ever figured that out. So, for all the others, I thank you right now."

The Bee bowed and with a wave of his arms, said, "Thank you, but now I must go back and get the others. Yes indeed, I'm sure that is right. I'll go back and get them. Yes. That's what I should do. In the meantime, you two go on along this road until you find someone who can direct you to a storehouse, yes, to a storehouse, where we can get new clothes for you and all of these, the once Invisible Children."

Amal looked at Binji, who shrugged his shoulders, then to the Spelling Bee, and asked him, "Why do we need to go to a storehouse?"

"Ah, yes. You may not know about that. You come from a world that uses money. Here in Oz, we have

Deliverance

no money anymore. Centuries ago we devised a plan whereby everyone works for half a day at whatever job he or she finds attractive. The other half day is for pleasure, recreation, study, exploring or whatever one wants to do. What one produces during the work time that is beyond one's own needs is then donated to the nearest storehouse. Then, if you need anything, anything at all, you can go to the storehouse and pick out what you need. That is why you need to find a storehouse, to pick out new clothing."

"Wow!" said Amal. "I haven't had anything new for over a year. You bet I'll look for a storehouse!"

With that the Bee flew off, back toward the Invisible Children, and the two visible ones turned and headed west down the little path. Amal said, "Looks like we'll be together for a while, so I suppose we should introduce ourselves. My name is Amal."

"Yes, I know," said the boy. "I've heard the Spelling Bee call you by that name."

"Yes, but we had not formally been introduced."

"I see. But then, if your name is 'M-L,' I suppose mine should be 'B-J,' but it's really Binji." Then holding his arm out beside Amal's, he said, "Gee, I look kind of pale compared to you. Is my memory wrong? I seem to remember that the few people coming through here look more like me."

Amal did not quite understand what he meant by "B-J," but skipped that and said, "I don't know what Oz people look like. You're the first person I've seen in Oz. But most of the people where I come from are about

The Spelling Bee of Oz

my shade, although I've occasionally seen paler ones like you."

"You're not from Oz, then?"

"No. I come from Mogadishu . . . on Earth," and she took his hand in hers and skipped on forward, saying, "Come on. We need to get going."

He did not resist her hand and for a while they skipped along until they slowed down and dropped hands, but continued walking along, anxious to reach the next town.

Chapter 12

Welcome

It was still over an hour before they saw any signs of humans. They had just topped a small hill when, on the other side, they saw a fair sized town. They pressed on a bit faster now and soon had found that it did, indeed, have a storehouse, the only one in many miles. They started, then, to turn back, but Amal stopped, saying, "Hey, it's not going to get them here any faster if we meet them sooner rather than later!"

Binji stopped too, and scratching his head, said, "You mean we should go in and choose our clothes now?"

Amal said, "You bet," and led the way into the storehouse. It only took about five minutes for Binji to pick out a pair of blue suede shoes, bright blue shorts and a white tee-shirt with wild blue designs all over both front and back. He looked at the various hats, even tried some on, but finally said, "I've never worn a hat in all my life. This is no time to start," and did not get one.

It seemed like years ago since Amal had done any shopping—five years to be exact, almost half her lifetime. Nonetheless, she remembered very well how to do it. She fingered the various dresses, blouses and skirts,

The Spelling Bee of Oz

classifying the material in her mind, enjoying both the tactile and visual stimulation of shopping. Eventually, she began picking out ones she would choose between. A long blue formal dress was just for the fun of trying it on.

It was nearly an hour by the time she had made up her mind and put on a dark blue satin blouse with short sleeves and a demure neck-line. She added a blue dotted white skirt with a wide hem and a pair of black patent leather shoes with a large blue bow on each. She topped it off with another blue bow in her hair. Turning before the mirror, she thought she looked every inch a little lady.

Done, the two decided it was time to back track to meet the Spelling Bee and the Invisible Children. But before they left the storehouse, Amal asked the clerk if she knew about the Invisible Children.

"Goodness, yes. We all avoid that area as much as possible. They are a bunch of wayward rogues, bothering everyone who goes through their land."

Then Amal asked, "Do you know about the Spelling Bee?"

"Of course," replied the lady. "Everyone knows how he saved Oz a few years ago."

"I was with him when we, unknowingly entered the Country of the Invisible Children. Pretty soon, I disappeared, but he walked me out of that area until I became visible again."

"Oh my! So it wasn't a curse on the children, but a curse on the land! A few of our own children have disappeared and now I know why. Oh my!"

Amal put her hand on the arm of the young lady and

Welcome

said, "Now the Spelling Bee is rescuing them, bringing them all out. But this means there will be twenty or thirty or more children looking for a place to eat and sleep tonight. Then we will go on to the Emerald City."

The lady's face shown as she said, "But some of those children will surely be our missing ones! They will be reunited with their own families tonight! How wonderful!"

"Oh yes, that it would be. Do you think that we can find enough homes to play host to the rest of them?"

Still smiling broadly, the lady said, "I'm sure we can. What time will the children be here?"

That stumped Amal, but she said, "That depends on how quickly the Bee can round them up and how quickly they can walk. There may be some pretty small ones among them. Will you be open long enough for them to pick out new clothes? You know they will all be in rags like we were."

"That doesn't matter. We will stay open until they arrive and have had time to pick out their new clothes."

With that, the young lady sent several of the other workers out to find people with room to take in the children for the night, and especially to call on parents whose children had disappeared.

For their part, Amal and Binji decided it was time for them to head back to meet those children and bring them into town. They moved along quickly, and it was well after noon by the time they could see the field of shocked corn ahead of them.

Binji stopped them then, saying, "Far enough. Ahead

The Spelling Bee of Oz

is where the Spelling Bee led us across the line to make us visible again. I, for one, am not getting any closer to the threat of becoming invisible again."

"I'm with you," responded Amal. "Besides, I'm getting hungry."

"So, let's look for something to eat," said Binji as he led the way toward a grove of trees.

They searched around in them for a while, found some berry bushes but not much more until Amal cried out, "What kind of trees are these?"

Binji wound his way through the other trees until he could see what she was looking at. "Hey! Great! You've found just what we need — lunch-bucket trees!"

"I hope that means what it sounds like," she replied.

"Sure does," he said, as he quickly picked two, a deep red one and a lighter red one. The darker one he put on his lap and twisted the stem so that the upper part split and revealed the contents. There was a peanut butter and dill pickle sandwich, a bowl of vegetable soup, celery stalks with a cheese-like substance in them and two big chocolate chip cookies.

When Amal opened hers in the same way, she found a peanut butter sandwich, but this one had jam on it and her soup was chicken noodle. Otherwise the contents were the same. Then Binji tore a couple leaves off the tree, stem and all, separated the stem from the leaf and showed Amal how the stem made a perfect soup spoon and the leaf was a more than adequate napkin.

They went back to the hillside overlooking the road, a hundred or so yards from the stacks of corn and had

Welcome

only just finished eating when they spotted the Spelling Bee walking along, arms extended, but apparently all alone.

They both hopped up and started toward him, but only for a few steps. Then they waited and called out, "Are the children with you?"

"Deedy, deedy, yes. Uh. At least I hope so. I have four of them hanging on to my hands, yes these hands right here," and he waggled them back and forth. Then he turned his head and said, "Are you all still here?"

There was a chorus of yeses, and he nodded his head and said, "All here." Under his breath he added, "I hope."

A few more steps and he was alongside the stacks of corn, and the children behind him were starting to pop into sight. There were cheers as they began to see each other and themselves for the first time.

They all moved rapidly forward, mostly to get further from the region of invisibility for children. However, all of them also stayed a good distance away from the Rattercobra. They knew that being in Oz, his otherwise deadly poison could not kill them, but it sure could hurt a lot!

Noticing what was happening, the Spelling Bee said, "You don't have to worry. Rattercobra is my friend and would not hurt any of you at all. Isn't that so, Ratter?"

There was a pause before he answered, maybe a bit too slowly, "Yesss. All your friendsss are alwaysss sssafe from me, dear Ssspeller."

This did not really satisfy many of them and the number that were willing to let him come close to them

The Spelling Bee of Oz

could be counted on one hand. They milled around a bit, talking with each other, but still keeping their distance from the Rattercobra.

They were grouping themselves by the voices they recognized the best. The only ones they had seen up to now were Amal and the Spelling Bee. Binji was a stranger to them until he started talking, when a few of them recognized his voice. There were many excited "Ohs" and "Ahs" as all of them began to identify the voices that belonged to the different bodies.

Amal interrupted their reunion by standing on the hillside and shouting for silence. Then she announced, "We need to make sure that everyone has made it out of that infernal area." This made the children begin to cut off their conversations. As things quieted down, she said, "It's a fairly simple process. Binji, here, will call out your names, and as he calls your name, you are to yell out, 'Here,' and come and stand behind us."

"Okay, Binji, start."

He did so and by the time he ran out of names that he could remember right then, most of the children were standing behind him. Then Amal picked the oldest boy still left and said, "Tell us your name and then start calling out other names that you remember."

He did so, and by the time he was done, there was just one little boy left standing by himself. He stood there with everyone looking at him and with his face growing progressively redder. Amal turned and asked all the identified ones, "Can any of you think of a name that hasn't been called out?"

Welcome

There was a chorus of nos, so she turned to the boy and said, "What is your name?"

He mumbled something so quietly that no one could hear what he said, so Amal asked him to speak louder. Then in a trembling voice which she could just barely hear, and as he twisted his toes in the dirt, he said, "Uthur."

Then Amal turned to the others and said, "Do any of you remember Uthur?"

There were a few hesitant yeses, and that was it. Uthur was not well remembered. One of those who did recall him said, "He was pretty bashful, afraid of saying or doing anything. But here he is now, one of us." And he went over and patted him on the shoulder. When he did so, Uthur smiled broadly and his face shone with a bit of red to it.

With that settled, Binji showed them where to find the lunch-bucket tree, the same type they had often eaten from in the Country of the Invisible Children, and everyone picked one and they all sat down under the trees to eat.

When everyone was satisfied, they all set out for the town, still keeping their distance from the Rattercobra. By the time they reached the town and its storehouse, it was late in the afternoon. But, for the children, it was the dawn of a new day when they saw the abundance of good clothing they could have.

Not all of them had come into the store. Three boys and a girl stopped out in front, for they were the local children who had wandered beyond the line and had

The Spelling Bee of Oz

become invisible and lost to the world of the visible. As soon as their families had heard of the once-invisible-children-made-visible, they hurried to the storehouse so that they could see if any of those children were their own. Fortunately, all four of the Lost Children were there and they all were more interested in reuniting with their families than in going after new clothing.

While host families were arriving and all were excited by the good fortune of friends who had found their lost ones, plans were being made to turn the evening into a celebratory community dinner. But inside, the rest of the children were busily searching through the tables and racks of clothing. Actually, most of the boys were done within fifteen minutes. Most of the girls took longer, but a couple of them were done almost as fast as the boys, and a couple of the boys were still making choices at the very end.

The children were told of the big celebration being prepared and that during the dinner assignments would be made as to which of them would stay with which family that night. Then off everyone went to the community hall to partake of a bountiful meal – for most of the children, the first really good meal they had had in all their memory.

Mayor Cadwallader made a speech welcoming the illustrious Spelling Bee to their community of Upper Stallingham and pointing out that they had many fine fields of flowers nearby if he should want to settle in the neighborhood. Others welcomed both him and the children to their community, and thanked the Spelling

Welcome

Bee for discovering that there was a line separating the Country of the Invisible Children from the visible.

The Spelling Bee told everyone that he was sure that when they got to the Emerald City, Ozma could help all the children find their own homes. And he introduced the Rattercobra to them, assuring them that they had nothing to fear from him so long as they did not step on him or try to harm him. The people of the town were no more reassured than had been the children.

The celebration went late, so it took a while to get organized the next morning. Many sleepyheads wanted to sleep in. The hostesses wanted to serve the children big and delicious meals. Some of them were loathe to let their young charges go and promised that if they could not find their own parents they would have a welcoming home with them.

However late the festivities of the night had gone, by mid-morning all were gathered in the town square and farewells had been said. The Spelling Bee led the way as he and the children left Upper Stallingham and headed for the Emerald City.

Beyond the town they found a good solid road, leading west, where they ran into occasional traffic. People kept asking them what so large a group of children were doing on the road. Each time they had to explain that they had been Invisible Children made visible by the Spelling Bee and now headed for home. Consequently their progress was slower than it might have been.

It was still before noon when the Rattercobra suddenly said, "I do believe thisss isss where my good

The Spelling Bee of Oz

friend Hooper livesss."

"Who is Hooper?" asked Binji."

"He isss a hoop sssnake."

"Hoop snake?" asked Amal. And making a circle of her arms, she continued, "Is he a big round snake, like this?"

"Actually, sssometimesss, yessss. When he wantsss to hurry he takesss hisss tail in hisss mouth and then flipsss himsssself up ssso that he isss a big, ssstiff hoop and the forcccce of the flip ssstartsss him rolling, and pretty fassst at that."

Then Rattercobra stretched himself up to about two feet high and shouted, "Hooooper! Hooooooper!"

No, snakes cannot really shout. Most of it would not have carried more than twenty feet. However, the drawn out "oooooo," though no louder than the rest, carried a long way and before long, sure enough, a big hoop came rolling, rapidly down the nearby hill.

It stopped right by the Rattercobra, broke its circle and flopped down as a beautiful shiny black snake with a bright red stripe down each side. At the same time, the Rattercobra slackened down to ground level and the two snakes intertwined, whispering soft assurances to each other. Then they disentwined and the hoop snake said, "Ratter! What on Ozzzeria are you doing with thisss mob of little children. There must be at leassst a dozen dangerous boysss there."

"Perfectly sssafe. We're friendsss," was the reply.

"Friendsss with children?"

"Yesss." And Rattercobra pointed his head toward

Welcome

the Spelling Bee as he added, "You know Ssspeller don't you?"

The hoop snake wiggled a little and stretched himself out a bit to look at the big bee and answered, "Not persssonally, but I guess that'sss The Ssspelling Bee, isssn't it."

"That'sss right, and I'm accompanying him asss he leadsss the children to the Emerald Cccity. Thessse are the Invisssible Children, made visssible by him and he hopesss that Princessss Ozzzma can help them find their homesss."

"Mind if I come along?"

"Join the crowd," said the Rattercobra as he slithered along after them with his friend beside him.

Chapter 13

Confusion

The very morning after their trip to make peace with the Live Wires, Zeebee and Korph had breakfast together back in the Nome Kingdom, and then headed through the Magic Gate toward the Emerald City. A whole army of Nomes accompanied them, bringing the special wheeled platform the King had had made during the night. It took a while for all of them to reach the top of the hole from the tunnel floor, but while the rest were coming, Korph pointed down the road, and told Zeebee, "Just follow this road until you reach the Yellow Brick Road. Then turn right, and after traveling most of the day you will reach the Emerald City. Be sure that you do not reach there before four-thirty this afternoon. Then, when you get there, you are to tell Jellia Jamb that Ozma needs the Magic Belt right away. As soon as you have it, say, 'Take me to King Korph.' Do you have that?"

"Yes. 'Take me to King Korph.'"

"Okay. Then off you go, little one."

Zeebee was pensive for a moment, then said, "All right, and I'm not supposed to arrive until four-thirty this

Confusion

afternoon." And she was off, skipping down the road.

In a few minutes, she came to a little bush with about a dozen or so raspberries on it. This seemed a little strange because, unlike a raspberry bush, it had large waxy green leaves. She quickly picked about half of them and continued on her way. Not being a native, she did not realize that red raspberries in the Emerald City area were a little unusual but ate them one by one as she began skipping along. On tasting the first one, she thought, That's strange. These leave a peachy taste in my mouth. It was much stranger than she thought, for what she had eaten were not raspberries, but speedberries.

Consequently, it was not more than fifteen minutes before she could see the gleaming towers of the Emerald City ahead of her

Out loud she said, "Whoa! How'd that happen?" Then she thought *How'd I get here so fast? I still have a whole lot of hours before I can enter the City. What can I do in the meantime?*

Then, seeing a path a short distance ahead, she decided to explore. It wasn't long before the path ahead divided and without particularly thinking, she happened to take the right-hand path. As she skipped along, she noticed that each skip took her rapidly many yards ahead.

What in the world is happening, she thought. Then her mind went on to, *That explains how I got to the Emerald City so fast. But it doesn't explain what gave me all that speed!*

Thinking about that she continued on, slowing to a walk, but then she found that each step, just like

The Spelling Bee of Oz

skipping, moved her rapidly many yards ahead. She stopped again and looked around. Nothing else looked out of the ordinary. Everything around her was green. The birds seemed to be flying at normal speeds. A rabbit poked its head out of the bushes nearby and said, "Hi Dorothy. Larry Cary is no berry. What're you doin' way out here by yourself?"

Startled, although she knew that animals talked in Oz, it still seemed so unnatural to her. She looked at the rabbit again, started to say, I'm not Dorothy, but realized she was supposed to be playing a part and merely said, "Just out exploring a bit. What are you doing?"

"Me? I'm just one ornery scabbletozer out looking for some nutty, sumsuty ol'nuts. My name is Hop-a-bop."

"Looking for nuts!" exclaimed Zeebee. "I thought rabbits only ate stuff like lettuce and carrots and such."

The rabbit began to cry. As it wiped at its tears, it moaned, "Blozzy, blozzy, artfulgazmee. Will people ever learn that a rabbit can live his life the way he wants to?"

"Okay," laughed Zeebee, "I'm willing. So you like nuts. Good for you."

"Amazement! You really don't object to my fondness for nuts, then?"

"Not at all. So where do we find them?"

"Right on down this road. That's where I'm headed now."

"Me, too. Let's go."

So saying she started skipping again and Hop-a-bop started hopping, but immediately, he said, "Hey you guntflipper, wait for me."

Confusion

Sure enough, Zeebee's two skips had taken her nearly one hundred yards down the road. She turned and took one step back toward the rabbit and cut the distance nearly in half.

"How come you're moving so fast?" asked the rabbit.

"I don't know. It never happened before, but this afternoon I had just entered the eastern Emerald City area and knew I had several hours before I would reach the Emerald City, but in just a few minutes I was on that hill looking right at the City."

"Hmm. Did you eat some small red berries off a green bush?"

"Yes, I did, about six of them."

"And, b'goree, how long did it take you to get here?"

"About fifteen minutes."

"Well, slap me silly, that means you have about another fifteen minutes of high speed in you. What happened is that you ate a handful of speedberries. Swishy, swishy. Each one will give you five minutes of high speed and about another minute or so of slowing down. So I'll say goodbye to you now as you zip away." And he waved one paw to the fast disappearing Zeebee as she did just that.

Exhilarated by the unaccustomed feel of speed, Zeebee turned this way and that as she came to side paths. Her second fifteen minutes was almost up when she noticed that she was now surrounded by blue grass, gravel, flowers and trees. She paused for a moment in her steady rush and thought, Hmm, from what Korph said, I guess I'm now in the Munchkin Country, the land where Dorothy landed when she first arrived in Oz. And

The Spelling Bee of Oz

I'm almost out of my time for rapid speed. I'd better head back or I won't make it today.

Then she wondered, But which way?

The sun was to her back so she must be headed north. Turn around and she'd be going south. Neither would work because what she wanted was west. For what little time she had of high speed, she might as well continue in the direction she was going until she found a west bound path or someone who could give her directions. No sense in retracing her steps.

In a few minutes, she could feel herself slowing down and after a few more steps, she figured her speed was about normal. It was then that she was pleased to see a man approaching on the path ahead of her.

With her last rush of speed she hurried toward him and called out, "Oh. I'm so glad to see you. Can you tell me how to get to the Emerald City?"

He looked at her and shook his head. Then he touched his ears and his mouth and shook his head again.

Zeebee looked at him a moment, then asked, "Are you trying to tell me you can't speak or hear?"

He shrugged his shoulders and repeated his previous movements. Then he pointed at the girl, with his right index finger, then quickly, with the same hand, a beckoning motion. Then, looking her in the eyes, moved his fingers rapidly at each other as though they were talking to each other.

Nodding, Zeebee said, "You're deaf and mute and want me to talk to you with my hands." Then after a little thought, she muttered, "But then you can't hear what I

Confusion

just said, can you? Let's see," and she started using her hands to try to ask him which way to the Emerald City, but she could not make him understand. She tried again and again, but nothing seemed to work.

Finally she gave up, smiled at him, nodded and waved her hand as she proceeded on her way, still not knowing the way to her destination.

Before long she saw a woman approaching. Dressed in a long, flowing blue gown, she strode rapidly, appearing to have something important to do. Nonetheless, Zeebee took her courage in hand and said, "Can you help me?"

Without pausing, the blue clothed lady replied, "I don't have time for you my dear," and turning her head as she hurried on, she said, "Goodbye."

After a while, she met a man talking a stream of words. Surprised at seeing her, he stopped in the middle of a sentence to try to help her. However, before she could say anything, he said, "My goodness, little girl! What are you doing out in this wilderness by yourself? Obviously you must be lost and you have come to just the right person, for I am Abner Dustworthy from Rigmarole Town and if there is anything that we Rigmarolers can do, it is to answer a question. If only I knew where you wanted to go, I could help you. Well, maybe that is true and maybe it isn't, for it may be that you're looking for some place of which I know nothing. In that case I could be of little help. On the other hand you may be looking for someplace that doesn't even exist. Now that would be a tragedy, for then no one could show you the way. Now that is a big question: the existence of someplace that

The Spelling Bee of Oz

doesn't exist. Is that even possible? Some would say that it is because anything that it is possible to imagine has to exist someplace. Personally, I think that is a fatuous claim, for then, flying elephants would be …"

Finding it quite impossible to get anything out of him that might help, Zeebee continued on her way with his voice humming on. Before she had gone beyond range of hearing him, she saw a road sign pointing to her left toward a small town on a hill. The sign said, "Rigmarole Town," and she thought, *That's right. That was sure some rigmarole he was giving me!* Within a few more steps, his tiresome voice had faded beyond her hearing.

Zeebee thought to herself, *That round-about way of speaking reminds me of Mr. Cartier.* That was the Warrens' neighbor a couple miles down the road from their home in California. He was wealthy beyond anything the Warrens could even think of and he had an airplane. When he needed to go to town, he'd have his pilot fly him to the airport and then take a taxi into town where he would have the taxi wait on him as he met with someone, or made some deal and then take him back to the airport. What reminded her of him was that that was the long way around. The airport was way on the other side of town and it would have been quicker to have the chauffer drive him into town in his big Rolls-Royce.

In thinking of him, Zeebee remembered that her father had said, "He puts on airs. I've known him a long time, and as a child his last name was simply Carter."

Thinking of Carter/Cartier, another half-hour went

Confusion

by before she came across anyone else. This time it was a curiously dressed young woman. She seemed to have about equal parts of all five of the Ozian colors. As they approached, the other one waved her hand in a friendly way and said, "Hi there. Aren't you Dorothy?"

"Ah, yes, I am. And who do I have the pleasure of meeting?"

"My name is Dee, Dee Tortia."

"Well, I'm lost and would appreciate directions back to the Emerald City."

"It's quite easy. Just keep going the direction you are, and take the first branch to the right."

"But, wouldn't that take me further from the Emerald City. Isn't it to the west, that is, to the left from here."

"Quite right, but the branch to the left curves back and becomes a south bound path." Just a little sternly, she added, "Just do as I say. All these roads do so much curving that the right branch is the only one that will actually take you to the Emerald City."

"I don't know how I can thank you enough, for, left to my own resources, I certainly would have taken that first left-bound path."

As she headed on the curiously dressed young woman said, "Don't mention it. Always glad to help."

During the next couple hours, Zeebee saw no other people or animals with whom to check the directions. But at last, she saw a group of children, led by a brown-skinned girl of about her own age and a giant bee coming toward her. The size of the bee scared her half to death, and she turned and started to run, but the little brown-

The Spelling Bee of Oz

skinned girl ran forward and said, "Don't let the Spelling Bee scare you! He's really very nice."

At the same time the Bee was saying, "Why, Dorothy, why are you running from me. I'm just your old friend the Spelling Bee."

Zeebee stopped and, realizing that she must not give herself away, said, "I'm sorry. I guess I'm so tired, I wasn't thinking straight. All I could see was what looked like a big monster to me."

"I'm so sorry. Oh, indeed, Dorothy, I am sorry to have frightened you," said the Bee. "Do forgive me."

"Oh!" said the girl next to the Bee. "Excuse me. I haven't introduced myself. You already know the Spelling Bee," and then bowing slightly, "and I am Amal."

Zeebee giggled softly and then said, "My nickname is Zeebee, so, I guess the three of us are quite a trio."

"Why so?" asked Amal.

"You're M-L and I'm called 'Zeebee,' and here" she waved her arm towards the Spelling Bee, "is 'zee Bee.'"

Some of the other children laughed at that, but Amal was puzzled as she merely said, "Hmm?" and then said, "I get Zeebee, but why do you say it twice and where do I fit in?"

"Z-B and M-L," said Zeebee.

Amal shook her head and just looked puzzled.

By this time, Zeebee was realizing that she may have made a mistake in even mentioning her nick-name. After all, that was from her real life, not from Dorothy's life.

However, the great Bee was already saying, "I believe my specialty is required here." As both girls looked at

Confusion

"... so, I guess the three of us are quite a trio."

him in puzzlement, he continued, "I am a speller and the problem here is spelling. I don't believe that you," and he turned toward Zeebee, "understand that this girl's name," and he turned toward Amal, "is spelled A-M-A-L. However, it is pronounced as though one was simply spelling out 'M-L' in English."

Zeebee nodded slowly and then gasped and put her hand over her mouth to stop another giggle, and the Bee turned to Amal and said, "Whereas, you, my dear friend, spelling everything in the Arabic script, do not realize that your name is pronounced just like the two English letters 'M' and 'L.'"

Amal stood there for a moment, scratching her head

125

The Spelling Bee of Oz

and furrowing her brow. Then she, too, laughed and said, "Oh! I get it," and looking at Zeebee, said, "So from your point of view, it is 'M-L' and 'Z-B.' But still, why did you say 'Z-B' twice?"

Raising her hand quickly, Zeebee said, "My turn. When the French try to speak English, they frequently pronounce 'the' as 'zee.' So we, in jest, sometimes will say 'zee' when we mean 'the.' Thus," motioning toward the Bee, "he is 'zee bee.' Get it?"

Amal now began to laugh lightly. "Yes, I get it. It is funny," and she laughed a little more, which made Zeebee and the Bee laugh all the more and all the other children, as well.

Soon people were crying from laughing so hard. Then the laughing died down and one of the children who had been laughing the hardest said, "What were we all laughing about?"

One of the other children explained and the first one said, "Well, I don't see that that is all that funny," but then he giggled, the one next to him giggled and then they both laughed and soon everyone was laughing again.

After they had all quieted down once more and resumed walking for a while, Amal asked Zeebee, "So why do they call you 'Zeebee?'"

Zeebee, still afraid to admit that she was not Dorothy, explained about her brother as though he was Dorothy's brother and how the nickname 'Z-B' stuck to her. Then she stretched out her arms and started running around. Amal and all the others joined in. Everyone was running around and going, "Z-z-z-z," and laughing their heads off

Confusion

again until they all began sitting down, panting and out of breath.

That lasted for a few minutes with the Spelling Bee well entertained by it all. The children were beginning to tire, but some of the boys found water and everybody had a good drink.

The Spelling Bee tapped Zeebee on the arm and said, "But, Dorothy, ahem, I've never heard you tell about your nickname before. And, my now, what's this about, ahem, a brother? I thought you were living with your Uncle and Aunt, yes, your Uncle and Aunt in Kansas."

Thinking fast, she replied, making up a family history on the spot, "Yes, of course I was, but that was afterwards, after all the rest of my family died in the epidemic."

The Bee, fidgeted and brushed his face with his hands while saying, "I'm so sorry. My, oh my, I didn't realize. Goodness gracious, dear child, how hard on you that was."

Zeebee hung her head, actually for being ashamed of the lies she was telling, but pretending it was because she was thinking of the death of her family, and said, "That's all right. That was many years ago." Then wanting to change the subject, she said, "But, I really have to be getting on to the Emerald City. I may already be a little late. I got lost until I met up with Miss Tortia, and she headed me in the right direction, but it seems to be taking an awful long time."

"Miss Tortia?" asked the Spelling Bee. "Dee Tortia?"

"Yes. That was her name. Why? Do you know her?"

The Spelling Bee of Oz

"Know her? Indeedy deed, I do. Her name should give you a clue. Dee Tortia. Ha, ha ha! She distorts everything she says. You cannot trust a word that comes out of her mouth."

"Oh my!" And Zeebee suddenly sat down on the ground, wringing her hands and looking up at the Bee, she asked, "Did she send me on a wild goose chase?"

"To say the least. That's probably why, looking for the Emerald City, you were taking the road away from it. But, I would have thought that you would have known where to find the Emerald City on your own."

"Normally, yes, but actually, I've never been in this particular part of the Munchkin Country before." Then, shaking her head even as it rested in her hands, Zeebee exclaimed, "Oh! What a mess I'm making of everything." Then looking up at the Bee again, she asked, "Can you help me?"

"Oh, deedy dee, of course I can. It just happens that the Emerald City is where we're headed."

Jumping up, Zeebee said, "So let's get going," and she started walking again. Amal fell into step beside her and the Spelling Bee.

Pretty soon, Zeebee asked, "Then, are you friends of the people in the Emerald City?"

"Yes. That we are, or, that is, I am, anyway," replied the Bee. "I'm taking young Amal here to see Ozma so our Princess can send Amal back to her home in Somalia."

"And you think she's likely to do that?"

"Of course she will! She is always helpful in any way she can be."

Confusion

This did not sound much like what Korph had told her, so she wondered, Which one is telling me the truth?

Wanting to stop thinking about that, she said, "But are you sure you know the way?"

The Bee responded, "After all, I am a bee. If I know where I started and where I'm going, I can find my way, easily."

"Is that true of all bees?" asked Amal.

"Oh, indeedey deed it is. 'Tis in the nature of bees," he answered.

"But," said Zeebee, "how did you get to be so big? How is it that you can spell just any word at all? Can you really perform all kinds of magical spells?"

"Yes," added Amal, "you started to tell me way back before we met Dorothy, but then the Invisible Children interrupted you. Please! Now, tell us all about it."

"My, oh my, but you are full of questions," he replied. "Let me see. Let me see, can I answer most of those for you? I'll try. Dear me, yes. I'll try"

Chapter 14

The Genesis of a Remarkable Bee

Back in 1461 O. Z. a remarkable bee was born in the far eastern part of the Munchkin Country, not far from the Deadly Desert. There was nothing remarkable about this hive. There was nothing remarkable about the bees in this hive. There was nothing remarkable about this bee when he was first born. He was named Buzzby and grew as other bees, educated in the same way by the same teachers. He ate the same food as the rest, but somehow along the line, some special enzyme crept into his diet and, instead of becoming a drone like all other males, he became a speller.

Like all males, he had nothing to do until he grew to maturity. And, of course, as a male, he had no stinger. Stinging was the duty of worker bees, who were female, or the queen of the hive. Also, as a male, if he had lived outside of the Ozerian planet, he would not have lived as long as a year. But, living in Oz, he was covered by the same magical charm that covered the humans. That is, barring some great catastrophe, like being stepped on and squashed, he would never die.

At first, all was normalcy for him. Then when he

The Genesis of a Remarkable Bee

came to his first reading lesson, it started. Immediately he could spell and pronounce every word that came up and not only that, but he also could give a concise definition. The first one was "Bee." Immediately, he said, "Bee, b-e-e, bee. That's me, a honey-making insect. That is a noun, but as a verb, it is b-e and means the state of existing."

Next came "Fly." He said, "Fly, f-l-y, fly. To move through air. Now that is as a verb. As a noun, it is spelled the same way and is a small winged insect."

And so it went with every new word. Sometimes he seemed to know the spelling and meaning of words he had never seen nor heard of before. Soon, everyone began calling him the Spelling Bee or Speller. And within a few years his original name had been entirely forgotten by all.

The bees of his hive were proud of the Speller. Yes, he was different from other bees, but he was also something very special. They showed him off to anyone who came by. Of course, everyone was a little afraid of bees, so this did not mean that a great number of people and other animals found out about his unusual ability.

Later, one other thing happened to make the Spelling Bee into the Spelling Bee we know today.

It actually started eighty-eight years before the Spelling Bee was born. Four Wicked Witches came to the Royal Palace of Winderhime that stood at the heart of Oz. They had recently stolen away the King, Oz VI. Since all the fairy rulers of Oz were named either Oz or, if a woman, Ozma, the disappearance of the one king

The Spelling Bee of Oz

left his son as the ruler, Oz VII.

It was this Oz that was in the throne room of the old Palace of Winderhime when the Four Wicked Witches invaded and destroyed first him and then the great Wizard Wam.

Technically, this made his younger brother, Pastoria, the King, but before anything could be done about declaring him to be the new king, the Witches had taken control. They immediately proceeded to make life miserable for anyone who displeased them. They took turns, a month at a time, in occupying the Royal Palace of Winderhime, but each of them mainly worked at keeping her own area subjugated to her own absolute rule.

However, in less than a year, Glinda, the Good Witch, met Dizateroo, the Wicked Witch of the South, in a fateful confrontation. In the course of it, Dizateroo attempted to hit Glinda with her Power of Destruction. But Glinda, using a magical cape provided for her by the fairies, succeeded in turning that destructive power back against the Wicked Witch, thus putting an end to the most powerful of the Four Wicked Witches.

This alerted the three remaining Wicked Witches to the fact that Glinda was the chief danger to their wicked rule. It took them awhile to concentrate their thinking, but before the passage of another year, they began developing plans to attack Glinda and conquer her.

Gingema, the Wicked Witch of the East, thought that making use of gigantic animals might help. If they stationed abnormally large and fierce animals between

The Genesis of a Remarkable Bee

themselves and Glinda, they could both protect the Wicked Witches and attack the Good one. So she began working on a spell to do just that and soon was ready to try it out.

She began by trying to create new creatures by combining the forms of a couple different kinds of animals. Her first attempt was in combining a hippopotamus and a giraffe. However, her Hip-po-gy-raf turned out to be a failure since its great hunger was for straw, and that was a threat only to farmers.

Her next attempt was more successful. This time, she tried to combine a tiger and a bear. The result was the savage Kalidah. A number of them still persist as a danger to travelers in the Great Munchkin Forest, and sometimes wander out of it to threaten others.

After that success, Gingema decided it was time to try gigantesizing animals. Her first attempt was on a mouse she found in her house. It just fell over dead. So she went back to work on her spell until she thought she had developed what she needed.

When she tried that on a second mouse, it tripled in size for a few minutes, then shrank down to nothing. Again she went back to work. This time it was a rabbit and it quadrupled in size and stayed that way – for a while, at least. But five minutes later, with the rabbit frantically hopping around, wondering what had happened, it shrank back to its normal self, and made a dash for its hole.

However, the giant spider that Gingema created on the morning that Dorothy's house crushed her was much

The Spelling Bee of Oz

more successful. She had sent it off to destroy the animal army that was defending Glinda's northern frontier and it might have succeeded if the Cowardly Lion had not decapitated it. But that came after the day that all Oz celebrates, the day Dorothy arrived, June 22, 1493 O. Z.

However, it is the day before the big celebration day that the Spelling Bee remembers best. It was late that afternoon that he had wandered far and was buzzing around in the heart of the Munchkin Country, looking for good nectar-filled flowers. And that was the day that Gingema finally succeeded with her gigantism spell.

In the back of a poorly kept house, the Bee found a great growth of blue nasturtiums that he busied himself in for a few minutes. Then he heard a voice saying, "Come here, little bee. I have a gift for you."

Not knowing who was speaking, and with his curiosity piqued, he tipped his wings in just the right way to turn him to face the voice. He saw an old and wrinkled woman in a gray dress with silver-colored shoes and black and white stripped socks.

Gingema, the Wicked One, he thought. *I've got to get out of here.*

But before he could even get started, he could already hear her beginning a chant.

He sped away at top speed, which he could only sustain for a few moments. By the time he had covered a hundred yards, he had to slow down and could still hear her chanting away. *What's going to happen if I don't get away?*

Another twenty yards and he knew. He was suddenly

The Genesis of a Remarkable Bee

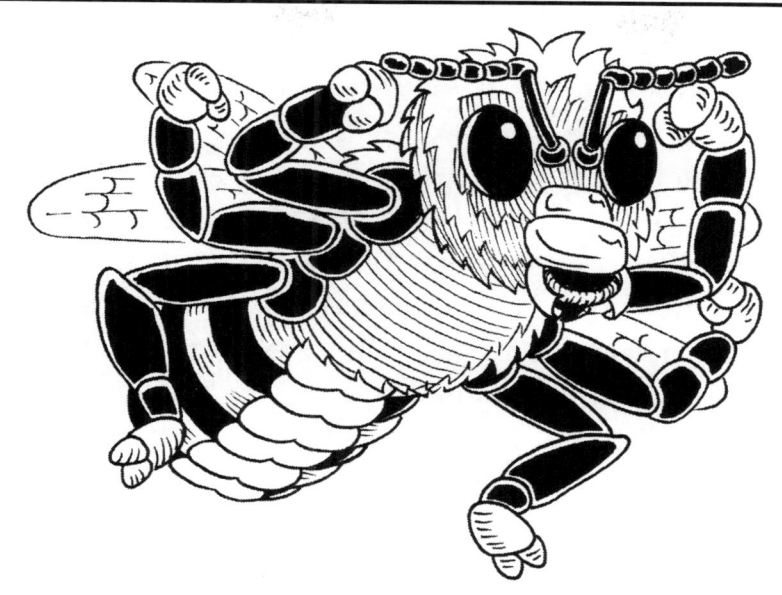

He was suddenly . . . a three-foot-long bee!

nearly one hundred times his normal size – a three-foot-long bee!

Behind him, he could hear the Wicked Witch yelling, "Come back here! Come back! I need you! Oh, please, big bee. You can help me conquer that terrible Glinda!"

That only made him fly the faster until he could no longer hear her outcries. Then, realizing he was running out of energy, he slowed. He would have to find some nourishment fast. Fortunately, a large meadow was just ahead. But as he started to settle toward the many flowers it contained, a desperate thought assailed his mind: *With my new size, will my proboscis still be small enough to insert into the throat of the flowers?*

It was a strange sensation, now. He no longer had to flutter his wings to stay stationary high in the air in front

The Spelling Bee of Oz

of a flower. He could simply stand or sit upon the ground, lean over and, now, he tried to put his proboscis into the nearest flower. He extended it tremblingly. He had real difficulty getting into the first flower that he chose. But then he thought, I'm shaking. Maybe if I can be more steady, and he took a deep breath and then, slowly and carefully tried again. He was steadier this time and found that when he wasn't shaking, his proboscis went in just as easily as ever. The very tip of it was still as small as it needed to be, but along the new long course of it, it grew wider and wider to fit his new large size.

He drank his fill of nectar in that field, taking of course, far more than he did as a little bee. At last, his thirst was satisfied, but while he drank the nectar, he had been thinking. He decided that it would be best if he did not go back to his hive. In fact, he had probably better stay away from everyone as much as possible. His great size would seem a deadly threat to others and make him a social outcast amongst bees and all insects. Somehow, he had to find the means of shrinking back to a normal bee size.

Finished with his feeding, the Bee began to lift off, but realized that the sun was touching the horizon and he had best find a place to sleep for the night. No hive would fit him now, so he went toward a group of three great blue oaks. Near the middle of the largest one, he found a convenient roost where three branches came together at the trunk.

There he settled down for the night, and slept soundly until morning. He woke up and stretched his

The Genesis of a Remarkable Bee

wings and arms and legs, then started off to find a large patch of flowers in the meadow a little further south. While sipping, he thought, If Gingema wants me to help her defeat Glinda, she will probably be looking for me. I'd better get out of her territory. Since she had never subjugated the south part of Munchkinland he thought that would be the best place for him to go, and so south he went, following a major north-south road.

He was approaching the eastern extension of the Yellow Brick Road when he heard a raucous crowd coming along it from the west. A farmhouse stood at the intersection of the two roads and the crowd paused as one of their number approached the house calling out, "Halloo, Rothene! Come out and join us! We are carrying the news across the country. The Wicked Witch is dead. The mighty sorceress, Dorothy, dropped a house upon her this morning and the evil old hag was crushed and turned to dust!"

By this time a chubby woman, dressed in blue like all the others, had come to the doorway and was now practically bouncing out to join the celebrators. As they all went on down the road, the Spelling Bee thought Gingema dead! She put this terrible bigness spell upon me. Maybe there's something in her cottage that will remove it. I've got to get there as fast as I can and start searching, and off he flew to the west, going at his top sustainable speed.

When he reached her house, he found a crowd of people gathered around. Some were near the witch's house, but most were on the other side of the Yellow

The Spelling Bee of Oz

Brick Road, around a slightly out-of-line and badly weathered house. He could hear some voices talking about that house killing old Gingema and how Dorothy was now following the Yellow Brick Road to find the Wizard.

This was too many people, so he settled down behind a group of trees off to the side of the house and waited. Night came and the people made bonfires and continued their celebrating. He moved up into one of the trees where he would be out of sight and went to sleep. In the early hours of the morning, the stillness must have awakened him, for all was quiet. At first he just sat there in the tree trying to go back to sleep, then he thought, Maybe as the morning goes along the people will gather again. I'd better go in there now.

So in he went. He dared not turn on any lights for fear of attracting some of the people who would wonder why there was light in the witch's house. He could see well enough to rummage around a bit. He could locate certain things, places where the old witch had kept clothing, dishes, food, decorations and other non-magical equipment. The house was fairly well kept, but there were dirty dishes in the sink. In the process of exploration, he also noted where he found the things that might be magical potions, instruments or recipes as well as books and papers with formulations for spells written in them. He was very thorough, so that by the time daylight was beginning to show in the east, he had searched only about one-third of the house. But with broad daylight, people began to show up again, so he

The Genesis of a Remarkable Bee

retreated to his tree.

Having been awake a large part of the night, it was easy for him to sleep for much of the day. It was late afternoon by the time everyone had left. Now it would be safe for him to return to the old witch's house.

Thus, he spent the next several weeks combing what had once been the abode of one of the most powerful witches in the land. Someplace in here he might find the means of making him small again. There was plenty of just ordinary things – chairs, tables, a bed, dishes, flatwear and pans for eating, clothing and all such. These he passed over quite quickly. His main interest was written material that would give him a shrinking charm, but he also inspected all labels on bottles, boxes and vials, in case shrinking was accomplished by powders and liquids.

Early in his search, he ran across a little tablet of paper with various things written on it. A few were some recipes for magical potions or the words and motions needed for this or that spell, most were things to do that had been crossed out. Some were not crossed out, like, "June 23 – Up early – search for true shimeji mushrooms in meadow by creek beyond Yellow Brick Road. Don't fail!!!"

He hummed a bit and went to the window where he could see Dorothy's House sitting in the meadow as he thought, *Meadow by creek beyond Yellow Brick Road? That is where the house fell on her. Boy! Just her bad luck that she didn't fail to go over there!*

Among the spells was one entitled, "For Lighting."

The Spelling Bee of Oz

Curious, he thought, but he had better not try anything that he was not certain that he really wanted to. This discovery prompted him to start a stack of things he wanted to save. The first thing in that stack was that little tablet. As his search continued, the stack grew.

On the second day, he came across a paper with the notation, "To cancel any spell" with the necessary words and motions entered beneath it. He started to toss it on the pile, but stopped himself: This might be a time to try that Lighting Spell. So he started looking for that first little tablet he had found, but in the process, he realized, I don't need the tablet. I can remember the spell all right, and he gestured toward a bookcase as he recited:

"Ramble kabamble, hosh melalee.
Fido, fa faddo, fell and beetauw.
Light may it be,
And light it is now."

Instantly, the bookcase glowed with a light strong enough to illuminate the entire room.

The Spelling Bee rose from the floor and buzzed merrily around the room, saying, "I did it! I did it! I'm a Spelling Bee! A Spelling Bee!" And he was laughing all the time.

Chapter 15

Spellings

After three circuits of the room, the Bee settled down upon the floor, thinking that he should cancel the spell. But, at the same time, he thought Ummhm. This is fun. I think I'll try some other spells. But he delayed while he looked around at the now brilliantly illuminated room.

Finally he decided to look up some other spells and soon came across a pair for Self-Washing Dishes. One of them was labeled "Initiating," the other "Continuation." The Initiating spell was long and complicated, but the Continuation spell was brief and simple.

Certainly, he thought, that old witch has already made it easy on herself and all I need this time is the Continuation Spell. These dishes probably know what to do, all right.

So he stretched out one hand, pointed it at the sink full of dishes and said, "Commence!" Immediately, the dishes sprouted little arms and hands and legs.

One of them, toward the bottom of the stack, put the stopper in place in the sink.

A couple others stood on top of each other and

The Spelling Bee of Oz

turned on the water.

A big pan scrambled down into the cupboard under the sink and soon came back up lugging the soap, which it squirted under the flowing stream of water. Then it took the bottle back below and returned to hop into the sink with the others.

As the suds built up, dishes, cups, glasses, pans and flatware began scrubbing themselves and each other. The two that had turned the water on, now turned it off and began their own scrubbing. Before long, job completed, each brightly shining dish, pan or utensil clambered up onto the drain board and placed itself in perfect order in the draining rack with all the rest.

All the time the Bee hovered, watching in amazement as the job was quickly, thoroughly and professionally done. Humming his approval, he then returned to the various spells to see which other ones to try.

He found a Spell to Activate the Immobile, and thought, I think I'll try this on the chair over there. So he did. He then watched the chair for a moment. It didn't move, so he thought, I guess that's not what it does. Then, just as he started looking for a different spell, the top of the chair bent over, and it started dancing around the room. Although he could see no eyes on it, it seemed to be quite able to avoid all obstacles.

After a few minutes, the Bee said, "Ahem! You can stop now." That made no difference. The chair continued dancing.

He seems to be able to see without eyes, but maybe he can't hear without ears.

Spellings

So the Spelling Bee yelled at the chair, "Stop that dancing around, right now!"

The chair kept right on dancing.

I guess I won't use that spell again until I find one for managing those newly given mobility, but I'll bet that Dis-Spell I saw would do the trick, and he thought for just a brief moment, then started waving his arms in a mystical way while he chanted:

"Away and gone, the spell is wrong.
Let what's been done be now undone."

And the chair stopped dead still right where it was.

"That's better," said the Bee and then he thought, What's next?

Glancing over spells, he saw one for making things immobile and thought, Ha, I should have had that earlier, but I'll remember it now.

A little further on, he spotted a Chicken Soup Spell. Apparently, you could use it to make chicken soup out of anything. Aloud, he said, "I think I'll try that." The instructions were carefully laid out:

1. Pick out something from which you want to make chicken soup.
2. From here on we will call the "something" the "object."
3. Put object in a container.
3. Be sure container is bigger than the object, or you'll have soup all over the floor (or ground or wherever you

The Spelling Bee of Oz

are).

4. If you want it hot, build a fire; if not, you don't have to build a fire.

5. Put left hand on top of your head

6. Point at object with right hand

7. Stamp your right foot.

8. Keep on stamping your right foot.

9. As you circle the object and container counter-clockwise.

10. But wait! Don't start circling until you are also saying "Oona booma kroona, chicken *dit*!" as you do so.

11. Emphasize the "*dit*" each time you come down with your right foot.

12. Do a complete circle, saying "Oona booma kroona chicken *dit*!" six times in the process.

13. When you have completed the circle, you can stop walking.

14. You can also stop stamping.

15. You can also stop chanting.

16. If all of the object has turned into chicken soup, you're done.

17. For that matter if it has not all turned into soup, you're done. You'll just have to wait a little longer. It will all become soup eventually.

18. Now you're ready to eat. Cold or hot? It's your choice.

Carefully, he went through each step. Surprisingly, it was quite simple and did not take as long to do it as it took to read about doing it. When it was all done, he stuck his

Spellings

proboscis into the cold soup, and since anything other than nectar was a new experience for him, he tried to judge the taste in an unprejudiced way. The result was that he thought it really was pretty good, but probably better if heated.

Now to heat it. He remembered noticing a spell for starting a fire, so he went to his stack of papers and fingered through them until he found the spell he was after. He read it once and then, pointing at the logs in the fireplace, he performed it. A nice blaze flared up and he hung the soup pot on the hook that could swing over the fire.

In a few minutes the soup was hot and he dished himself up a helping of fragrant soup with a number of unexpected vegetables in it. Of course, he had no teeth with which to chew on vegetables, so he avoided them, since they could well stop up the flow through his proboscis.

Yes, he thought, t*his has an interesting flavor. I miss the sweetness of nectar, but I think I could learn to like other foods. Maybe not as well, but interesting has something to offer.*

Then as he sipped at the soup he began thinking about what had happened. Spelling. Spelling. Two different things, but there were similarities. Spell a word. Cast a spell on a thing. Instantly, remember any word, to spell it. Instantly remember any spell to perform it. Apparently my spelling skill has two facets to it. How interesting!

His reveries were interrupted by a harsh voice in the

The Spelling Bee of Oz

doorway demanding, "What are you doing here?"

The Spelling Bee twirled around, fully expecting to see the revived wicked witch framed in the doorway, but was surprised to see a wiry and not very big man standing there with his arms akimbo.

So surprised was he that he answered a question with a question: "Who are you?"

"I am the Good Witch Gingema's assistant. My name is Urfin Djus, and I repeat, 'What are you doing here?'"

The Bee thought it best to ignore his appellation of the witch as "Good," and simply answered, "Gingema made me big like this, but was killed before she could return me to my normal state, so I have been looking for a spell to make me small again."

"Go ahead and look," growled Urfin Djus as he strode over to the fireplace and picked up the heavy poker. "Just don't look in Gingema's house. Go someplace else, and I mean now!" His voice lowered in pitch and rose in volume as he spoke.

The Bee started to try a magical spell, but realized that before he could complete one, the man could be flailing at him with that big poker in a most deadly way. So instead of doing anything at that moment, he tilted his head and said, "Just let me pick up the papers I have already gathered."

The man jumped toward him, swinging the big poker around his head and crying out, "No! Don't touch those. Leave here now."

In response, the Spelling Bee quickly rose into the air and flew out the door and around the corner, to a place

Spellings

about twenty feet from the house where he could see Urfin Djus through the window. The man was standing, hands on hips, looking at the stack of papers that the Bee had gathered. As he picked one up, the Spelling Bee held out his two top hands and started moving them forward and back, pointing toward Urfin Djus chanting just loud enough to be heard outside, but not inside, "Sleep, sleep, sleep …"

After the fourth repetition, the man suddenly collapsed onto the stack of papers. Satisfied, the Bee flew back into the house and continued his searching. By the end of the day he was done. He gathered up all his papers and left the house. But, just before he left, he turned to the immobile Urfin Djus, waved his arms in the necessary way and chanted:

"Away and gone, the spell is wrong.
Let what's been done be now undone."

Then he closed the door and started flying west, leaving the now awakening man wondering what had happened.

Chapter 16

In Search of a Spell

The Spelling Bee flew over roads, towns, forests, fields and prairies. He spent the rest of the day examining every likely place he found, looking at large trees, dark forests, isolated hillsides and an occasional deserted building. He paused in his search only twice in the day, each time stopping long enough to fill himself with the nectar of flowers he found in out-of-the-way meadows. Then he was on his way again, continuing until late in the afternoon.

At that point he decided to return to a deep and dark forest where he had seen a hill with a small cliff on one side of it. Swooping close, he had found a small cave high on its face. Hovering before it he could see that it might make a safe retreat for him. Now he returned to it and found that it was certainly large enough for the needs of a three-foot-bee and it was dry.

The next morning, after filling himself with the nectars of a field of flowers above the cave, he decided to work on the Chicken Soup Spell. The vegetables in it had been wasted so he thought there might be some way to eliminate them from the process. So this time when he

In Search of a Spell

made it, his chant went, "Oona booma kroona chicken broth dit!"

After he had finished the circling and stomping and chanting, he waited expectantly. Sure enough, when he was finished, he had an excellently flavored broth with no extra materials in it at all.

He spent the next few hours reading over the various spells that he had collected. Actually, he marveled at the fact that it only took one reading for him to have mastered each spell.

The next day he decided to try some other uses of the Chicken Soup Spell. The first thing he did was to try substituting beef broth for chicken. That worked deliciously. Then he tried cream of tomato. *The next time*, he thought, *let's go wild*, and he tried a flavor he had heard people praise - peanut butter. Again, it was a very interesting taste, not at all familiar to him.

During the next few days, he decided to try some of the more innocuous spells on various rocks, trees and bushes. He became quite adept at changing one to the other, to making them jump around, to set them on fire (even rocks), to make them sing or talk, to giving them arms and legs and giving them many other magical experiences.

The only thing he did with sentient creatures was to temporarily change their colors or put fur on birds, or feathers on mice and other magic that would cause no harm to the recipient, but he always, then, removed those spells.

He was always aware of the problem he was having

The Spelling Bee of Oz

with being made permanently large without his consent. In the back of his mind, and sometimes in the forefront, he was thinking about finding a Get Small spell.

Otherwise, his days were filled with experimentation, food hunting and relaxation. That is until he thought of Dizateroo, the Wicked Witch of the South who had been destroyed and whose castle might hold other spells he could use. Especially he hoped that Dizateroo's store might include one to make something be smaller.

So he headed to the southwest. When he reached the Quadling Country, he started looking around for someone to give him directions. He did not want to scare anyone, but, on the other hand, he had no idea where the Wicked Witch's castle had been. He had to talk to someone.

After by-passing a couple towns and many farmhouses, he finally decided he could delay no longer and slowed down as he neared a particular town. There was no one on the road, so he settled down to the ground and walked when he was only about four hundred yards from the first house.

Just beyond that house, he saw his first person. He slowed down even more. Then, bowing as he approached her, he said, "Dear lady, I am perplexed. Ahem. That is, I need directions."

The lady, dressed in a long red dress and bonnet, not an unusual sight in a Quadling town, stepped back a bit. She looked at the Bee and said, "You seem to be a little larger than most bees I've seen."

"Ah, yes. Yes, I am, and that is the problem. I would

In Search of a Spell

like to resume my normal, that is, yes, my normal size."

She replied, "I'm afraid I can't be of much help in that. Neither I nor anyone else in this town knows anything about magic."

Quickly, the big Bee responded, "No matter. That's not what I need right now. I want directions to Dizateroo's old castle."

"What in the world for?"

"She was a most powerful witch, and in her personal effects there might be a means of undoing this terrible charm that has been put on me."

"Ah, yes. That makes sense. No problem, then. Just do not continue on your present route. If you do, you'll end up at the Mountain of the Hammerheads, and they won't let you go beyond them. Instead, you'll have to fly over the thick forest you see to the south of us," and she pointed in that direction.

"And what do I do when I get there?"

"Go clear past the Hammerhead Mountains and to the west of them you'll see a little stream leaving them. It will grow as other tributaries join it and eventually wind its way into the Winkie Country. But you don't go that far. A few miles after it leaves the Hammerhead Mountains, you will see an old gray castle standing on a cliff overlooking the stream. That is it."

So the Spelling Bee set off and at last came to that old castle. Instead of the isolated and deserted ruin he expected to find, here was a bustling community living within its walls and flowing on beyond them. As he stepped through the gates of the old castle, he was

The Spelling Bee of Oz

surprised to find that it had been cleaned up, repaired and divided into comfortable apartments. These were occupied by the lonely from all over Oz. Colors of all kinds were everywhere.

He stopped to look around for a while. He could see that the town that surrounded the castle was mostly occupied by local Quadlings, families serving the needs of the castle. Many of the castle's occupants were elderly people, beyond the age of doing much constructive work, but still able to give advice and to train the younger ones in the various arts and crafts that support a society. Others of them were younger and for one reason or another, left alone in life. They willingly contributed their part to the various jobs needed to sustain the social fiber of castle and town.

After a little study of his surroundings, the Bee approached the nearest person. To his surprise, this stalwart man did not recoil upon being confronted by an outsized bee, so he went ahead and told the man that he was looking for the effects of the Wicked Witch who had once lived here.

"I wouldn't know anything about that," replied the man. "You'd better talk to Yarna. He's the Chairman of our House and can be found in the room to the left of the entrance gate."

The Bee thanked him and went to the room he had indicated. A large man, both in girth and height was busy looking over some maps on a high table, and the Bee asked, "Are you Mr. Yarna?"

Startled by the voice, the man jerked around, saying,

In Search of a Spell

"Yes, I am Yarna," only to be startled again as he faced such a large bee.

To forestall any problems, the Bee said, "Sorry to frighten you. I guess a bee of my size is a bit daunting."

"Not so much that, as just surprising," and coming out from behind his desk, he said, "What may I do for you?"

"A lot, I hope, although it is only one thing. I am the Spelling Bee and it is not actually natural for me to be such a big and scary bee. It is my hope that in the files of old Dizateroo I might find some antidote for this condition with which Gingema cursed me."

The man answered, "In the first place, I don't think you need to worry. You are more interesting than scary. Seems to me a bee can be any size it wishes."

"Thank you, but what I wish is to be a normal bee."

"Okay then. The second thing is that I would have no idea where any of her papers are."

The dejected look on the face of the Bee, prompted him to add, "But I could take you to see Kladaborn. Come, let us go." And he led the way out the door and up a single flight of stairs.

As they went, the Bee said, "Why Kladaborn? Who is he?"

"He was the first person who started using this old castle as a home and dividing it into apartments for others."

The man paused at the first door he came to and knocked on it. There was the sound of footsteps slowly approaching the door and it was opened to reveal a

The Spelling Bee of Oz

man, elderly, but vigorous, tall and wiry. Standing back, and opening the door wider, he said, "Welcome, friend Yarna. You bring an interesting visitor."

As they stepped through the door, Yarna, speaking to each in turn, said, "This is the Spelling Bee and this is Kladaborn." To the last, he said, "It may be that you can help him."

The Spelling Bee explained his need to the old man, who replied, "An interesting request. Your size is obvious, but your need for concern is less obvious. However, the fact is that I have never seen any magical implement or books around here. They were all gone before I arrived."

In response to the great disappointment that showed in the Bee's many-faceted eyes, Kladaborn put his arm across the Bee's shoulder and said, "I know that must be a great disappointment to you, but let us sit down and see if we can think what to do next. I'll go out and get some cookies and Ozade for all of us."

He headed for the kitchen and then turned back, saying, "Oh, Mr. Bee, you probably do not eat cookies. Would some honey do?"

"Would honey do? Would honey! My goodness, yes. I haven't had any honey since I left the hive. Oh, would honey do!"

Stifling a laugh, the host went on into the kitchen and was soon back with a plate full of cookies, three glasses of Ozade and a bowl of honey.

Again the Bee expressed his thanks as he put his proboscis into the honey and the others started on the cookies and Ozade.

In Search of a Spell

Within a few minutes, Yarna said, "As I understand it Mr. Bee ..."

The Spelling Bee interrupted, "Oh please, just call me 'Speller.'"

"All right then, Speller, as I understand it you are seeking for a means of dispelling the Spell of Gigantism that has been ..."

Suddenly, the Spelling Bee dropped his honey dish, looked at Kladaborn and shouted, "Dis-spell! Why have I not thought of that before? Of course. I'll do it now."

The other two looked with surprise at this sudden outburst, but the Bee proceeded:

"Away and gone, the spell is wrong.
Let what's been done be now undone."

And then there was no bee at all. Or rather, so it seemed to the two men until the now very high pitched voice of the Bee could be heard saying, "It worked! It worked! I'm a normal bee again." Then they saw the little bee, zooming around, doing circles in the air.

When finally he settled down on the table where the food had been placed, he looked at Kladaborn and said, "Oh my friend, I don't know how to thank you. What you have done for me is beyond imagination. Thank you! Thank you, thank you."

"Thank you for your thank yous, but I don't know just what I did."

"You spoke of dispelling, which made me think of the Dis-Spell, which will reverse any spell in all the

The Spelling Bee of Oz

world. Oh, woe is me, I cannot understand why I did not think of it before." And with a little bow, he added, "And I thank you again, oh dear friend."

The three continued with their conversations, although, to tell the truth, it was mostly the two men who were conversing with one another. Because he was so small, the Bee was not often addressed.

Finally, the Spelling Bee bade farewell to his two new friends, having decided that, now that he was a normal sized bee, he ought to head back to his home hive. That night, he slept in the protected crotch of a big red tree.

His trip this time was slower, for he had only about one-thirtieth of the power he had had when he was so big. Over the next three days, as he made his way to his old hive, he had much time for thought. He had noticed that people were impressed with his size when he was big, but not as afraid of him as he had expected. He remembered the feeling of bigness, that it was a good feeling. Especially, now as he remembered how much faster he could travel, covering more ground than he could as a normal bee. *Maybe I should return to my large size*, he thought. *But no. I will at least wait until I have returned to my home hive.*

So it was that on the fourth day, in the evening, he arrived at his old home in the eastern part of the Winkie Country. Those that he had been closest to wanted to know where he had been, but most of the hive had not even known he was missing. That was a bit disappointing. When he told about what had happened to him, many, even those he had not previously really known, wanted

In Search of a Spell

to know what it was like to be so big.

As he told them, he realized, *I could make any one of them, or all of them, big like I was, but I think it would be better if it is only I who return to my larger size.*

So, after a while he announced, "Since so many of you wonder about me as a large bee, let's go outside and I will restore myself to that size."

To his surprise, virtually the whole hive swarmed out. One of his old friends said, "But how can you restore that size. You are no wizard, are you?

"No, not a wizard, but, as you well know, I am a Spelling Bee, and apparently that includes the casting of spells."

His friend, and all those who were nearby, exclaimed at that.

Once all were gathered outside, the Spelling Bee stepped well away from them, and as many tried to follow him, he said, "No, you need to keep a good distance from me so that my sudden expansion does not harm you." Then, exaggerating the required motions for the fullest dramatic effect, he recited the words and motions he had found recorded in one of Gingema's books, the very words he had heard her pronounce:

> O, aim of my art,
> Make like a dart.
> Little though I be
> Big now make me.
> Big.

The Spelling Bee of Oz

Bigger.
Bigger!

And throughout the chant, he was growing until with the last flourish of his arms, he was finally, just as big as before. The mass of bees all exclaimed at his sudden change, many of them retreating away from him, even back into the hive.

He strutted around in front of those who were left, saying "I am the Spelling Bee. I can spell all words and I can cast all spells. Great is my power, great as I now am."

In that moment, he decided that he would remain large and live a solitary life, gathering together all known spells and using them whenever needed, but always only to help people.

It was not long before he discovered that he was not the first insect to practice magic. That made him uniquely suited for some spells he found that required the use of antennae and extra arms and legs. Other discoveries about spells continued to grow and he became a true spell-master, even able to make new ones on his own.

Content at last, he decided to live alone in an isolated part of the Winkie Country, store his own honey and do what good he could.

Chapter 17

The Truth Will Out

By the time the Spelling Bee had finished telling the tale of how he came by his great size and his marvelous spelling abilities, the sun was moving low in the west. He, Amal, Zeebee and the once Invisible Children, had also long since moved from the blues of the Munchkin Country to the greens surrounding the Emerald City.

The Spelling Bee looked up and said, "Oh my! See how low the sun is! We must prepare to sleep. But first we should spread out to look for food, yes, good food. There should be plenty of nuts and fruits available, and for me, there are all these flowers, beautiful flowers."

Before long everyone had gathered lots of different kinds of food and brought it all back to where they could sit down and share it. After dinner, they found a stream that provided them good, pure, clear water and then each child found a comfortable place under the trees and bushes where he or she could lie down and sleep.

As they were doing so, Zeebee took Amal and the Spelling Bee aside. Once she was sure they were out of earshot from the others, she said, "I don't know how to

The Spelling Bee of Oz

say this, but, here goes. From what you were saying this afternoon, before you started telling about how you got so big and all, I do believe I've made a mistake."

"Why? What is that?" asked the Bee.

For moments they both looked at Zeebee with anticipation. She obviously wanted to say something, but did not, at first, seem to know what to say. At length, she simply broke out, "I'm afraid I've been lying to you."

"Lying!" both of them exclaimed.

"What do you mean? Yes, yes. What do you mean?" asked the Spelling Bee.

There was silence again for a moment. Finally, Zeebee said, "I'm not Dorothy Gale from Kansas. My name is Elizabeth Warren, and I'm from a farm in the Santa Clara Valley of California."

The others stood there, open mouthed, not sure they had heard aright.

Finally the Spelling Bee said, "But you're Dorothy!"

"No. I was picked because I do look so much like her, and, at the time, I just happened to be dressed as she was when she first came to Oz. It was a costume day at home, and I had chosen to dress like Dorothy."

For a while, the other two were not convinced. They questioned her more. She insisted. Finally, Amal said, "Then if you're not Dorothy what are we supposed to call you? Do we call you Elizabeth or Zeebee?"

"My friends mostly call me Zeebee. Yeah. That's what you should call me, too. You are my friends now."

Both of them said, "Okay, Zeebee," pronouncing the name rather strongly.

The Truth Will Out

Then the Bee said, "You said you were picked. What do you mean by that?"

"That's another part of the lie," she replied. "The new Nome King, Korph, needed a Dorothy look-alike to help save Oz."

"Save Oz!" exploded the Spelling Bee.

"That's what he said, and he sounded so convincing, I believed him."

"You believed, you actually believed the Nome King? Tch, tch. My, my, but you do have a lot to learn about Oz, that you do."

"Did I do really bad?"

The Spelling Bee put two of his arms across Zeebee's shoulders and said, "There, there, little one. Nothing bad has happened yet. Don't worry, we'll soon be in the Emerald City and Ozma will check and be sure everything is hunky-dory. Yes. Yes, that she will."

"Korph would say things that didn't seem to quite fit and I started thinking maybe he wasn't leveling with me. But his version of truth was all I knew."

"Oh dear, oh dear," said the Spelling Bee. "People who lie can sometimes be very convincing."

"He certainly was that," answered Zeebee. "And that's another thing. He assured me that he did not put Pak in any danger."

"Pak? Who's that?" asked Zeebee.

"He was a young Nome that Korph sent into danger. Oh dear. How do I explain it? The Nomes have Magic Gates that if you step through one of them, you appear miles and miles away where the other half of the Gates

The Spelling Bee of Oz

is. Does that make any sense?"

The Bee quietly nodded his head, knowing much of magic, but Amal frowned a bit and then said, "I think I see what you mean." Then she held her hands wide apart out in front of her, and flipping one after the other, said, "You enter a Gate here and come out at a Gate over here."

"That's right. So, a long time ago there was a tunnel the Nomes used to invade Oz, but Ozma filled it up with dirt, and in the process covered the Magic Gate the Nomes had used at the Oz end of the connection. This meant that if anyone entered the Gate at the Nome end, they would find themselves immobile in the thick dirt of the tunnel at the Oz end."

"Just a minute," said Amal, "let me get hold of that idea." After a moment she said, "Okay, go ahead."

"So, when Korph decided to come to Oz, himself, he had to get the dirt out from around the Magic Gate in Oz. First he threw some dynamite through the Gate at his end of it so as to clear some of the dirt away. But he did not know how much had been cleared, so he sent this little boy, Pak, through to see."

"And," said the Bee, "if not enough had been cleared away, Pak would have been suffocated. Typical Nomish disregard for others."

"But," said Zeebee, "Korph convinced me that he knew that Pak was at no risk, but then afterwards, I realized he had told Pak to come back immediately. That was because if he did not step back through the Gate without even trying to turn around, he would not be

The Truth Will Out

able to do it at all. So Korph really did not know for sure whether there was room for the little boy. 'Disregard for others,' just as you said, and a liar to boot."

"Not a very nice guy," said Amal.

"I'm ashamed that he was able to flummox me so."

"Nomes are not much to be trusted," said the Spelling Bee, "but they have their reasons. At least they think so. They are great diggers. They live under ground and they claim everything that is anywhere underground. So they do not like it at all if any of the others of us dig up anything from underground. And that's true even if they had no idea it was there."

"Yes, he did seem rather possessive about things underground," said Zeebee.

The Spelling Bee said, "Since all of us do some digging, that means Nomes do not much like any of us, so they feel justified in doing anything they want towards us. Frankly, the truth is, we cannot trust a thing they say."

"I guess I was pretty stupid."

"Oh no. No, not at all. You just knew nothing about Nomes and you simply had to take things as they came to you. Now you know more than you did."

At this point, Amal, who had been listening with her eyes practically bulging out of their sockets and her ears wide open, said, "So this Nome King thought you looked a lot like someone named Dorothy who is quite important here? Is that it?"

The Spelling Bee laughed and said, "My, oh my, yes. Dorothy is very important here. Oh, she is. She is our ruler's best friend and is a national hero because she

The Spelling Bee of Oz

killed, yes I say, she killed the last two of the Wicked Witches that use to run our land with considerable cruelty, cruelty, I say. Yes, Dorothy is important in Oz."

"And does, ah, Zeebee really look like Dorothy?" asked Amal.

"Look like Dorothy? I should say. Didn't she fool me? Yes she fooled me, even when she didn't seem to recognize me. Dorothy not recognize me? I should have known then. But there you are. Deedy, deedy, yes she looks like Dorothy."

"So what do we do now?" asked Amal.

"We go on to the Emerald City. Yes. That is just what we should do," said the Spelling Bee. "I suppose our Zeebee needs to tell Ozma about the Nome King's plan or do you know what he has in mind?"

"Oh, do I ever! He has made a deal with the Transformer that is the King of the Live Wires for them to attack the town of Insulaville. Then he sent his messenger, Knunk, to tell Ozma about it. He doesn't really care about that. He just wants to get Ozma out of town, knowing that Dorothy will go with her. Then I am supposed to come rushing into the palace saying that Ozma needs the Magic Belt. Then I am supposed to take the Magic Belt to King Korph so that he can, as he said, 'save Oz.'"

"Ah ha! So that's what he thinks he'll do. That little scamp may be assuming too much. Ha! I bet he's going to be surprised." Then the Bee looked at Zeebee, "You're not going to do it are you?"

"I don't think I am," answered the girl, a bit slowly.

The Truth Will Out

"That's a good girl. Of course you're not. Tomorrow we will tell Ozma all about it."

"That may be too late," replied Zeebee.

"What on Ozeria do you mean?" demanded the Spelling Bee.

"Knunk was supposed to deliver that message to Ozma promptly at four this afternoon and I was supposed to arrive about an hour later."

"My, Oh my!" exclaimed the Spelling Bee. "So the message has long since been delivered."

"I am sure it has."

"Then there is nothing, I say nothing, we can do about it now. So I suggest that we all get to sleep and start out as early as we can in the morning. Yes, early is a good idea. We should be in the Emerald City by mid-afternoon.

Attack!

Chapter 18

Attack!

Very possibly, the most beautiful city in the world is the lustrous, green Emerald City in Oz. Its beautiful towers and spires reach for the sky. Its rounded domes add contrast. Its gracefully curving streets and lanes are lined with attractive homes and civic buildings. The jewel of the city is the Royal Palace sitting in its center and thus, in the very center of all Oz.

This palace is occupied by a varied group of people and other beings. First among them all is the Queen of Oz, the fairy Princess Ozma. She has lived in Oz for over 150 years, but appears to be only about seventeen. Although she has the sensibilities of a seventeen year old, she has all the maturity in judgment and wisdom of her many years.

Her best friend is the Princess Dorothy, who is not a native of Oz, but had come there from Kansas over one hundred years ago. Ozma made her a princess of Oz even before Dorothy had settled permanently in that wondrous country. Despite her many years of life, she appears to be only about eleven.

There is another young lady who is their friend: Jellia

Attack!

Jamb, a native of Oz who is officially Ozma's personal maid. However, she is more friend than attendant. Princesses generally have several maids, but, unlike most princesses, Ozma does not need all kinds of personal help, so Jellia is also in charge of the upkeep of the palace and has a considerable sized staff to assist her.

Dorothy's Aunt Em and Uncle Henry also live in the palace and have been in Oz just as long as she has. Oddly, they look even younger than they did when they first arrived. The only magic in that is the magic of relaxation, for they had lived hard, hard lives in Kansas. Trying to eke out a living on a hard-scrabble farm had caused them to become tired and worn looking. The more relaxed living in Oz allowed many lines of care and labor to disappear. They were not lazy, for Henry liked to work in the gardens of the palace and Em busied herself in the kitchen and helped Jellia in the upkeep of the palace. When they first arrived they lived right in the palace. Eventually they moved to a farm out in the country, but soon moved back near the palace to occupy a new home that Henry built right in the shadow of the palace. Here he could have his own small garden to tend part-time and Em could do a certain amount of sewing, knitting, tatting and house cleaning.

Two other "young" girls are also residents and close friends of Ozma and Dorothy. Both have lived in Oz for about one hundred years but Trot, who came from California, appears to be about ten, and Betsy Bobbin, who came from Oklahoma, appears to be about twelve.

Besides these seven, there are many other people.

The Spelling Bee of Oz

There is Button-Bright, a young boy, appearing to be about six years old, who came originally from Philadelphia. However, he got lost so often that he finally settled in Oz, where he also gets lost, but also, always is found again. There are also a good number of courtiers, living both in the palace and in the city proper.

There also are animals living in the palace, such as the Cowardly Lion and the Hungry Tiger and the Woozy, and there are created beings like Scraps, the Patchwork Girl, the Wooden Sawhorse and Tik-Tok, the mechanical man.

All these and many more live at the palace so that there is always someone to talk to and to do things with. But besides them, there are frequent visitors. On this

Ozga was in the middle of a two week stay . . .

Attack!

particular day, Ozma's cousin, Ozga, was in the middle of a two week stay. Her husband was here, too. Like Ozma's parents, Pastoria and Arabeth, this was a mixed marriage, for of course Ozga was a fairy, but Jo Files was a normal Ozian from the Winkie Country of Oogaboo.

This was the same day that Zeebee met the Spelling Bee, Amal and the once Invisible Children. It was about four in the afternoon and Ozma and Ozga were out in one of the palace gardens. Although there were gardeners to take care of everything, the two young ladies were checking on the condition of the various plants and flowers. They were dressed appropriately. Ozma had on a pair of shin-high blue jeans with an old white shirt with gold crowns scattered over it. Appropriately for the Rose Princess that she was, Ozga had on an older pair of rose colored shorts and matching blouse, both with golden stripes on their edges. The blouse was tied a little above her waist. Both of the women had on sneakers. They were about half way through their task when Jellia Jamb rushed up, saying, "There is a Nome here with a message for you from his King."

Yes, Knunk had arrived at the Emerald City. A little before four o'clock he had been nearing the City and, in order to reinforce the urgency of his message, he decided to run the last couple miles. Thus, he arrived at the East Gate panting hard so that it would seem that he had come as fast as he could.

Faramant, the Guardian of the Gate asked him his business, and Knuck said, "I have an urgent message for Her Majesty, Queen Ozma."

The Spelling Bee of Oz

"And just why does a Nome have any message for Queen Ozma?"

Prepared for such a question, Knunk said what the Nome King had told him to say: "Things have changed. We have a new King of the Nomes. He knows what a bad reputation we have and he is out to improve that. So when he found out that the Live Wires were getting ready to attack Insulaville, he knew he should warn Ozma. That's why I am here."

"That may be. Nonetheless, I will have the Hungry Tiger accompany you. We will wait for him to arrive."

The Guardian picked a little square box off a shelf at the back of his cubicle. It had a wire extending out its bottom to the wall and another jutting out from its top. He turned a crank on its side, then punched several buttons beside the crank, and when a raspy voice speaking out of thin air, said, "Palace," he put his mouth near the wire on top of it, and said, 'I need the Hungry Tiger here at the East Gate to accompany a young Nome in to see Ozma with what he says in an important message for her."

The disembodied voice replied, "At once, Guardian. Palace done."

Then Faramant said, "Gate done," and put the box back on its shelf.

They waited. In a few minutes the great stripped beast arrived and he said, "We will go faster if you sit on my back."

Knunk just stood there for a moment until the Guardian shoved him right up to the Hungry Tiger and then boosted him up onto its back. Then off they went

Attack!

in great bounds toward the palace, with Knunk clinging tightly to the Tiger's fur.

Ozma was waiting for them in the throne room with the Cowardly Lion at the foot of the throne and the Wizard and Ozga standing on either side of her.

When the Nome dismounted from the Hungry Tiger, he bowed before the Queen who said in a pleasant voice, "Welcome to Oz. I am Princess Ozma, Queen of Oz. What is your message?"

Standing straight, the little man said, "I am Knunk, a messenger for the great King Korph of the Nomes. He realizes that the Nomes have not dealt well with you in the past and wishes to make amends." Then he handed the sealed envelope to Ozma, saying, "This is the communication from my King, Korph."

Ozma opened it and read it, then she said, "Live Wires attacking Insulaville. This is serious." Then she turned to Knunk and said, "I thank you and your King very much for this warning, and I hope we may be the friends that he indicates in his letter. But, for now, you and I need to go up and take a look in my Magic Picture, and all the rest of you should come as well."

So off all of them went, including Knunk. In Ozma's grand apartment, all decorated in green with touches of gold and silver, they went into a room with a large picture on one side. It showed a red scene of trees lining the edge of meadow with red cows grazing in it.

Ozma walked up to it and said, "Show me the town of Insulaville."

Immediately, the red scene disappeared, to be

The Spelling Bee of Oz

replaced by a purple scene of a small town in the Gillikin Country. It was carefully laid out, but it was apparent that a struggle was going on in the streets.

The two sides were quite obvious. It was a fight between two totally different kinds of people who looked so bizarre that we might not think of them as people at all. We already know what the Live Wires look like. The homeowners were of two basic types.

First there were the shiny white ones. And they too, were of two types. There were the long rod-like ones. They appeared to be anywhere from a few inches to several feet long, some standing straight up on two spindly legs, looking rather unsteady, but still, expertly, keeping their balance; others of them bent at various angles, with one part parallel to the ground and running around on four of those spindly legs.

But besides the rod type, there was a considerable group that were dome shaped, rounded in all directions except for being flat on the bottom. They too were up to several feet tall, and came in two types: some of them were made of the same shiny white material as the rod-like ones, others were made of a translucent blue-green material. All of these ran around on four very short, thin little legs.

Curiously, the faces of all of these Insulavillers seemed to be painted on, but mouths and eyes opened and closed, so they were definitely a part of the structure of these individuals.

Everywhere the attacking Live Wires were reaching out to touch the big white or translucent people. As we

Attack!

know, every time a Live Wire touches someone, sparks fly, but in this case, their shocking ways seemed to have no effect.

"Ha-ha," laughed the Wizard, "That's fooling them! Those are the biggest insulators I ever saw."

"What's an 'insulator'?" asked the Cowardly Lion. "Should I be afraid of it?"

"No. No. Not at all," was the quick response. "An insulator is something that is used to prevent electricity from going through."

"Then it was pretty dumb of the Live Wires to try to attack them," said the Hungry Tiger.

"They probably did not realize what an insulator was," said the Queen.

"Or maybe," said Ozga, "they didn't even know that the name Insulaville meant it was occupied by insulators"

Even as they talked, the attacking group of thin, little Live Wires was beginning to regroup at a distance from those they had expected to be easy victims. Their ruler, however, was undeterred. The Transformer's magic was still effective. Every time he touched one of the town's inhabitants, that creature would be changed into a flower, a dish, a book or something. Quite a few such objects lay around the town already.

Ozma said, "I've seen enough!" and walked over to another wall where she pulled out a drawer, took from it a wide, jeweled belt and put it around her waist. Then she said, "Wizard, I think you should go up to your workroom and get someone to help you bring your Magic Door down here. Then using the Magic Picture,

The Spelling Bee of Oz

you can keep an eye on what we are doing in Insulaville and come to help me if I need it.

"As for you, Knunk, you have delivered your message. I understand what it involved and it is time for you to head for home. Give Korph my greetings and tell him I look forward to our being able to work together in friendship from now on."

Her tone was such that Knunk left immediately.

The Wizard had waited until the Nome had left and then said, "Do you really think the Nome King can be trusted to work fairly with us?"

"Not really, but he was being courteous in his message, so I thought I should do likewise. Courtesy costs nothing, and who knows, it wouldn't be hard to be easier to work with than Ruggedo ever was."

The Wizard laughed and said, "Indeed," as he hurried off to his workroom. Ozma thought for a minute or two before conferring with Ozga. Then, taking her cousin's right hand in her own left, she put her right hand on the Magic Belt and said, "Take the two of us to Insulaville," and they disappeared.

Chapter 19

Insulaville

A large number of the Live Wires were pushing their King around on his platform. He was vainly trying to touch the Insulators in order to change them into whatever he wished. However, by this time, the Insulators had learned to stay out of his reach. It was easy for them to move faster than the little Live Wires could push him. The rest of the Live Wires were trailing around behind their King, dejected because they could not shock the Insulators.

Suddenly Ozma and Ozga appeared, standing side by side. When the Live Wires saw this, they started to rush toward the women, and the Transformer called out, "Bring them to me. I will make one into a big emerald and the other into a rosebush."

With both hands on her Magic Belt, Ozma said, "No, you will not. All of you will stop right where you are," and they did. Then she said, "I am Ozma, ruler of all the Land of Oz, and I would like to know what's going on here."

All the Live Wires began chattering and looking at each other and at the Transformer. Finally the Transformer

The Spelling Bee of Oz

said, "We have just come to visit our neighbors here in Insulaville. You can see that we are on a friendly visit."

Pointing around the street where they stood, Ozma said, "So, what is this flower and this dish and this book and this bush and this wooden box and this kettle?"

"You seem to have named them quite successfully."

"Have I?" asked the Queen. Then she went around, touching each of them in turn and saying, "Resume your natural form," and five Insulators stood where the other things had been. "You see King Transformer, I saw you changing these people into inanimate things. What was your reason for doing that?"

"I was simply trying to add a little beauty to the place."

"By taking life away from them?"

"Oh no. They were quite alive when I changed them."

By this time, a number of Live Wires that had been on other streets began edging onto the scene and moving toward Ozma. Ozga did not like the looks of this and reached into the front of her blouse and pulled out her magic wand. Then whispering a few words, she waved it at the advancing Live Wires and they all stopped.

Ozma had seen what happened and she said to the Transformer, "So what was the intention of that group of your subjects?"

"Intention?" he said. "I know nothing other than that they wanted to hear what was going on."

Ozma nodded at Ozga to go ahead, so she addressed the Live Wires she had stopped, "Why were you creeping so furtively up to Ozma?"

Insulaville

"That's right. Our leader said it," replied several of them.

Ozma looked at them and said, "I'm curious. Why are you called 'Live Wires?'"

"Because we are so lively," was the answer.

"Creeping around doesn't seem so lively to me," said Ozga.

No one said anything more until Ozma said, "Your leader says he was only beautifying things here. Let's see," and she walked over to a barrel that was sitting on the sidewalk. She looked at it and walked around it. Then she spoke to it, saying, "Would you move down the sidewalk for me?"

Nothing happened.

"Please answer my question: what is your name?"

The barrel said nothing.

Then Ozma stepped over to a tree that was only a foot or so from the barrel and repeated the same procedure.

Still nothing happened.

"I suppose that is enough examples," said Ozma as she looked at the Transformer. He did not react, so, with her hands on her Belt, she said, "Let these last two I spoke to return to their normal selves," and there were two more Insulators who each gave a little jump and waved their arms around joyfully.

"I don't believe they were enjoying themselves in the forms you gave them Mr. Transformer," said Ozma.

He shook himself a bit, but said nothing.

"Now," said Ozma, "are there any other Insulators to whom you have given other shapes."

The Spelling Bee of Oz

"No, that is all."

"Let us see." With her hand still on her Belt, Ozma said very loudly, "let all the Insulators that were transformed by the Transformer resume their natural shapes," and a dozen more items changed back into Insulators.

"Aha! So far I have heard seven untruths from you. I want to hear no more. So now I will ask the Insulators," and turning to several of them, she said, "Why were the Live Wires and their Transformer here?"

A very large Insulator spoke up: "Those vicious little monsters were trying to shock us. Ordinarily they have to stay in their own vicinity because they have to be close to the Transformer in order to be energized. There, they waylay any stranger unwise enough to pass through their land. But somehow they got wheels under the Transformer and so were able to come here to attack us."

"You say that previously the Transformer did not have wheels?" asked Ozma.

"That's right."

Ozga whispered something to Ozma and she said, "I agree." Then speaking to the Transformer, she said, "How did you happen to get wheels at this particular time?"

There was silence for a moment, then, hesitating as he spoke, the Transformer said, "Forgive me your majesty, but may I ask you one question before I answer yours?"

"Certainly."

"All right then. How did you happen to come here just as we were inv ... ah, in Insulaville?"

Insulaville

"I received a message from King Korph of the Nomes, telling me you were attacking Insulaville."

"Yes. I should have known. He was just trying to trick us. I couldn't believe he was really being so generous as to do that. He was just getting even with us."

"What do you mean?" asked the Queen.

"A few days ago we shocked him when he trespassed into our territory. He escaped and then came back with this generous offer to give me a platform with wheels so we could attack our neighbors if we would let him and his Nomes pass by us unattacked. The villain!"

"I figured he had some nefarious reason for telling me about your attack on Insulaville. So since you were tricked by him, I will not make your punishment very big. I will simply send all of you back to your home, minus the wheeled platform. However, King Transformer," and here she placed her hands upon her Magic Belt, "you will also find that you can no longer transform people however you wish. You will transform only those that wish to be transformed. All other transformations will fail you."

With her hands still on her Belt, she whispered a few more words and in a moment all the Live Wires and the Transformer had disappeared.

Then turning to the Insulators, she said, "Forgive us for leaving so soon, but I believe you have all been restored and I fear that the wicked Nome King may have drawn me here so he could do some further mischief in the Emerald City."

The large Insulator stepped forward, bowed to her

The Spelling Bee of Oz

and said, "I am Dielectro, King of the Insulators, and I thank you most sincerely for your assistance just now. You can always count on me and my people anytime you need us. We are, as you might guess, completely immune to electrical shock."

Then all his people also voiced their thanks, and Ozma and Ozga disappeared, only to reappear immediately in front of the Magic Picture in Ozma's suite.

The Wizard, the Cowardly Lion and the Hungry Tiger were all still there. Ozma bowed to the Wizard and thanked him for keeping watch, but then said to the Magic Picture, "Show me what Korph, the new King of the Nomes is doing right now."

The Picture switched to a room that was basically dull and gray, but it was lit up by hundreds of jewels sparkling everywhere, on walls and floors and ceilings, but especially on the great stone throne in the middle of the room. There sat a rotund Nome whom Ozma had never seen before, wearing a crown on his head. It was, of course, Korph. He was doing nothing in particular, just sitting, looking a bit bored, if anything.

Ozma watched him for only a short time before she said, "He does not seem to be causing any trouble just now, but I'll keep my eye on him." Then she looked around and asked, "Has anybody seen Knunk?"

Everyone looked at everyone else and finally, the Wizard said, "I don't think anyone has seen him since you sent him home."

"Just checking. It may be that he stayed around, hid himself, and is planning to make some trouble."

Insulaville

"Wouldn't be surprised," said the Hungry Tiger.

Ozma said, "Think I'll check with Faramant." So she went to the wall, opened a little door and out popped a device just like the one in the Guardians shed. She turned the crank, pushed some buttons and a voice was heard to say, "Guardian here."

Ozma said, "Ozma here. Did the little Nome, Knunk, leave the Emerald City yet?"

"Yes. Not long ago."

"Thank you. Ozma out."

"Guardian out."

Ozma turned to the others, "So, that's settled. He's on his way home."

Yes. Knunk, the messenger, was on his way home at that moment. However, later, trotting steadily along the Yellow Brick Road, he began thinking about the situation. It occurred to him that humans were not very reliable and their children especially. What if that little girl did not show up and ask for the Magic Belt? He hurried on for a while, but finally decided to stop to sleep and think about that a bit. When he woke up in the morning, he had decided that he should return to the Emerald City.

That evening, he stopped, just within view of the Emerald City's beautiful towers and found himself a hiding place at the edge of the woods where he could see and yet not be seen. Being to the northeast, he could keep an eye on both the north and the east roads leading into the City. However, it was already too late, for earlier in the afternoon Zeebee and the other children had been led into the Emerald City by the Spelling Bee.

Chapter 20

The Children Meet Ozma

As they approached the City, the children that were with the Spelling Bee were overcome with excitement. The sight of the gleaming towers and great walls was a new experience for all of them. As they moved closer, their wonder increased. Inside the gate, they found much to see that none of them, save the Spelling Bee, had ever seen before. Yes, Amal had known the city of Mogadishu back when it was pretty much intact, but at its best it was no match for this wondrous city. Zeebee had seen San Francisco, but although that city had taller towers, nothing could rival the beauty of the emeralds and the flowing lines of these towers. All of them were talking and pointing, sometimes shouting over all this that was so new to them.

The commotion they made attracted enough attention that they were soon surrounded by crowds of people, especially children. The crowds slowed their progress, for they were not only following along beside and behind them, but also in front of them.

At last they came to the palace. The Soldier with the Green Whiskers came down to the foot of the steps to

The Children Meet Ozma

greet them. Here was one more thing for them to exclaim about. He was so tall and his whiskers were so green and long.

Then he spoke: "Welcome to the Emerald City, Mr. Spelling Bee, you have not been here for quite a while and you bring so many with you."

"Yes. We have come to see if Ozma can help them," replied the Bee.

As in the streets, a crowd had, by this time, gathered on the stairs of the palace. Of course, all the famous people living in the palace were just as curious as all the others. One of them, Dorothy, came forward and said, "My, Speller, but you have certainly grown a big family."

The Spelling Bee was flustered and answered, "Ah, b-b-but, you see, these aren't actually my children. I have, ah, I guess you might say, I have just picked them up along the way. Yes, that is, along the way."

Dorothy and the others laughed. She said, "Of course, but where did you find all of them?"

"The first was this charming little girl, Amal," and he pointed her out. "The second was Zeebee." That brought another round of laughter form many who thought that should indicate the Bee, himself. So he said, "Or maybe it would be better if I introduced her as 'Elizabeth.' That is her proper name, you know."

At the introduction of Elizabeth, many of the important personages gathered around, saying,"That's incredible," "Imagine that!" and "She's a dead-ringer for Dorothy," and other such comments.

Dorothy looked at Elizabeth, shook her head and said,

The Spelling Bee of Oz

"She's a dead-ringer for Dorothy!"

"Just because she has blonde hair and a blue gingham dress doesn't mean she looks like me."

Everyone laughed and several said, "But she does look like you, even so."

Again Dorothy shook her head and, looking hard at Elizabeth said, "No! That's not what I look like."

Zeebee joined in with, "I don't see anything more than a slight general resemblance. Like Dorothy says, yes, we're blondes and of about the same height and age, but I'd say that's about as far as it goes."

Again, people were saying, "But you do."

Finally, it was Aunt Em who said, "Land sakes, we're gittin' nowhere here. We'll settle this when we git inside and you stand side by side before some big mirror. That'll

The Children Meet Ozma

settle it down, all right!"

Before she had finished, a large rag doll spoke up, in a sing-song voice:

Enough of this,
That's two we know.
For sure it is,
But there are more
Be that or this.
How name them so?

Fluttering his wings a bit, the Spelling Bee said, "Ahem. Ah yes. Thank you Scraps for reminding me that these others all deserve to be introduced." As he spoke, he bowed and swept his two left arms toward them, then continued, "But, ah, well, I don't know the names of most of them. But, yes, yes, this is Binji and this one is Alora, but I'm afraid each of the rest will have to introduce themselves. You see I only picked them up day before yesterday."

He turned to the children and one by one, they gave their names.

After they were done, Dorothy said, "My, what a lot of names! I'm sure we can't remember them all right away, but as we get acquainted, the names will stick a little better. But come. You say you want Ozma to help them, so I suppose we had better go in to see her."

So saying, she led the way in through the great front doors of the palace and down the hall a ways until they had come to the throne room. Along the way, she and

The Spelling Bee of Oz

Zeebee were talking to each other, agreeing that they really did not look a lot alike. But Dorothy said, "The Spelling Bee gave two names for you, so which should I call you?"

Zeebee replied, "Whichever you like, but most everybody except my teachers call me Zeebee."

"All right then, Zeebee it will be."

And hand in hand, they continued into the throne room.

When everyone, both the new visitors and the residents of the palace, had entered the room, there was a good-sized crowd, nearly filling it. No one was talking loudly, nonetheless there was quite a bit of noise, for everyone was saying something. The residents were all wondering who these children were. The children were commenting about their surroundings – the brightness of the many jewels, the beautiful pictures of Ozian landscape and the many pictures of famous Ozians.

At the front of the room was the giant carved emerald that was the Royal Throne of Oz. For this occasion it had only been raised one step above the floor of the throne room. To the left of it sat the famous Cowardly Lion, looking nervously around the room. On the other side of the throne was the Hungry Tiger, a rather frightening sight for the children as he stared at them and licked his lips. In front of the throne stood the Soldier with the Green Whiskers, looking over the gathering and with his long musket held rigidly in front of him. And right in front of him stood the Spelling Bee with Amal on his left and Zeebee on his right and all the once Invisible

The Children Meet Ozma

Children ranked behind him.

By this time, Dorothy had gone up the one step of the throne to stand beside the Cowardly Lion and running her hand through his great mane, comfort him a bit.

Finally, the door behind and to the right of the throne opened and the Soldier pounded the butt of his gun three times on the step of the throne. With each stroke a reverberating, mellow sound rang out from the throne. Also, with each stroke he intoned, "Make way for the Royal Queen of Oz, Princess Ozma."

Behind him a very beautiful black-haired girl emerged through the door. She was slim and dressed in a lovely long dress consisting of many hues of green. On her head was an emerald and diamond encrusted coronet, and two large red poppies rested on either side of her head. Her dark eyes were dancing with excitement as she seated herself in the throne, looking out over the crowd.

Following her another young woman, almost as lovely as the first, walked, but she had light red, almost pink hair and was wearing a long dress much like Ozma's except that it had a generous amount of yellow mixed into it. On her head rested only a small coronet. This was Ozma's cousin, Ozga, the Rose Princess, now married to Jo Files of Oogaboo. She followed Ozma around the throne. But, while Ozma sat down on it, Ozga sat beside the Hungry Tiger, one hand resting on his great paws, the other, occasionally, scratching him under the chin causing him to utter a low purr.

Once they were both settled, Ozma spoke, "What

The Spelling Bee of Oz

a fine group of young people. I welcome you to the Emerald City and hope you find it to your liking, Mr. Bee. But how did you happen to bring so many children with you? And oh, wait! That one I would say was Dorothy if I did not see our own Dorothy right here with the Cowardly Lion."

So the Spelling Bee introduced Zeebee to Ozma and she had Dorothy and Zeebee stand side by side and exclaimed that she was not certain that she could tell the difference.

After a few moments of talking about the resemblance, the Spelling Bee said, "but the interesting thing is how she happens to be in Oz at all."

"More interesting than the resemblance?"

"I should let her tell you," said the Bee.

So Zeebee said, "It this apparent similarity that brought me to Oz."

"How is that?" asked Ozma.

"The Nome King used magic to bring me here from Earth because I did look so much like Dorothy," and she stepped up to where she could take Dorothy's hand in her own, then continued speaking to Ozma. "He wanted me to come here while you were gone and say that you needed the Magic Belt. And, since I appeared to be Dorothy, I could take it, but not to you. I was supposed to take it to him. And he had me completely fooled. He had convinced me that you were a wicked witch ruling Oz meanly and that you had enchanted the Tin Woodman and the Scarecrow and the Cowardly Lion so that they would obey your wicked commands. Then, when he

The Children Meet Ozma

had the Magic Belt, he would use it to set everything right in Oz!"

"My! My!" said Ozma. "He certainly had ambitious plans. So that is why he made it possible for the Live Wires to attack Insulaville."

"And you outwitted him there," said Ozga.

"I guess so," said Ozma, "but Nomes are too devious for their own good. He did not think of the fact that his method of tempting me out of town assured that I would take the Magic Belt with me. He missed the obvious. Even so," and she turned to Zeebee, "by that time, you realized what the truth was and you did not even try to steal the Magic Belt."

"Nonetheless," said Zeebee, "I really apologize for having been so gullible. If I had not met the Spelling Bee, no telling how bad things might have been. Dear, oh dear."

Ozma stepped over to where the young girl was standing, put her arm around her shoulders and said, "That's all right. You had no way of knowing and those Nomes can be very convincing. I have experienced it myself."

Then, putting her other arm around the great Bee, Ozma said, "So my old friend, you have played a part in the saving of Oz once more by getting Zeebee to tell the truth. Thanks then, to both of you."

Embarrassed, the Bee decided to change the subject and said, "This other young lady also comes from Earth. Her name is Amal and she comes from a wonderful place called Somalia."

The Spelling Bee of Oz

"My," said the Queen, "what an unusual day this is. Two young ladies from Earth at the same time."

"Two very sweet young ladies," added the Spelling Bee.

"Yes," said Ozma, "and now, my dear, come forward that we may talk more easily."

Amal did so with a kind of curtsey and said, "I am most pleased to meet your Royal Highness and I thank you for welcoming us to your city." Then she curtsied again.

"You don't have to use honorifics here, Amal. You can just call me 'Ozma.' What brought you to Oz?"

Again Amal curtsied and said, "There was an explosion on the streets of Mogadishu and the next thing I knew I was walking on a purple road in Oz. Now I want to get back home."

"I am sure we can do that for you."

"Oh, would you, Princess?"

"Yes, I would, but, like I said, no honorifics, just call me 'Ozma.'"

"I'm sorry. Something is mixed up here. I called you by a common name in Somalia which, now that I think about it, does actually mean 'Princess,' but I thought it would come out as I meant it to, as ..." but the word she said, still sounded to the ears of Ozma and everyone else as "Princess."

Ozma told her as much and she responded by saying, "Now I don't know what to do."

"I think I do," said the Spelling Bee, and turning to Ozma, he asked, "Do you have a blackboard around?"

The Children Meet Ozma

"I don't, but the library does," and she led the way, through her study and then unlocked a door that led them into the library.

The librarian took them to a side room with a blackboard on one wall. Then the Spelling Bee picked up a piece of chalk and said to Amal, "If you will spell out the word you are using, I will write those letters on the board."

So Amal began. Of course, she used the Arabic names of the letters, but everybody heard them in the Ozian form. As she named them, the Wizard wrote them on the blackboard, "A-M-I-R-A."

The he said, "I would pronounce those letters as 'Amira.'"

"Almost," said Amal, "but in the middle, change that 'ee' sound to an 'i' sound."

This time the Spelling Bee said it just the way Amal wanted it – "Amira."

"That's a beautiful name," said Ozma. Then sweeping the others with her gaze, she added, "You may call me that anytime you wish. You know it's the first time in one hundred and – let me see, ah¬ – one hundred and fifty-one years that I've had a new name."

Amal, curious, said, "You mean you had a different name before they called you 'Ozma'?"

"Yes and no. When I was born, I was to become the next Queen of Oz, so they named me Ozma. All the Queens of Oz are named Ozma."

"Aren't there ever any Kings of Oz?"

"Yes, there are and they are always named 'Oz.'"

The Spelling Bee of Oz

"So, there have been other Ozma's before you?"

"Yes. I am actually Ozma VI."

"And several Kings, I suppose."

"Again, yes. My grandfather was Oz VI. He was captured and hidden by the Wicked Witches, which made my uncle King as Oz VII. But those same witches killed him that same day, so his brother, my father, became King Pastoria. He was never intended to be king, since he was the second born and of course had to have a different name from his brother."

"Yeah, I understand. Well, pretty well, at least. But what I don't understand is: if you were born Ozma and are still called that what did you mean about not having a new name for one hundred and fifty-one years?"

"Oh, that. While I was still a little baby, the Wicked Witch of the North, Mombi, stole me, changed me into a boy so no one would know that I was the lost Ozma, and gave me the name of 'Tippetarius,' shortened to 'Tip'."

She laughed then and said, "I guess we might say that we are now acquainted with each other and it is time to give our attention to the rest of the children."

"Ah, great Ruler" said the Spelling Bee, "I am only too happy to introduce to you," and here he turned and swept his two left hands toward them as he continued, "the Invisible Children of Oz."

"'Invisible'?" said Ozma, "they look plainly visible to me."

"Oh yes. Yes, indeed. Visible they are, but they were not always. Until a day ago, they were quite invisible. They were the Invisible Children, or if you would, the

The Children Meet Ozma

Lost Children."

"And now they are not even lost, for you have found them and brought them here."

"Indeedy so. There is a place in the Munchkin Country with firmly defined borders, not too far from here, where all children become invisible. And once they have become invisible, they cannot escape that country unless someone pulls them out of it." And he explained their experiences in the Country of the Invisible Children, ending with the fact that four of the children had already been reunited with their families in Upper Stallingham.

When he had finished, Ozma turned to the green-haired maiden standing near her which prompted that young woman to leave the room with al dispatch. Then Ozma said, "We certainly must do what we can to reunite these children with their parents. And we need to put up signs, warning people of the danger of that area."

"Ah, yes, wonderful Queen!" exclaimed the Bee. "That is exactly, oh so exactly, just what I was hoping you would want to do."

Then, raising her voice, Ozma called out, "May I have your attention, please?"

As the crowd grew still, she said, "We need to find the homes for all these children, but that will wait for tomorrow. For now, we need to find them rooms in the palace."

She clapped her hands, and as the green-haired young woman came in from the hallway, she said, "This is Jellia Jamb. She is in charge of running this whole big

The Spelling Bee of Oz

palace and will assign rooms for each of you children." Then with a flourish of her hands toward the Chief of the Household Staff, she said, "Jellia."

The Chief of Staff stood on the step of the throne and, raising her voice so she could be heard by all the children, said, "Welcome to the Royal Palace! We have rooms for all of you. If you want, you can have a single room, but I imagine most of you would prefer pairing up with two or three others. So, group yourselves however you want and once you have your own little cluster formed, come on out into the hall and my helpers will take you to your rooms. There you can clean up from your long trip and there will be fresh clothes for you to put on. Any questions?"

One little girl, standing with three others, raised her hand and when Jellia nodded at her, she said, "Can four of us share a room?"

With a broad smile, Jellia said, "I think that would be just fine."

Since there seemed to be no other questions, she said, "All right. I'll see you in the hall," and went out through the nearest doors.

While the others were organizing into their groups, Dorothy took the hands of Zeebee and Amal and said, "We'll have our own little company of three, and we already have a suite of our own. C'mon!" and off she ran, pulling the other two along with her, all of them laughing.

The first thing they did when they reached Dorothy's suite was to go and stand in front of Dorothy's full length

The Children Meet Ozma

mirror.

All three of them stood there, side by side, and then both Dorothy and Elizabeth gasped and said in unison, "You *do* look just like me!"

Then they broke into laughter and hugged each other.

Dorothy said, "We're like twins!"

And Zeebee added, "Who've just found each other after being separated at birth."

Then they all laughed again and Dorothy said, "Come along. We need to get cleaned up for dinner."

But, before they cleaned up, the two newcomers had to inspect Dorothy's apartment. Then all three took their turns in the tub and the last, Dorothy, was just getting into her fresh clothes when a bell sounded.

"That's the dinner bell," said Dorothy. "Let's go," and she led the way downstairs.

When they reached the Dining Hall, youngsters were streaming in through all the doors. A number of the more famous of the regular occupants of the palace were with them, all talking together and getting acquainted. Excitement ran high: for the Lost Children it was the fact that they would soon, at long last, be going to their own home; for the palace residents it was the very presence of those Lost Children.

In all that great crowd, it may have been only Uncle Henry, Aunt Em and the Shaggy Man that were thinking about the fact that the meal was being delayed. They talked among themselves, wondering why Ozma had not yet arrived. What was holding her up?

The Spelling Bee of Oz

The answer was simple. On the way to the dining hall, the Spelling Bee had taken her aside and said, "I have something I have to say." Those words were followed by a confession that kept them talking for more than just a few minutes. As a result, when they did arrive, Ozma tapped on her glass and in a few moments there was silence. That was also a signal for the Spelling Bee.

He stood up and said, "Ahem. The honesty of Elizabeth Warren, yes, her honesty in admitting how the Nome King had deceived her has led me, in my own turn, I must say, to be honest with all of you. I have told the Lost Children this story. Harrumph, ah. Now I must tell all of you. I have always said that I did not know how I happened to be so big, so big, that I always had been. That is not true. I do remember how it happened and now I will tell you the truth.

"Harrumph, umm. Ah, a sad story, indeed," and he proceeded to tell them the same long story he had told the Lost Children the night before.

When he had finished, Professor Wogglebug, who had come up from his Royal Athletic College of Oz when he heard about the Lost Children, stood up and in his pompous though squeaky voice said, "My dear sir, I never did believe that you had always been such a big bee. After all, I have experienced being a small bug transformed into a large one. It happened ..."

Ozma interrupted, saying, "Perhaps, Professor, after dinner you might want to tell the Lost Children all about your transforming experience. The rest of us are well acquainted with it.

The Children Meet Ozma

"And now, let us get on with our meal."

With that announcement waiters began bringing in trays filled with hot food. The chef, Baluol, had prepared them a delicious dinner of lasagna in a tasty marinara sauce with a green salad and plenty of garlic bread. At the end there was chocolate cake smothered in chocolate sauce with a generous dollop of whipped cream on each one.

It was a long dinner, full of excitement, but afterwards the Emerald City Symphony Orchestra played a number of quiet pieces that encouraged a general relaxing of the wild tensions the young people felt from being in this glorious city and its wonderful palace.

After that the residents retired to their own rooms but the Lost Children stayed in the dining room to be regaled by Professor H. M. Wogglebug, T. E's tale of his beginnings.

Chapter 21

Going Home

After breakfast the next morning Ozma called for quiet and then told the Lost Children, "I have a plan. I think we can soon have you all back with your families. Then we will put up the signs to warn people of the danger of the Country of the Invisible Children.

"However the first thing is: Are there some of you who already know where to find your families?"

Three hands went up.

"Very good," said Ozma, "You may go up to the library." Then she turned to Betsy Bobbin and asked her to be the one to take them there. "Also," she added, "while you're there, write down their names, the names of their parents and their home towns and locate those towns.

"Now, I believe some of you must know the name of your home town or area, but don't know where that is. Raise your hands?" And when eight hands went up, she responded, "Oh, that's good. So, you may join those going up to the library with Betsy Bobbin and give her all that information."

As those eleven headed out the door with Betsy,

Going Home

Ozma said, "Now, the rest of us will go up to the throne room and proceed further. As we are going, I want you to be thinking about anything you can remember about your home: colors, distinctive features, names of people around you, whatever you can remember."

All the way up two flights of stairs and to the library the children were talking excitedly, trying to remember things about their homes. What one remembered frequently inspired the memories of others. By the time they reached the library there was quite a hubbub, so it took a while to quiet down. Once it had, Ozma said, "So, do any of you remember anything that might help locate your home?"

Immediately so many answered that Ozma could not tell what any of them was trying to say, so she said, "Wait, wait! One at a time."

And she pointed to a little boy near the front who said, "There was the biggest tree I've ever seen, right in front of our house and it was purple."

"Ah, a very good clue," said Ozma, "so I want you to go over and stand by the north wall, here. Do you all know why I want him by the north wall?"

Everybody said, "North is the direction of the Gillikins whose national color is purple," or something along that line.

"All right then, if the only thing you can remember about your home is the color, go to the appropriate wall," and she pointed them out, north, east, south, west, "And for those who remember green houses, stand right in the center under that big chandelier."

The Spelling Bee of Oz

It took quite a while for those children who could remember their native color to reach the right part of the room, for the room was fairly full and they had to make their way through crowds of people who were all trying to move out of the way.

When the process was completed, there were still five of the children that did not know where to go. Ozma told them, "Don't worry, with the others, we have a particular area to send their pictures to. Your pictures we will send all over Oz."

Then she whispered something to Dorothy, and that young lady hurried out of the chamber. Next Ozma went around talking to a number of those new young friends who were nearest to her, and by the time she had finished and everything was settled down, Dorothy was back with a young man carrying a large briefcase and she had a big tablet of paper in her arms.

A word from Ozma to the Soldier with the Green Whiskers, who then pounded the butt of his rifle upon the emerald step twice and everyone ceased their chatter so Ozma could speak again.

She announced, "Everything is organized now. I have here Norjil, the finest artist in Oz. He will make quick portraits of each of you. These we will circulate in your home area until we find your parents. We will start with the Gillikin Country."

There was a cheer from all those along the north wall and groans from most of the other children.

"That's all right," said Ozma. "All of you will get your turn and none of the pictures will be ready to go out until

Going Home

tomorrow. It will take a while, so I have arranged for games and other fun activities for all of you. Four of the Gillikins should stay here with the artist All the rest of you should follow the Soldier with the Green Whiskers, and he will lead you out to where some of my friends have games ready for you and other ideas for having fun.

"Then, as soon as Norjil finishes one picture, that child will go out in back and tell another from the Gillikins to come in, and so on through all five areas until everyone has been drawn.

"Okay. Any questions?"

There were none, so Ozma signaled them to go and off they romped. However, she had to stop four of the Gillikins or everyone would have gone out to play.

She also held back Amal and Zeebee. The Gillikins she herded toward Norjil while she brought Amal, Zeebee, the Spelling Bee and Ozga up to her own apartment. There she poured lime punch into five glasses, put out a plate of cookies and a jar of nectar so the five of them could talk.

The young ladies sat in comfortable chairs. The Bee was more content simply sitting on the floor. He commented on the delicacy of the nectar and asked where it had come from. Ozma's answer was, "I do not really know. I simply asked the Magic Belt to fill that pitcher with nectar."

"Did you do it long distance? You're not wearing the Belt."

Laughing, Ozma said, as she held up her left arm, "But the Belt automatically adjusts to fit anything it is put

The Spelling Bee of Oz

around. See my colorful bracelet? That is the Magic Belt."

"Will miracles never cease?" said the Bee

"Oh I should hope not," said the Queen. This time everybody laughed.

Just then the doorbell rang and Dorothy ran to answer it. After a moment, she said, "Come on in. Ozma is expecting you," and she brought with her the eleven children whose homes had been located and Betsy Bobbin who had all their information written on cards.

As soon as Ozma heard the bell, she stood up and took the colorful bracelet off her wrist, which she then started putting around her waist. Everyone was surprised

Everyone was surprised to see that small band expand...

Going Home

to see that small band expand, both to be long enough to go all the way around her waist, and to be as wide as it was once it was around her waist. Even the jewels on it expanded to cover the whole big Belt.

By the time the Belt was in place, Dorothy, the eleven children and Betsy were coming into the sitting room and Betsy handed to Ozma what she had written down about each child's memories of home. While Ozma was looking over the notes, the doorbell rang again and in walked Jellia Jamb.

Ozma asked her, "Do you have anything that will demand your attention for the next hour or so?"

Jellia's answer was simple: "Nothing at all." Now you may think that a servant should be more respectful in talking to the Queen of an important fairyland, but as we have noted, Ozma and Jellia are close friends and there is no need for formality between them.

"Good," said Ozma, "for I will soon need your help. These eleven, I will be sending back to their homes in a few minutes, each one accompanied by one of my long-time friends. That is so they can explain the child's long absence to his or her parents. The children themselves might be too excited to be able to make a coherent explanation of what had happened to them. While this is being done, I'll need to be with Amal and Zeebee. So I'll need you to watch the Magic Picture for our friend's signal that they are ready to return, and you'll have the Magic Belt to bring them back."

"I understand, and I presume it is the usual signal."

"You're right, of course, and I thank you. So now

The Spelling Bee of Oz

we'll all go back to the room with my Magic Picture."

It was only a matter of moments before they were all crowded together in front of that Picture. With all in place, Ozma instructed it to show first one house, then another. In each case, the child concerned said, "Yes! Yes! That's my home," or words to that effect.

So she proceeded to send first one to her home, then another and another, until the last child had reached his home. With the first, she sent Dorothy, with the second, Betsy and others of her friends with each child until the last, when she sent Ozga along. Of course, each of the children thanked Ozma effusively before she or he left.

By now it was time for lunch, so any further work on sending children home would be delayed until the afternoon. While they ate, Zeebee said to Ozma, "My parents must be mad with worry over my absence. I just hope they have not given up on ever seeing me again. Can you send me back really soon?"

"Of course, I can do that as soon as you want me to."

"Fact is: I'm torn. I really have been enjoying my friends and adventures here." At this point she put an arm around Amal and continued, "I wish I could have both, but I know I do have to go home." Tears were beginning to form in her eyes.

Ozma reached out to put an arm around both her new friends, saying, "Long ago, the first time that Dorothy went back home after we'd met, I made an arrangement with her for a special sign she could make and I would check on her every Saturday, and if she made that sign, I would bring her to Oz."

Going Home

Dorothy nodded and said, "But later, after I nearly died in the Outback of Australia, she changed it to every afternoon at four."

"Yes," said Ozma, "Dorothy always seemed to be getting in trouble on Earth. And I'm not sure that you two are any less danger-prone, so I'll share that same sign with you, and check with each of you every day at four p.m."

Both girls jumped at the chance, saying "Oh! Would you? Would you really?"

"Of course, and here it is." With that Ozma held her right hand up in the air, crossing her fingers a certain way and said, "It's that simple."

"Wow!" and Amal and Zeebee jumped up from their places on either side of Ozma, and taking their two hands across, they danced around in a circle, saying, "We can come back any time we want to!"

After they settled down and were back in their places, Ozma said, "So Zeebee, before you leave could you tell us a bit about your home?"

"Nothing special. I live with my parents and my little brother, Alvin, and my cat, Valentine, in a standard California ranch house."

"You have a ranch? Many years ago my cousin was here and he lived on a ranch in California near Gilroy."

"No, no. No ranch. A ranch house is a very common type of house in California, rambling like houses on ranches supposedly do."

Then she continued, "I'm eleven years old and in the sixth grade at Franklin Delano Roosevelt Grade School.

The Spelling Bee of Oz

My favorite subject is geography and I play on the soccer team and I play a clarinet in the school band. That's about it in a nutshell."

After lunch was over, Zeebee pulled on Ozma's sleeve and said, "Much as I hate to leave, I think it's time to send me home now. But first, let me say goodbye to all the Lost Children."

So, she worked her way around the table, saying goodbye, to each of them individually. She told them how much she had enjoyed meeting them and hoped that soon all of them would be going home, even as she was. Binji, she took by the hands and said, "You've been a good comrade."

Then she went back to her place by Ozma and the two of them with Amal, the Spelling Bee, Ozga and Dorothy went up to Ozma's apartment. As they entered the Spelling Bee said to Ozma, "Dear Ruler, may I have a, ahem, a private, I say a private word with you for a moment?"

Ozma looked at him with puzzlement on her face, but said, "Of course. Dorothy, would you lead the others on into the Magic Picture Room? We'll be with you in just a moment."

When they were alone, the great Bee said, "Ahem. We use magic in many ways here. Yes, in many ways. But on Earth there is no magic. Well, that is, humph, not any of our kind. Their magic is of, what is it? Ah yes, of the mechanical and chemical kind."

"That's right," agreed the little Queen.

"But," continued the Bee, "we know that Oz magic

Going Home

does, ahem, work on Earth. Button-Bright's Magic Umbrella works as well on Earth as in Oz. Yes. The magic of your Magic Belt has extended to Earth to, so cleverly, pick up Dorothy and bring her to Oz."

Ozma nodded her head at each example and then the Spelling Bee said, "So, might it be that I can place a spell on these young ladies, yes, young ladies, that will work on earth?"

"But we should not interfere with things on Earth."

"Quite right, your Majesty. Quite Right. Ah, no, I do not plan to interfere. I have a Spell for Communication. Yes, communication. I could cast it between them and any one object on Oz so that they could affect it. Yes, they could affect it."

Ozma raised her left eyebrow and cocked her head to one side as she looked at the Spelling Bee.

He went on, "Ah yes. Strange it is, indeed. But say you had a little glass bell sitting by your bedside, glass, yes, or brass or ceramic. Yes. Whatever. And when it rang, you would know that one of those girls was trying, indeed, trying to reach you. That would be good. Yes? Any emergency, any time, they could call upon you."

Ozma answered, "That does seem like a good idea. It is something you can do right now?"

"Of course. Find the bell you want to use. Oh! But it can be anything that would make a noise."

"I know the very thing," said the young queen as she began rummaging in the nearby closet. Soon she came out with a horn in her hand, the kind of metal horn used for celebrating the dawning of a new year.

The Spelling Bee of Oz

Handing it to the Bee, she said, "This would do very nicely."

They rejoined the others in the Magic Picture Room where the Spelling Bee explained what he had in mind. Then he held the horn in one hand and Zeebee's hand in another hand. Then waving the other two hands in mysterious ways and his antennas as well, he chanted:

Between these that are two,
May connections accrue.
That in a true halloo,
If she whispers;
It shouts.

Then the Spelling Bee repeated the same procedure with Amal and in the end he said, "Now all you have to do when you want to contact Ozma is to say, 'Horn blow,' and it will. Yes, it will. It will keep on blowing until Ozma picks it up. Yes. Then it will stop blowing. Indeed!"

"But she won't know what I want," objected Zeebee.

"No, no indeed, she will not, but she will then summon you with her Magic Belt and then you can tell her whatever you need to."

"Sounds like fun," said Amal.

"That seems to take care of everything. So, Zeebee, are you ready to go?"

"Yes and no," replied the little girl. "My parents need me to be at home, but I wish I could stay here, and at the same time I'm anxious to be home and telling everyone

Going Home

about my wonderful experiences here."

Ozma smiled upon her and said, "So, we are ready, but before sending you home, we should take a look at where we're sending you. Have to be sure that I send you to the right place. Tell me what your father's name is and where your home is."

"My father is Douglas Warren," and then gave her address in San Jose, California.

Ozma gave the Magic Picture that address and in a trice it was showing a brown and white ranch house at the end of a country lane.

"That's it," cried Zeebee. "Beautiful, beautiful home."

"Are you ready to go now?" asked Ozma.

"Yes, oh yes," and taking Ozga's hands in her own said, "you are such a lovely woman and have been so helpful in all this. I hope to see you again on my next visit."

Then Zeebee stepped over to Dorothy, giving her a hug, saying, "Now, when I look at you, I see myself! I never would have had this great adventure if we had not looked so much alike." Then she gave Dorothy a quick kiss on the cheek and moved to the Spelling Bee. To him she said, "How can I ever thank you? You saved me from serving the purposes of that dreadful, lying old Nome King."

Next she gave a big hug to Amal, and said, "Oh, I wish I did not have to leave you behind. I think you are one of the best friends I've ever had." Tears came to her eyes as she gave Amal a firm kiss on the cheek, a kiss that was returned on her own cheek.

Finally, she stood in front of Ozma and said, rather

The Spelling Bee of Oz

formally, "I want to thank you for everything, hospitality, sending the Invisible Children back to their homes, and especially for sending me back now."

Ozma smiled a broad smile, took Zeebee in her arms, and, planting a kiss on her cheek, said, "You are always welcome here, and you should treat me, not as a queen, but as a friend. After all, you have given me an important new nick-name." Then smiling and giving Zeebee a kiss on her other cheek, she said, "Now, if all is ready, I will send you home. Just repeat that address again."

Earlier Jellia Jamb had returned the Magic Belt to Ozma and so, with merely a touch and a wish, Zeebee disappeared from the room. At the same moment she could be seen in the Magic Picture, standing on the front step of her own home. A big, fluffy, black and white cat came out from under a bush by the door. He looked up at her and meowed a quiet little meow that she could not resist, so she bent over and picked up the willing cat, cuddling it as she continued into the house.

Although the people watching in Oz could not hear what was happening, they could see as she opened the front door, called into the house and her mother's head poked around the corner from the kitchen. There was a crash as she dropped the pan she had held in her hands, and shouted "Elizabeth! You're home!" and ran to embrace her.

Almost immediately a little boy came running from the back of the house, yelling, "Zeebee! Zeebee!" And he also threw his arms around his big sister.

In a worried tone her mother said, "What happened

Going Home

to you?"

"Oh Mother, Alvin, you wouldn't believe the wonderful time I've been having!" and she began telling all about her adventure in Oz. She had not told the half of it when her father arrived home from work and she had to go back and start over.

The people in Oz felt that this should be a private reunion and had stopped watching as soon as Zeebee's little brother had run into the room. As the Picture turned to a pastoral scene in the Quadling Country, Ozma and her friends went back down to join their friends in the Dining Hall.

By the time all that had happened, it was getting late, so everyone went off to bed.

Ozma, although she did not know it at the time, was going to need her sleep more than anyone, for she would be awake for quite a while during the night, all because of Knunk.

Chapter 22

Knunk Meets Ozma

By the time the sun was up on the next morning after his return to the forest beyond the Emerald City, Knunk had devised a plan. He hid himself by a stream, back in the woods, but alongside the road. Although many carts went by through the day, it was well into mid-afternoon by the time one of the drivers stopped to water his team, Knunk slipped into the back of the cart and hid himself by burrowing into the blue turnips that was its payload.

Thus he returned to the City without anyone knowing he was there. When the cart stopped at the market, Knunk waited until all was clear, and then crawled out from his hiding place and scooted down back alleys until he was close to the palace. By this time it was already dark and he could safely creep along the grass to the side of the palace. There he looked for an unlit window in the basement, and taking out his knife, he pried it open.

He found himself in a store room stacked with boxes and bundles. There were still people moving around in the halls and rooms above him, so he passed his time inspecting his immediate surroundings. Like all Nomes,

Knunk Meets Ozma

being accustomed to working in underground tunnels, he could see as well in the dark as any cat. His inspection revealed a number of boxes of clothing among many other things in this basement room. Checking them over, he found some children's clothing that was both suitable and a good fit for him, so he put them on. By keeping his face somewhat hidden, if anyone saw him, he would appear to be just another child.

When everything seemed quite quiet above him, in his child's disguise, he snuck out and up the stairs. He went straight to Ozma's room, having seen no one along the way. However, he found her door was locked, so he made his way up the stairs and back down the hall to a room that would be just above her suite. Being as quiet as possible, he turned the doorknob very slowly and the door opened. Entering the room, he closed the door with the same care, he then slipped through the rooms of this apartment. There was a bedroom with two children in bunk beds.

As quiet as a mouse he went to another room, which had a window, cut the cords from several curtains, tied the cords together and then to a doorknob near the window. He then lowered himself down beside one of Ozma's windows. He took out his trusty knife and began working at the window until he had it open.

Once inside, with great care, he crept through Ozma's rooms. He had seen where Ozma had gone to get the Magic Belt and that was where he was headed. When he reached what he remembered as being the right place, he tried to open the drawer, but it would

The Spelling Bee of Oz

not budge. He got out his knife and worked to try to pry open the drawers.

Then a soft and gentle voice behind him said, "May I help you?"

He jumped in the air, turning as he did so to see Ozma standing there in her green robe. He threw his knife at her, but it bounced harmlessly aside. Of course she had her magic wand in her hand. Waving it a bit, she said, "Now, now, little one. Don't be so impulsive. Little boys should not play with knives. They can be very dangerous," and the knife flew back, nicking his throwing hand and then returning to rest in the palm of Ozma's hand.

Pitching his voice high, Knunk said, "I was just investigating."

"And why were you investigating the safe of the Queen of Oz?"

"I didn't know. I was just investigating."

"And what did you expect to find?" By this time she was standing between him and the drawer he had been working so hard on. She pulled out the drawer, reached in, held up the Magic Belt, and said, "Was it this that you wanted, Knunk?"

"I'm not Knunk," he said, continuing with his high pitched voice.

Ozma turned on the light that illuminated that part of the wall and said, "I knew it was you all along, Knunk, from the time you came in my window. And I knew what you would be after."

In his normal voice, he said, "Since you know who I

Knunk Meets Ozma

am, I want to ask how you could open that drawer and I could not?"

In answer, Ozma waved her wand, saying, "It takes magic. But now what am I going to do with you?"

"Just send me home."

"Yes. That is going to happen. But first, how did you get here and how were you going to get back past the Deadly Desert?"

"We Nomes have our magic, too."

"I will not send you back until I know how you got here. I do not want any more invasions by Nomes."

"Oh, we'd never try that again."

Ozma put her hands on her hips and stared hard at Knunk for a long minute. While she did, he lowered his eyes, and then, very firmly, she said, "Tell me."

"I dare not. Korph would throw me to the seven-headed dog."

"You would prefer that I just toss you onto the Deadly Desert?" and she put the Magic Belt around her waist, leaving her hands resting on it.

Shaking his head and speaking quickly, he said, "No! No! Oh! This is terrible. Please don't even hint to Korph that I might have told you! Oh, please, please!"

Her hands still on the Belt, Ozma said, "All right. I promise I will not tell Korph that you told me how you got here."

Heaving a sigh of relief, the little Nome said, "All right, then. We have Magic Gates. They come in pairs. If you put one in one place, and the other someplace else, when you step through one, you step out through the

The Spelling Bee of Oz

other. Korph has a Magic Gate just outside his throne room, and the other one is in the eastern edge of your Emerald City area. One step from the Nome Kingdome to that spot. One day from there to here."

"I see. So what I will do is to send you, myself and several of my friends to that spot. Then you can go through the Gates just as you would be expected to."

The Nome looked worried as he shook his head.

Ozma continued, "You wouldn't want to suddenly show up in the Nome Kingdom, not having used the Magic Gates. Your King might ask you some embarrassing questions if that happened."

"Um, yes, I guess so, but I shouldn't show you the Magic Gate."

"Actually, you have no choice. We will take care of that in the morning. But in the meantime, what's this about Korph? Last I knew Kaliko was your king."

"That has changed."

"Apparently. But how?"

"When Kaliko resigned, Korph became our King."

Focusing her eyes right onto those of the little Nome, Ozma said, in a firm voice, "All right, now, quit beating around the bush. I want you to tell me exactly what happened."

Shifting his eyes away, Knunk finally said, "After General Guph failed to conquer Oz when he had the tunnel built under the Deadly Desert, he was sent to work in the mines, under guard, of course. Then Korph was elevated to Commanding General. After many years he decided that he had enough loyal followers that he

Knunk Meets Ozma

could stage a coup.

"So one day he walked into the throne room, where Kaliko was sitting on his throne with his crown upon his head. Reports say that he said to Kaliko, 'It is time for you to yield your throne to me.'

"Kaliko said, 'I think not,' and pounded on the gong beside him. Immediately, the back door opened and in came Alklank, Steward to the King. But he ignored Kaliko and went straight to Korph, where he bowed and said, 'What is your majesty's desire?'

"Korph said, 'Bring in the guards and have this interloper sent to work in the mines, under guard, of course.'

"Soon the guards hustled Kaliko out of the room, and Korph was sitting on the throne with the crown upon his head.

"Thus has it been ever since."

"All right" said the Queen. "You have nothing to fear from Korph. When we drove that rascal Roquat/Ruggedo out of your Kingdom, I installed Kaliko in his place. If Korph took the throne from him, I will have the two exchange places." Then looking at the clock on her bedstand she said, "I need to finish my sleep and so shall you."

She touched her Belt and waved her Fairy Wand, and the Nome disappeared from Ozma's Magic Picture Room only to reappear on a sofa in her Reception Room, fast asleep. She went back to her bedroom and slept soundly until morning.

Chapter 23

Ozma Visits the Nomes

In the morning, when Ozma awakened, she first dressed and then went in to wake up Knunk, saying, "You can have breakfast with us and then we'll go to the Magic Gate."

At breakfast there was a full score of the most famous inhabitants of the Royal Palace. She told them the story of the previous night's occurrences. When she had finished, Dorothy said, "You would not really have dropped him in the Deadly Desert, would you?"

"Of course not, but at the time he did not know that." She looked then, at Knunk and said, "Would you have answered me if you'd known I would not carry out that threat?"

"Umm, ahh, well, ah." By this time he was visibly shaking, but he continued slowly, "I don't suppose I would have."

"No. I don't think so either. I'm glad you did tell me the truth and in a few minutes you and Ozga, Dorothy, the Wizard, the Cowardly Lion, the Hungry Tiger and the Spelling Bee will be going through that Magic Gate you told me about."

Ozma Visits the Nomes

"Let me go too, Amira," said Amal.

"I don't think you should," replied Ozma. "This will be a dangerous trip."

"I've been in lots of danger. But anyway, I'll be safe if the Spelling Bee is there. And besides, there'll be you and Ozga and the Wizard, all with magic, too, and the fierce Cowardly Lion and Hungry Tiger. It's the Nomes that'll be in danger."

"Yes," spoke up the Spelling Bee. "I'll protect her."

"So will I," said the Cowardly Lion.

And others joined in.

"All right," said the Princess. "You have lots of protectors – and advocates. You may come, too."

"So, what's this about a Magic Gate?" asked Dorothy.

That question led to explaining the whole matter to everyone. "But that is only one thing we have to do," said Ozma. "There are other things. We have to complete the task of returning the Lost Children to their homes. We have to return Amal to her home. And we have to put up signs warning people about the dangers of the Country of the Invisible Children."

"That's a lot of important things," said Ozga. "What comes first?"

Ozma answered, "Since Korph may be planning more trouble for Oz, it is imperative that we get to him as soon as possible."

"Yes," said the Wizard, "and you should probably tend to that right away."

"I agree," said Ozma, "and while those of us I just named do that, those that remain here should proceed

The Spelling Bee of Oz

immediately with sending the Lost Children to their homes. Then, when I get back from the Nome Kingdom several of us will seed to putting up of the warning signs around the Country of the Invisible Children."

Speaking hesitantly, Amal said, "But, Amira, when do I go back home?"

Smiling and putting her hand upon the girl's shoulder, Ozma said, "That's entirely up to you. When you're ready to go I'll send you. Is it time yet?"

Amal looked at the Princess and said, "Er, not yet. I certainly want to be around for the return of the Lost Children and probably the punishment of that Nome King."

"Very good. So it shall be. Just tell me when you're ready."

And Amal said, "Okay. I will."

By this time, the meal was over and Ozma said, "Before we leave the table, I need to make some assignments.

"I have already named those who will go with me to the Nome Kingdom. But, Dorothy, I think it would be a good idea if we had Billina along with us, don't you?"

Dorothy jumped up as she said, "It certainly would be!" and off she ran to fetch her pet hen.

"Join us in my apartment," Ozma called after her. Then, looking down the table at all the others, she said, "Those of you not going with us, and probably some more that you will recruit, will stay here and see to reuniting the Lost Children with their families. Uncle Henry, will you take charge of that?"

"Sure as tootin'," replied Dorothy's Uncle. "I reckon

Ozma Visits the Nomes

I've got the operation down pat."

"All right then, you get to your work and, Shaggy, I have a task for you."

The Shaggy Man rose from his seat and headed down the table toward Ozma, saying, "Tell me what and I'll do my best, Amira." After that last word, he was just passing Amal and whispered, "Did I get it right?"

As she smiled and nodded, Ozma was saying, "We need signs to warn people of the dangers of the Country of the Invisible Children. Will you go out to the shops behind the palace and ask Broman to make as many as he can before we get back in the early afternoon?"

"Immediately," replied the Shaggy Man, and he hurried out of the room.

Now Ozma left her seat, saying, "Ozga, Wizard, Cowardly Lion, Hungry Tiger, Amal, Spelling Bee and, of course, Knunk, all of you, follow me up to my apartment."

When they reached there, she led them straight to the Magic Picture. Standing in front of it, she said "Show me to Korph!" and there he was, sitting on his throne. He was giving orders to a number of Nomes, each of whom left through various doors from time to time.

"He seems to be tending to the business of his Kingdom right now, so maybe there is no immediate worry. Let's go to that Magic Gate," and looking at Knunk she said, "Can you tell me where it is located?"

It took a few minutes to describe, for Knunk could only say that it was a little north of the Yellow Brick Road near the Munchkin border of the Emerald City area. But eventually, by using the Magic Picture to follow his

The Spelling Bee of Oz

memory of the path he took, the entrance was located and Ozma transported the whole group, including Dorothy and Billina, to a point right in front of it.

As soon as they were there, Knunk pushed the greenery aside and said goodbye. But Ozma gripped his arm with a surprisingly firm hold for a young lady, saying, "Not so quick. We're going down there with you."

Quivering, Knuck said, "But you surely don't want to go through the Gate, too?"

"As a matter of fact, we will. I need to take care of Korph's usurpation of power. So, you and I will hold hands as we go through the Gate."

"Me, hold hands with a fairy?"

"Me hold hands with a Nome?" and Ozma laughed as she took his hand firmly in her own. "Let's go."

As he started down the stairs, Korph said, "These stairs are rather dangerous. Be careful. Holding on to me could cause you to fall."

"I'm a fairy," said Ozma. "How could I fall?" Then with her voice growing stern she said, "That's enough of that Knunk. Stop trying to keep us from going with you." Then she let go of him and put both hands on her Belt and said, "Any more of that and I might turn you into a chicken!"

With the Nome's abject fear of death from eggs, Knunk cringed and said, "All right, come along!"

But before anyone could move the Cowardly Lion groaned and said, "I'm afraid I'll fall." He just stood on the edge of the pit and shivered.

Beside him, the Hungry Tiger said, "Here now, old

Ozma Visits the Nomes

friend. The Nomes will give trouble to Ozma. She's relying on your fierce strength to protect her. You can't let her down."

"You're right. I have to go down," and the great Lion took a first step, but then stopped and said, "But it's dark down there."

Dorothy said, "Take courage."

The Lion replied, "That's easy for you to say." But, as the little Nome led Ozma down a few more steps, the lights came on, and the Lion said, "Whew. Okay, that's better," and followed him, as did all the others, one by one with Dorothy carrying Billina.

As soon as Knunk stepped on the bottom step, Ozma reached out her hand and took his. He started to shrink away, but Ozma said, "Chicken?" And he relaxed and let her take his hand.

Ozma turned to the others and said, "There's not room for all of us in this space, so be prepared. As soon as Knunk and I go through the Magic Gate, I want each of you to follow on our heels, one after the other as fast as you can. He tells me it's a large enough room on the other side to accommodate thirty times as many people as we are."

Having spoken, Ozma led Knunk through the gate and instantly they were transported hundreds of miles away to a huge chamber with many gates lining the walls. They were in the middle of the Nome Kingdom and were quickly joined, first by one and then another of their party until finally the group was completed with the arrival of the Spelling Bee and Amal.

The Spelling Bee of Oz

Each of the Magic Gates had a label saying where it led, but there were two that were unlabeled. Knunk pointed to one of them and said, "That is the door into the throne room where you may well find Korph."

Ozma took a step toward the throne room's door, but then she stopped and, pointing to the other unmarked door said, "Where does that other door go?"

"To the main hallway."

"Let us take a look there," said the young Queen.

The Wizard was nearest to it and reached over and opened the door. Sure enough, a long and wide hallway stretched before them."

"All right," said Ozma, "we will go on into the throne room," and while the Wizard closed the hallway door, she put her hand on the doorknob of the throne room door. Before she could open it, she saw Knunk reaching for the doorknob to the door into the hallway. Putting her hands on the Magic Belt, Ozma called, "Knunk stop!"

He did. Very suddenly, with one foot in the hallway and one in the Magic Gate chamber.

"Where did you think you were going?" she asked. "We will need you until we actually are talking with Korph."

"But I dare not bring a group of surface dwellers into his presence, especially not with a chicken along."

"If you continue being so recalcitrant, I will make you carry the chicken! Come along now," and Ozma took his hand and opened the door.

The room was empty except for the big stone throne with a scepter on it, the gong standing beside it, and

Ozma Visits the Nomes

the thousands of glistening gemstones in the throne, and the huge walls which curved upwards to form the ceiling high above.

As everyone stood, enchanted by the gleaming gems, Amal murmured, "Flying genies! What a display!" And she stood in one place, but kept turning in order to see it all.

While she was doing so, Ozma went to the gong, took its drumstick off its hook and pounded on the gong. Once. Twice. Before she could hit it a third time, a door behind the throne flew open and a little scraggly Nome rushed in. On his second step, he stopped and cried out, "Get out of here, you upsiders! You have no right being here and you brought a chicken, to boot! Get out!"

Speaking softly, Ozma said, "Calm down. We mean you no harm. As Queen of Oz, I am here for a state visit with the King of the Nomes. Is that you?"

"Oh, no. I certainly am not the King! I am just his Steward, Alklank, but you must leave at once."

"I am sorry, but we do have to speak to your King." Then putting her hand out to the Nome, Ozma said, "Pleased to meet you, Alklank. As Steward, I presume you can lead us to your King."

He did not take her hand, but said, "Of course I can. The question is: Should I?" Then he looked at Knunk and said, "Or is this why King Korph sent you to Oz?"

Nodding his head and pursing his lips, Knunk, like most Nomes, feeling no particular need to be honest, said, "Yes. That's right. I'm to bring Ozma to see him."

Humping his shoulders and scowling, Alklank said,

The Spelling Bee of Oz

"All right, come this way," and he led off.

Ozma slipped back a bit so she could whisper to Knunk, "You may want to leave us now. If Korph were to see us together, he would think you had told me of his plans."

Knunk let out a wail, "But I did."

"Not until after Zeebee had told me most everything. Actually, more than you did. Don't blame yourself."

Brightening, Knunk said, "Yes, you're right! Korph would be after my scalp if he saw me with you. Thank you," and off he went, away from where Alklank was leading the Oz party.

Chapter 24

Korph or Kaliko

The route Alklank took them through was filled with passages and entrances to other passages. He took them around pits and through caverns until they finally came to a particular pit. There was a large sign in front of it that said:

PIT B

SMELTING

A number of Nomes were gathered there by the protective railing. The one with the crown on his head was studying the work going on below him with considerable attention. All the others were paying more attention to him than to the work below.

The Wizard whispered to Ozma, "I guess we know which one is Korph."

She giggled and nodded.

Not noticing their interchange, Alklank said, "If you will excuse me for a minute, I will go over to inform King Korph that you are here. That way he can determine whether he wants to see you or not."

The Spelling Bee of Oz

"No, Alklank, we will not excuse you. This is a state visit and he will see us."

As Ozma moved toward Korph, the Hungry Tiger stepped in front of the Steward who had started to take a step, then looked at the Tiger's wide open mouth and stood still.

The King of the Nomes was so engrossed in watching the work in the smelting pit that he paid no attention to Ozma and her friends as they approached him. However, the other Nomes did not miss the advance of the strangers and they warned him. At first he shook his head, but finally turned when Ozma was no more than four feet from him. His recognition of her was immediate and, scared though he was, he raised his hand and his voice, almost shouting, "Be gone, you interlopers! You belong on the surface! Go back to where you came from!"

Without raising her voice, Ozma said, "Now, don't get so excited. This is a state visit. I am here to confer with the Ruler of the Nomes."

But then, the King caught sight of Billina, the hen, in Dorothy's arms and said, "How dare you bring a vile chicken into my presence? I'll call my army of thousands and drive you all out," and without hesitation, he blew on a whistle that was hanging around his neck.

All the Nomes below dropped their tools and ran faster than imaginable toward hallways that could be seen at the edges of the great cavern, and, as they disappeared, others armed with pikes and swords and clubs began to appear in the passages behind the visitors from Oz.

Korph or Kaliko

Seeing them, the Spelling Bee began waving his arms and antennas as he recited:

Still you are
And still you will be,
Until this charm,
I, myself, undo.

As he said, "undo," all of the Nomes stopped and stood stock still in whatever pose they had been at that moment. Really, it made a rather humorous scene.

Once the Bee had begun his chant, Ozma just stood there with her hands on her Belt, but saying nothing. She wanted to see what his spell might do before she used the power of the Magic Belt to accomplish the same thing.

With the Bee's charm complete, Ozma spoke to him, saying, "I need to have a conversation with Korph. Can you release just him from this spell?"

"Of course," and while touching the King with one hand, he waved the other three and chanted,

From this one only,
Let the Statue Spell
Be lifted.

Then Ozma, standing right in front of Korph said, "Answer my questions and we'll leave as soon as we have taken care of all the answers."

The Nome replied, "I'm not doing a thing until he

The Spelling Bee of Oz

releases my Nomes from that dreadful spell he put on them."

"Would you prefer that I turn them all into eggs?"

"You wouldn't!"

"I do not trust them so long as they are free to attack us, so they shall remain immobilized and you will talk to me." Putting her hands on the Magic Belt, she continued, "Which will it be?"

The Nome King shuffled his feet and turned this way and that before answering, "All right. Let's talk."

"Are you the King of the Nomes"?

"Yes."

"How can that be? I thought Kaliko was King of the Nomes."

"Ah, yes. He was, but about two months ago the Nomes decided they wanted a new King, and I was elected."

"The Nomes had an election?"

"Yes, and it worked!"

"I still have someone else to question. Where can I find Kaliko?"

Looking off in the distance, Korph said, "I really don't know."

"Well I do," and Ozma touched her Magic Belt and said, "Bring Kaliko here," and there he stood right beside her.

He was covered with a layer of dirt, his clothes were somewhat torn and he was trying to grasp with his hands something that was not there. His mouth was open he had a mystified look. Slowly he said, "Where am I? What

Korph or Kaliko

happened?" By this time he began to take in the scene around him - Ozma, Korph, the big cats, the chicken - and a shiver went up and down his spine.

Ozma spoke to him, saying, "Kaliko, everything is about to be put right again if you answer my questions truthfully."

The Wizard reached out and put a hand on Kaliko's shoulder, as he said in gentle tones, "Pull yourself together now, old man, and do as she says."

Kaliko first shook his head and then he nodded, paused a moment, and said, "All right, I will answer your questions, and truthfully."

Before doing so, Ozma whispered to Ozga, "Have the Cowardly Lion and Hungry Tiger stand on either side of Korph, and you behind him. He will either try to run away or interfere. Stop him in either case."

Ozga did so and Korph looked from one of the great cats to the other. As he did, each smiled at him, only making him all the more nervous.

Ozma then said to Kaliko, "My first question is: Where were you just before I brought you here?"

"I was in my prison cell."

"Why were you in prison?"

"Korph sent me there to keep me from taking the throne back from him."

"Reasonable enough, if he came by the throne honestly. Did he?."

"No. He brought a score of soldiers with him and forcibly took the crown from me. Then he sent me to prison."

The Spelling Bee of Oz

At first, as the questioning proceeded, Korph cowered between the two great cats, but then his resolution returned and he said, "No! No! That is not the way it was! The Nomes wanted a new King, and asked me to be it! I had to take some soldiers with me to see Kaliko, knowing he would resist."

Ozma smiled at both of the Nomes and said, "So I have two stories, only one of which can be true. The other is false. Which is which?"

Both Nomes insisted that his was the true version.

Still smiling, Ozma turned to where Alklank stood behind everyone else and said, "Alklank, summon all the Nomes to the assembly hall. We will meet you and them there." Then, turning to her friends, she said, "Come, and be sure that Korph is with us all the time."

With Kaliko beside her, she led the way to that same huge assembly hall that she had seen on her first visit to the Nome Kingdom, long years ago.

It took a while for all the Nomes, or at least a major portion of them, to assemble. When sufficient numbers of Nomes seemed to be present, Ozma called for quiet. There was little response, so the Cowardly Lion and Hungry Tiger both roared their loudest and with utmost ferocity until the walls shook. Then, in a soft voice, the Cowardly Lion said, "Quiet now, if you please."

There was silence.

Ozma, standing at the railing of the balcony with Korph on her left and Kaliko on her right, said, "There seems to be some confusion about who your king is. Both of these men claim it. Which one do you want as

Korph or Kaliko

. . . but mostly it was pandemonium.

your King? Or should it be someone else?"

There was a total confusion of answers. Many shouted, "It should be me!" A few other names could be heard along with "Korph," or "Kaliko," but mostly it was pandemonium.

After a while, Ozma called for quiet again. This time they did quiet down without her resorting to the Lion and Tiger. Then she said, "It is hard to tell by the voices, so I ask you to divide; all those for Kaliko on this side," and she motioned to her left, "and all those for Korph on this side," as she motioned to her right "and all those who want someone else to the back of the room," as she indicated the far end of the great cavern.

The Spelling Bee of Oz

It was nearly an hour before the decision was clear. In the beginning, Nomes began moving rather haphazardly, one way or the other. Many were simply milling around in the middle. But the largest number had gone to the back of the room.

After a while, it settled down, and Ozma said, "It looks like the majority would like someone else to be your king. Let me confer with my colleagues for a moment."

So saying, she gathered all her friends close around her and said, "A majority seem to want someone else, but I don't imagine there is any large number interested in any one person."

"Right," said the Wizard. "Knowing the nature of Nomes, I suspect that ninety percent of them would vote for himself."

Several snickered and Ozma said, "Exactly. So I think I can sort this out rather quickly," and she returned to the balcony overlooking the great cavern.

After calling for attention again, she said, "All right, those of you who want some other than Kaliko or Korph for king, if you want that to be someone other than yourself, raise your hand."

About thirty hands out of thousands went up.

"I thought as much. So there are thousands of single votes for thousands of different people. None of those count. And there are around thirty votes that are for various people other than oneself — not enough to elect. So the contest is now, only between Korph and Kaliko and I want all of you at the back to range yourself on this

Korph or Kaliko

side for Korph," and she indicated her right, "and all of those for Kaliko to this side," and she indicated her left.

In a short time, many of them had moved to one side or the other, but the majority were just milling around, seeming to move one way, then the other. Quite soon though, more seemed to be moving toward Kaliko's side and then in a surge, many who had headed for Korph's side turned and went to Kaliko's. As more and more moved to the left of Ozma, there was a new crescendo in the noise of their voices.

Korph had tried to flee several times as the rush to Kaliko's side had begun, but each time there was the wide smile of one of the two great cats to greet him and he stayed put. Finally, when everyone had gone over to Kaliko's side, the noise of those talking about it grew exceedingly loud.

When the Tiger and Lion roared for silence, the crowd hushed very quickly and Korph could be heard to say to Ozma, "They have chosen wisely. I was tired of the job anyway." Then taking it off his head, he added, "Here's the crown." Handing it to Ozma, he bowed to her and Kaliko and walked away.

Ozma said to Kaliko, "When we get back to the throne room, you may occupy the throne again and I will place the crown upon your head."

This was done with much pomp and ceremony. But when it was over, Ozma said, "You may not be aware that, while he had the throne, Korph reopened your Magic Gate leading to Oz."

"How could he do that?"

The Spelling Bee of Oz

"I have no idea, but he did it. You might ask Knunk about it. He was the one that, under a bit of duress, told me about it."

Kaliko turned to Alklank and said, "Fetch Knunk for me."

Feeling this must mean that he was still Steward, Alklank smiled broadly, bowed low and went out. As he left, Ozma said, "We cannot have any gateway that allows anyone to come into Oz whenever they wish. Oz must remain cut off from the rest of the world. People should come to Oz only by invitation."

It took a while, but Ozma finally convinced him that the Magic Gate had to be closed. She ended by saying, "I see four options. First, I could just fill the hole where it is with dirt and anyone coming through the Gate would be smothered in it. Secondly, it would be a simple matter for me to put the Gate that is in Oz out on the Deadly Desert, giving a horrible death to anyone using it. Thirdly, I could simply destroy the Gate at our end, making the other useless. Finally, I could place this Gate someplace where it would be useful to you. I will leave the choice between those four options up to you."

"Kaliko looked at her for only a very short time, frowning and then said, "If you will not allow me to keep that Gate into Oz, the choice is simple. The first two alternatives would be simply awful. The third would be useless. So, of course, I would choose the one where we put it in some useful place."

Then there was another delay as they tried to come to agreement as to where that should be. Kaliko kept

Korph or Kaliko

suggesting places where other countries had their own mines, but Ozma absolutely refused to help him invade other countries. Finally they agreed on putting the Gate at the end of the Nome's longest tunnel, one that currently required a walk of five days to the mine and a longer time to return with a cart full of jewels.

Using the Magic Belt, Ozma took Kaliko and the Cowardly Lion there so that she could see the situation, then back to the location of the Magic Gate in Oz. Using the Magic Belt, she commanded that the Gate be moved to its new location and it was gone.

Next, she took the three of them back to the Nome Kingdom where she and the Cowardly Lion joined their friends, said goodbye to Kaliko, and returned in an instant to the Emerald City.

Chapter 25

Upper Stallingham

The trip of Ozma and her friends to the Nome Kingdom had taken six hours and all were as hungry as tigers, one of them most fittingly so. Thankfully, Baliol, the Head Chef for the palace, was prepared and he set out a quick cold lunch for them. Not only that, but before they were done, he was even able to add a few hot things to their repast.

While they ate, Aunt Em came down to report on the progress being made by Uncle Henry in returning the Lost Children to their homes Everyone in the palace had willingly pitched in to help do the job. Most of a process that could easily have taken weeks was already three-quarters finished.

Each picture that had been sent out to be posted throughout the land had instructions on it. This included directions for signaling at particular times whenever a person could identify a child. Twenty-four hours a day someone was stationed at the Magic Picture, checking each posted picture on schedule. Betsy Bobbin had the first turn and she had four successful reports of a lost child being identified. Later viewers reported similar

Upper Stallingham

results.

With the early successes having been reported to her, Ozma told her friends gathered around the table, "After we finish eating, we're going to have to put up the warning signs around the Country of Invisible Children. Can all of you help me?"

Everyone agreed without any delay, so then Ozma said, "However, someone has got to take a considerable risk. In order to identify the borders of that Country, we will need to see a child disappear." Then, looking at Dorothy and Amal, she asked, "Is either of you willing to risk it? We'll all be right there, and you will be holding my hand as you disappear. The risk should be minimal so long as you don't drop my hand and run away."

With no hesitation, Dorothy responded, "That's good enough for me."

Amal took a little longer, but then said, "Sure. Why not?"

So, out they all went, stopping along the way to get the Wooden Sawhorse and a wagon to carry the signs. Reaching the shops, they found that the Shaggy Man and Broman were just finishing the ninth warning sign

"These should suffice for now," she said. "Why don't the two of you join us and we'll leave right away." She still had the Magic Belt on, so they loaded up the wagon, all stood close together, and Ozma said, "Let us all be in the town square of Upper Stallingham."

And they were.

Of course, their arrival drew a crowd. Everyone was excited about actually having their nation's Ruler in

The Spelling Bee of Oz

their own town, and with her, there were other famous people and creatures, as well. The citizenry wanted a big celebration, so Mayor Cadwallader spoke for them, saying, "We must celebrate this auspicious arrival with a great festal board."

Before he could start giving orders, Ozma interrupted, "Not just yet, dear Mayor. First we have to get these signs put up all around the Country of Invisible Children to warn people of the danger."

From the lowliest Upper Stallinghamer right up to Mayor Cadwallader himself, all agreed to that and volunteered to help. Then everyone followed Ozma and the Spelling Bee down the road to the cornfield that marked the boundary of the Country of Invisible Children.

Along the way some of the local children, having heard what Dorothy and Amal were going to do, volunteered to do the same if their parents would hold their hands. With the help of all these good people, it did not take long to get signs put up about every thirty feet along the border of the Country of Invisible Children, but the nine signs they had were not enough to go all the way around.

Ozma said they should go back to the Emerald City to make more, but Mayor Cadwallader said, "Upper Stallingham is blessed with as capable sign makers as you will find anywhere in the fair Land of Oz. Rest assured, most gracious Ruler, that we will do the job ourselves."

"That is very good of you," she replied. "In that case, we will leave now."

Upper Stallingham

"I will not hear of it," said Cadwallader. "Not at all. We promised you a great meal and we will produce the greatest spread imaginable. You and your friends will be our honored guests." And he began giving orders to people to prepare the food, to rearrange the assembly hall into a dining room and to bring chairs and tables and all that would be needed.

While he was doing so and the citizens of Upper Stallingham were hopping to his every command, Ozma used the Magic Belt to send a note to Jellia Jamb, telling her what was happening and that she would continue the process of sending the Lost Children home in the morning.

During the great banquet, the Shaggy Man asked, "Where is Lower Stallingham or Middle Stallingham, or whatever?"

Mayor Cadwallader laughed and then said, "There are no other Stallinghams. Upper is all there is, all there ever has been."

"So why is it 'Upper'?" asked Ozma. "It is not even located on top of a hill."

"That story will take a bit of telling."

"Go ahead then. We would like to know," she said.

"Many centuries ago, actually, only a few years before the Enchantment of Oz, there was a man, his wife and all their possessions carried in a cart pulled by two oxen. All their possessions, that is, except for a grubbing of pigs that followed the cart. The place where they lived had grown too crowded, so they were looking for a new home. They were following the very road upon which

The Spelling Bee of Oz

our town is located when the pigs got tired of walking and refused to budge another foot.

"Tangell, the husband, said, 'I do believe the pigs have found us our new home.' So they unloaded their goods, covered them with a tarp, set up their own temporary tent and the good man began to build their new home."

Waving his arms around, the Mayor said, "And that home was located right where this very building is now. Then, even before he was finished,, Tangell said, 'We have to have a name for our little villa. I don't think "Pigstop" sounds quite right.'

"After a few minutes thought, the wife, Pansy, said, 'This is where the pigs stopped us, so, how about "Hamstall"?'

"'Yes. Much better. We will call it …. No, no. Wait. Reverse it. We will name it "Stallingham"!'

"And so it was called, and the husband put out a sign in front of his home, naming it, 'Stallingham.'

"Tangell and Pansy were friendly people and they enjoyed entertaining visitors. So, it was not long before another family decided to settle down near them. Then another and another. By this time, the name 'Stallingham' had come to be applied to the whole village and so large signs were placed at either end of the one road through town, saying,

STALLINGHAM
A choice village
Your choice of villages

Upper Stallingham

"More and more people were attracted until, one day, one of the newcomers, Quimpy, suggested, 'Stallingham is a nice name, but I think we would have more class if we added "Upper" to it.'

"Someone else said, 'Stallinghamupper'?"

"'No, no, no!' was the response, "Upper Stallingham."

"Several others approved of the idea and both signs were amended to put 'Upper' in front of 'Stallingham.'

The Mayor concluded, "And so that is how we came to have our name."

"What an interesting story," said Ozma. "I doubt if it can be found in any of the annals of Oz, so I'll rectify that oversight immediately." Then turning to the Shaggy Man, she asked him, "May I send you to Hoeborn Tower to fetch Terwilliger."

"Assuredly. This certainly would be of interest to the Royal Hoztorian."

Then she said, "I want him to come here, stay overnight and record the names and dates we have just heard and any other information pertaining to this town's hoztory and geozophy. Of course he will include their marvelous help in warning people of the dangers of the Country of Invisible Children."

"I'd be pleased to do that ," he said.

"Would half an hour be enough time?"

"Should be, I'd say," replied the Shaggy Man.

With that, Ozma touched her Belt and he disappeared. The meal continued and half an hour later, she touched her Belt again and there stood the Shaggy Man and Terwilliger.

The Spelling Bee of Oz

The latter, unlike most people in Oz, wore a bi-colored outfit, part blue and part purple, for he lived high in the mountains on the border between the purple country of the Gillikins and the blue country of the Munchkins.

In his tower-castle he had a vast collection of every known document dealing with the hoztory of Oz. Isolated though his castle was, he was not lonely for he had a wife and three children and 123 loyal followers. They were not so much servants as friends and there existed in his domain a strong sense of fellowship, for everyone was considered equal to every other one.

Terwilliger being a rather large mouthful, his friends, everyone in Hoeborn Tower at least, called him "Lee," or, sometimes for the fun of it, "Double Lee." He was a tall, rangy, bespectacled man, the picture of the scholar, but one should not be fooled into thinking he was a weakling. He was very athletic and each winter spent some time at Professor Wogglebug's Royal Athletic College of Oz where he was the player-coach of the basketball team. Of course, basketball in Oz was a little different from that played on Earth: since there were sapient flying species in Oz, it was necessarily a three-dimensional game.

The first team that used a flying creature was impossible to beat because it scored every time it got the ball. It was the Munchkin Blues that played a giant blue eagle named Hilda. Just toss the ball to the flyer and she would fly over the goal and stuff it in. Also, she could hover near the basket and so long as she hit it on the way up, she could knock the ball away from the basket.

There were many parties and celebrations. Every

Upper Stallingham

national holiday was an excuse for a big celebration as was each of the 128 birthdays. Of course there had to be a division of labor, and Terwilliger was unquestionably in charge, but he always listened to what anyone else had to say. Some people were cooks, some waiters, some grew vegetables and fruits, some cared for animals, some were craftsmen and craftswomen, but the menial and servile tasks were shared equally by all.

Over dinner Ozma told him what she wanted of him. He took notes and by the time the banquet was over, Mayor Cadwallader had invited him to stay the night with him so they could discuss the hoztory of Upper Stallingham at their leisure.

After dinner, the rest of the people from the Emerald City returned home. By the time they got there, they were all so tired they went straight to bed. But in the morning everyone was up, breakfasted and working hard before nine.

The process of finding the homes for the Lost Children went more smoothly even than expected, so that only this last day was needed to reunite all the children with their families. Each time a home was located, everyone wanted to go to the room of the Magic Picture to say farewell to the one going home. However, at the beginning, there was not that much space in the room, so only a few of their closest friends were able to accompany those getting ready to go home. Most of their goodbyes had to be said before they headed to the Magic Picture.

Now, on this last day, it was finally possible for all

The Spelling Bee of Oz

the children that were left to crowd into Ozma's room, as she sent each one home. They now had the luxury of being able to bid goodbye standing right at the picture and seeing their friends as they were welcomed by their families.

Finally, all the children had been sent to their own homes. That is, all but one. That one was Uthur. As usual, he had said nothing when all the others were talking about finding their homes. One who does not speak is not heard. But now, being the only one left, they knew he had been missed. So Ozma took the little boy in her arms and said, "Have we found no sign of a home for you?"

He shook his head.

"Do you remember anything about your home?"

Again, he shook his head.

Then Ozma said, "Tell me everything you can remember about your home?"

He shrugged his shoulders.

"What colors do you remember around your home?"

He shook his head.

"Do you remember any colors at all?"

Again he shook his head.

"Do you remember anything about your parents? Were they fat or slim, dark hair or light hair?"

Whatever she asked him, he just shook his head.

Running out of possibilities, Ozma gave up and talked with the Spelling Bee and Amal about it. In the end, they decided that the only thing to do was to take him back to Upper Stallingham. Ozma used the Magic Belt to take

Upper Stallingham

all four of them to the family that had fed and housed the boy that one night in the village. They were a young childless couple and they were pleased to have him join their home for good.

The next day they were back in the Emerald City where Ozma saw to it that Amal was assigned to an apartment of her own equipped with new clean clothes of the Ozian style and, as soon as she was spruced up, everyone gathered in Ozma's study to hear Amal tell of life in Mogadishu.

She began, "Somalia is a beautiful country, or at least it used to be. Of course never so beautiful as Oz. Somalia is much dryer. We have much bare ground, but also many trees, although different from yours. Ours are mostly palms and acacias.

Originally, I lived in a beautiful and comfortable large home. My father was a government executive with good pay, so we had many luxuries – fine car, exquisite gowns and expensive private schools. We led an easy life, but there was rebellion in the air and soon fighting broke out. One day I came home from school and found my home destroyed and my parents and all my brothers and sisters dead. I could find no one, none of our family's relatives or friends who could help me. Many were dead. Others were just as homeless as I. I don't know what the revolution was about, but it certainly had nothing to do with the rights of people. Everything had been turned topsy-turvy.

"From then on, I have lived in the streets of Mogadishu, sleeping in a little hollow in a bombed out

The Spelling Bee of Oz

building. My friends are a small group of other street children and several street merchants that help us. They provide us with some food, we beg for more and we scavenge for other food. It's really not such a bad life, but to be perfectly honest, I prefer the life I grew up with."

She stopped there and no one spoke for a while, until Ozma said, "How would you like to live in Oz permanently?"

"Oh, I would love that. It would be ideal!" As Ozma started to nod her head, Amal went on, "But no. I think I should go back to be with my friends at home. They need me. I need them. But, maybe a couple more days here."

"Of course," said Ozma, "and I have already shown you the signal to give at four p.m. any time you want to come back for a visit or to stay.

Chapter 26

Amal's Return

During the next couple days, Amal was shown as much of Oz as could be done. By using the Magic Belt, Ozma took her and the Spelling Bee to visit Glinda, the Tin Woodman, the Scarecrow and Jack Pumpkinhead. She took them to meet the King of the Munchkins and the King of the Gillikins. They visited Dorothy's old house where it had landed on the Wicked Witch of the East, now a National Monument of the Munchkins.

All of this kept Amal very busy during those two days, but it also kept her with her first Ozian friend, the Spelling Bee.

Finally the day came for Amal to go home.

"Praise Allah! I have had such a wonderful time here. I don't know how I'll ever thank you all for being such good friends to me."

"No more so than we have enjoyed your being with us," responded the young Queen.

Amal reached out and gave her a big hug, saying, "Really, part of me hates to leave here, but part of me is anxious to see all my old friends and tell them of my

The Spelling Bee of Oz

marvelous adventures."

"You might not want to tell your friends," said Dorothy. "After my first visit to Oz, when I tried to tell people about it, they thought I was just making up stories, maybe even dreaming."

"True. True," remarked the Wizard. "No one will believe you've been to Oz. They'll say you just dreamed it. Harrumph. That, I'm afraid, is the usual explanation among Earth people."

"My friends will believe me," countered Amal.

"Mine didn't," said Dorothy.

"Nor mine," said the Wizard, "but of course I had a reputation for stretching the truth a bit."

"If my friends think it's a dream," said Amal, "I'll just go along with them and tell them all my adventures anyway."

"That's the spirit," said Dorothy.

All that was left was another round of goodbyes, and for Ozma to touch her Magic Belt and say the words to send Amal home.

The moment she disappeared from Ozma's room, Ozma looked at the Magic Picture and said, "Show us Amal."

As in Oz, so in Somalia. It was a little past lunch time and Amal streaked away from the little depression next to the wall that was her home, running to find some of her friends. The first was Mona, who was so utterly surprised to see her that she jumped up, shouting "Amal! Dear one! You are alive," and rushed to hug her. The two celebrated for a moment and then Mona said, "When you

Amal's Return

did not show up at all the day of the hand grenade, we decided that you must have been killed, but here you are! Alive and well!" After a little more excited talking, they went on to find the rest of their friends and each one was surprised and so pleased to have Amal back.

It was Jamal who said, "You're not only alive and well, but you look better fed than I have ever seen you. Where have you been?"

"In Oz, and just wait until I tell you about all that happened there."

So the next couple hours was a mixture of rejoicing over her safe return and an account of her adventures in Oz. Everyone was jabbering all at once, but Ozma, Dorothy and the Spelling Bee could hear nothing of those happy sounds coming from all the children, only the expressions of glee upon their faces.

However, Amal found that things had changed in Mogadishu. No longer did the street orphans need to fear for their lives every moment. Streets were cleaner, electricity and water were available, libraries and schools were open again. All the advantages of civil government had been restored.

It would be a year after Amal returned to Somalia before the senseless killing that had been the way of life in Mogadishu truly came to an end. Many of the advantages of civil government were once more available.

When Amal returned, her friends were overjoyed to see her again and everyone celebrated the fact that she had not been killed, after all. But, within a few days, the children's lives settled back into the usual rhythm

The Spelling Bee of Oz

of playing together while searching for food for the day. However, there was a new sense of security, for the savage militia and rebels had been driven from the city, and the killing of children for no reason at all had ceased. The only danger was an occasional attack upon the city by rebels.

The months went by, but unknown to the others, Amal had a particular thought going through her head. Finally, in early July of the following year, she decided the time had come to do something about it, and she had a conversation with Ahmed and Mumino. Then she talked with Mona, Jamal, Abdul, Anab and Hawa. That afternoon at four o'clock, she found a place where she could be alone, raised her hand in the air with her fingers crossed in a particular way, and in an instant she was standing with Ozma and Dorothy in front of the Magic Picture.

Both of the young ladies threw their arms around Amal and she returned their hugs.

Ozma said, "Oh! It's great to see you again Amal."

"And it's great to see you two, Dorothy and Amira!" (She used the Somalian name she had given Ozma). "I think often of the good times we had, here and visiting around Oz."

"So, you're here to have some more good times?" asked Dorothy.

"I'm afraid not. I'll have to hurry right back. Everything has changed in Mogadishu. The fighting is over, stability is returning and my friends and I have come up with an idea."

Amal's Return

"What's that?" asked Dorothy.

"First, is the Spelling Bee around?"

"No," said Dorothy.

"But I can have him here in the snap of the fingers," said Ozma.

"I'd like to see him, too, while I'm here," said Amal.

It took but a moment to direct the Magic Picture to show him and then transfer him to stand beside them.

"Oh my! Where am I? My golden proboscis, what's happened?" exclaimed the flustered Bee as he appeared in front of the three young women.

Amal threw her arms around him as she said, "It's all right. I just wanted to see you again."

As he grew calmer, the Bee said, "Yes, yes, of course. Ahem. Everything is all right. I was just startled. Hello to you all, and especially to my dear Amal."

Ozma said, "It was at her request that I brought you here. She is only having a short visit this time."

"How fortunate I am. Oh yes. Oh yes!" replied the big Bee and then he asked Amal, "My dearest child, what is it then that brings you here?"

"I was just beginning to explain to Amira and Dorothy when I thought I'd like to see you before I return home."

"I am so honored that you wanted to see insignificant little — ah, maybe not so little — me," said the Spelling Bee.

"You're not so insignificant," said Ozma. "You are not only the biggest bee there is, you also have a great command of spells and spelling and once, not so long ago, you saved the Kingdom."

The Spelling Bee of Oz

"Ah now, you're exaggerating. I will admit that I helped, but you and Glinda and the others had a lot to do with it, too."

"You're right," returned Ozma. "But now, let's have Amal, continue with her story."

But, instead of going ahead, Amal suddenly said, "Hey! What's happened? My clothes suddenly feel kinda' loose on me."

Dorothy laughed and said, "The same thing happened to me once. You know we don't age in Oz unless we want

"Yes."

"But we do age when we're on Earth. So, each time we travel between Oz and the outside world, we return to our age in that world. In my case, I have come to Oz six times and gone back to Earth five times. At first, I didn't know I could stop aging, but when I moved here permanently, I learned I could, and stopped at eleven.

"About twenty-five years later, I happened to have sand from Wish Way in my pocket when, full of nostalgia, I wished myself back to America. Since I would have been thirty-six there, I soon grew to that size. Before long, I wished myself back to Oz where I was soon back to my eleven-year old size."

While Dorothy was talking, Ozma had rung for Jellia Jamb and instructed her to go to Amal's apartment and bring her a suitable outfit. Now she said, "You see Amal, that's the way it worked for you just now."

Amal said, "Will wonders never cease?"

"I hope not," said Dorothy.

Amal's Return

Amal continued, "Here I am as a ten-year-old again, and in a few minutes when you send me back, I will suddenly be an eleven-year-old once more!"

Ozma said, "You just said 'in a few minutes.' You will at least stay for dinner, won't you?"

Amal nodded her head rapidly and said, "Yes. I'd like to do that."

Both Ozma and Dorothy said, "That's good," and Dorothy added, "Now, Amal, you can go on with your story."

Squaring herself around, Amal said, "Okay, so things have changed in Mogadishu. Although there is still a lot of fighting, things are not as bad as they were and there is this merchant friend and his wife who would be willing to be the house parents for a group of orphans, and we'd have a school in the building too.

"Ahem. Pardon me," said the Spelling Bee. "I don't mean to be interrupting — Harrumph — but what would you call this building?"

"Since Amira is helping us with it, I would like to name it after her — 'Amira House.' To the people of Mogadishu, that would be 'Princess House'."

"Ay, yes, I see." said the Spelling Bee. "So then, once it is built, you and all your friends will live there instead of out on the streets?"

"That's right, but we need help in order to get it built."

"What kind of help?" asked Ozma.

"We can do the searching for a suitable place. In fact, just talking about it, we already know of several

The Spelling Bee of Oz

possibilities. But how do we manage to acquire one of them? We have no money. Is there some sort of magic you can use that might help us?"

"Magic?" asked Ozma. "Maybe not what you're thinking, but maybe the magic of jewels would work."

"What do you mean?"

"I understand that in your world, our rubies and emeralds are of great value, especially some of our bigger ones."

"That's true."

"So maybe I could give you a couple before you go back."

Dorothy interrupted at this point, asking, "Do you know how to get money for gemstones?"

"Not exactly," replied Amal, "but I'm sure that Ahmed would know how to do it. He's the merchant I just mentioned and he knows all about buying and selling everything."

"Oh, but my dear little one," said the Spelling Bee. "Are you truly certain that you can trust him? I understand that there are a lot of dishonest people in your world."

"We've trusted him with our lives more than once. I'm sure he will help us and be honest about it, too."

"All right then," said Ozma, "after dinner and before you leave, I'll give you a couple fine gems for starters."

Then it was time to go to dinner where all the famous residents of the palace joined them. It was a special joy for Amal to be with so many of them, just as it was a joy for them to be with her. She had become a favorite among the people of the palace. Her street adventures

Amal's Return

were quite an unknown kind of experience for most of them, except for the Shaggy Man and Button-Bright, both of whom had had spent much time on the streets.

During the dinner, the Spelling Bee said, "Now, dear little Amal, you have piqued my interest. I want to see you be successful with your Amira House. Yes, successful."

"We will be."

"I wonder," said Ozma, "if maybe we could watch you?"

"How could you do that?"

"Oh," replied the Spelling Bee, "you know, with her marvelous Magic Picture."

"Of course!" said the little girl.

"In that case," said Ozma, "if you stay overnight, then when I give you the jewels and send you back in the morning, we will not only watch you return, we can keep on watching to see how well you succeed in trading those jewels for the money to start your, ah, Amira House."

Amal agreed to this and after the dinner, when everyone went to their own rooms, Amal, too, had a room of her own to sleep in. When morning came, she dressed in the clothes she had arrived in, only by this time, they had been washed and well mended.

After breakfast, Ozma, Amal, Dorothy and the Spelling Bee gathered for one last time in Ozma's apartment.

The young Queen went to the wall, tapped it with her wand and out popped a drawer, surprising Amal, for it had not even been visible. From it, she extracted an emerald and a ruby and said, "These will be yours to use

The Spelling Bee of Oz

for your Amira House."

"I knew that, somehow, you could help us, but I don't know how my friends and I can ever thank you enough! You are such a good person, Amira."

Ozma smiled and said, "I do no more than anyone should for a friend."

The Spelling Bee, ruffled his wings in a nervous way and then said, "Ahem, you see I've been thinking. Yes. Magic will not work back in your home, that is it will not. But I may have something that will. Maybe a bit of a spell that is a blessing. Yes. This should be of some help to you.

> May your life be full of love, laughter, peace, adventure and inquisitiveness;
> May Amira House be always a place of secure refuge and passionate learning; and
> May you always remember Oz and sometimes return here to us who also love you.

With that, the great Bee threw his four arms around Amal and said, "Do come back again. You have been a blessing in my life."

All four exchanged hugs with one another, tearful ones with Amal, and then it was time for Ozma to touch the Belt to send their friend back to Mogadishu. The remaining three watched as she appeared in her old familiar spot in the corner of the destroyed building.

Amal looked about for a very short time and then ran straight to see Ahmed and Mumino. Although the adults

Amal's Return

had always been a bit skeptical of her stories about Oz, when she showed them the two large and beautiful jewels — a red, red ruby and a deep green emerald — their eyes bulged with wonderment. Then she explained how these jewels could build and equip what they needed for a home for all eight of them and a school for the six children and space to add others from the streets and money to pay a teacher.

Ahmed and Mumino were still somewhat doubtful about Oz, but the jewels certainly appeared to be real and when a reliable jeweler that Ahmed knew not only confirmed the great value of the jewels, but also made arrangements for them to trade them for cash, that was enough.

Back in Oz, Ozma, Dorothy and the Spelling Bee had been watching all that Amal was doing. Although they could hear nothing of it, the expressions on faces and in movements was enough for them to get the gist of what was going on.

Towards the end, Ozma said, "It looks to me like Amal is going to get her school and orphanage built."

"Thanks to you," said the Spelling Bee.

"But the greatest gift to her," said Ozma, "I'm sure, was your blessing."

The Oz Books

If you have enjoyed this book, you will probably be interested in the International Wizard of Oz Club. Not only does it publish *The Baum Bugle* three times a year, a magazine with much valuable information and opinion about Oz and things related to it; but it also arranges for regional meetings of people interested in Oz and tells you about other Oz events going on in the world.

Contact:
The International Wizard of Oz Club
P. O. Box 2657
Alameda CA, 94501, USA
or www.ozcub.org

What is an Oz book? A few people declare that only *The Wizard of Oz* is eligible. A few more limit them to the books by L. Frank Baum. Most people accept the Famous Forty, that is, *The Wizard of Oz* plus the 39 Oz books published by Reilly & Britton and its successor, Reilly and Lee. Many, including this author, add to that most of the other fairy tales by Baum (*Borderland of Oz* books), any other Oz book written by the authors of

The Oz Books

the Famous Forty and any published by the International Wizard of Oz Club by such authors as Dick Martin and Virginia Wickwar. Many others, including this author, would add to those any other Oz books written in the spirit of the Baum-Thompson books. Of course this latter is a highly subjective standard of judgment, but in the following list, that means the seven Shanower books, and some by Gjovaag-Carlson, Hess and Eichorn. Other people would include any book that has the word Oz in the title, extending the list to several hundred.

Most Oz books and Borderland of Oz books are available, used and sometimes new, from amazon.com or Books of Wonder, 16 W. 18th Street, New York, NY 10011 - www.booksofwonder.com.

Several, as noted, are more easily available from Hungry Tiger Press, 5995 Dandridge Lane, Suite 121, San Diego CA 92115, www.hungrytigerpress.com, or The International Wizard of Oz Club, P. O. Box 2657, Alameda CA, 94501, www.ozclub.org.

The Royal Historians of Oz

The first 22 books are by Baum and from there, on through number 41, by Thompson. From 42 on, the author of each book will be indicated by the abbreviations in parentheses in this list of Historians by order of their first publishing.

Authors
1 - L. Frank Baum (LFB)
2 - Ruth Plumly Thompson (RPT)
3 - John R. Neill (Neill)
4 - Jack Snow (Snow)
5 - Rachel Cosgrove Payes (RCP)
6 - Eloise Jarvis McGraw & Lauren McGraw Wagner (McG)
7 - Dick Martin (DM)
8 - Eric Shanower (ES)
9 - Karyl Carlson & Eric Gjovaag (C-G)
10 - Robin Hess (RH)
11 - Virginia Wickwar (VW)
12 - Edward Einhorn (EE)

The Oz Books

The Canon of Oz Books (as recognized by this author)

1 - *The Wizard of Oz*
2 - *The Magical Monarch of Mo*
3 - *Dot and Tot of Merryland*
4 - *The Life and Adventures of Santa Claus*
5 - *The Enchanted Island of Yew*
6 - *The Land of Oz*
7 - *Queen Zixi of Oz*
8 - *John Dough and the Cherub*
9 - *Ozma of Oz*
10 - *Dorothy and the Wizard in Oz*
11 - *The Road to Oz*
12 - *The Emerald City of Oz*
13 - *Sea Fairies*
14 - *Sky Island*
15 - *The Patchwork Girl of Oz*
16 - *Tik-Tok of Oz*
17 - *The Scarecrow of Oz*
18 - *Rinkitink in Oz*
19 - *The Lost Princess of Oz*
20 - *The Tin Woodman of Oz*
21 - *The Magic of Oz*
22 - *Glinda of Oz*
23 - *The Royal Book of Oz*
24 - *Kabumpo in Oz*
25 - *The Cowardly Lion of Oz*
26 - *Grampa in Oz*
27 - *The Lost King of Oz*
28 - *The Hungry Tiger of Oz*
29 - *The Gnome King of Oz*
30 - *The Giant Horse of Oz*
31 - *Jack Pumpkinhead of Oz*
32 - *The Yellow Knight of Oz*
33 - *Pirates in Oz*
34 - *The Purple Prince of Oz*
35 - *Ojo in Oz*
36 - *Speedy in Oz*
37 - *The Wishing Horse of Oz*
38 - *Captain Salt in Oz*
39 - *Handy Mandy in Oz*

The Spelling Bee of Oz

40 - *The Silver Princess in Oz*
41 - *Ozoplaning with the Wizard in Oz*
42 - *The Wonder City of Oz* (JRN)
43 - *The Scalawagons of Oz* (JRN)
44 - *Lucky Bucky in Oz* (JRN)
45 - *The Magical Mimics in Oz* (JS)
46 - *The Shaggy Man of Oz* (JS)
47 - *The Hidden Valley of Oz* (RCP)
48 - *Merry Go Round in Oz* (McG)
49 - *Yankee in Oz* (RPT)
50 - *The Enchanted Island of Oz* (RPT)
51 - *The Forbidden Fountain of Oz* (McG-W)
52 - *The Ozmapolitan of Oz* (DM)
53 - *The Enchanted Apples of Oz* (ES) [HTP]
54 - *The Secret Island of Oz* (ES)[HTP]
55 - *The Ice King of Oz* (ES) [HTP]
56 - *The Forgotten Forest of Oz* (ES) [HTP]
57 - *The Blue Witch of Oz* (ES) [HTP]
58 - *The Wicked Witch of Oz* (RCP) [IWOC]
59 - *The Giant Garden of Oz* (ES)
60 - *Queen Ann of Oz* (C-G)
61 - *The Runaway in Oz* (JRN)
62 - *Christmas in Oz* (RH)
63 - *The Hidden Prince of Oz* (VW) [IWOC]
64 - *The Rundelstone of Oz* (McG) [HTP]
65 - *The Salt Sorcerer of Oz* (ES) [HTP]
66 - *The Living House of Oz* (EE) [HTP]
67 - *Toto of Oz* (VW) [IWOC]
68 - *Toto and the Cats of Oz* (RH)
69 - *The Spelling Bee of Oz* (RH)

Index and Identification

Who's Who

1. **Abdul** – A Somali street orphan boy. 47-48, 51, 252.
2. **Abeh** – The Somali name for father is the only reference we have to Amal's father. 46-47.
3. **Abner Dustworthy** – A man from Rigmarole Town that Elizabeth meets when trying to find her way to the Emerald City. 121.
4. **Ahmed Abdulhi** – Scarf merchant, friend of the street gang that Amal belongs to. 47-48, 51-52, 54, 252, 255-56, 258.
5. **Alklank** – Steward to the King of the Nomes. (*Al* like *Al*, *klank* sounds like *clank*; *Al-klank*.) 48, 80, 217, 225-28, 232, 236.
6. **Alora** – One of the Invisible Children. (*A* as in *another*, *o* as in *old*, *a* as in *another*; *A-lor'a*.) 185.
7. **Alvin Warren** – Elizabeth's little brother. 126-27, 205, 211.
8. **Amal** – A Somali street orphan girl who gets blown to Oz by being too close to an exploding hand grenade. (Pronounced as if just saying the letters *m-l*.) 47, 50-51, 53-75, 77-78, 100-08, 110-11, 114, 124-126, 128-29, 159-64, 169, 182-83, 186, 189-91, 194, 201, 203-06, 208-09, 219-21, 223, 225, 239-

Who's Who

40, 246-58.
9   **Amira** – Name that Amal gives to Ozma because that is the nickname for Amran, which is Somali for Princess. (*A* as in *art*, *i* as in *machine*, *a* as in *another*; *A-mi'ra*.) 191, 219-21, 252-53, 255, 257.
10 **Amran** – A Somali street orphan girl. (Each *a* as in *art*.) 58.
11 **Anab** – A Somali street orphan girl; means *grape*.) 49, 51, 252.
12 **Baluol** – Head chef of the palace. (*A* as in *at*, *u* as in *use*, *o* as in *old*; *Bal'u-ol*). 197.
13 **Billina** – Dorothy's pet hen that came with her on her second trip to Oz. (From *Ozma of Oz*.) 220, 222-23, 228.
14 **Binji** – Name of first visible boy of the Invisible children. (*Bin* like *bin*, *ji* like *gee*; *Bin'ji*.) 75-76, 78, 100-11, 114, 185, 206.
15 **Blue Eagle** – See Hilda.
16 **Bouncy** – The red and blue stripped cat in the Munchkin cottage where Elizabeth and Amal stayed overnight. 27.
17 **Broman** - Head carpenter for the Palace. (*O* as in *old*, *a* as in *Cuban*; *Bro'man*) 221.
18 **Brother** – See Alvin.
19 **Brothers** – Amal had brothers who were killed by the rebels. 46, 247.
20 **Button-Bright** – A boy from Philadelphia that is often lost and spends a lot of time in Oz. 256.
21 **Buzzby** – The name given to the Spelling Bee at birth. 130.

The Spelling Bee of Oz

22 **Cadwallader** – Mayor of Upper Stallingham. 112, 240-45.
23 **Cartier** – Elizabeth's wealthy neighbor. 122.
24 **Catloo** – Next to youngest, a daughter of the Nornan family. (*Cat* like *cat*, *loo* like *lu*; *Cat'loo*.) 27.
25 **Cowardly Lion** – One of Dorothy's original friends from her first visit in Oz. Although King of the Forest located north of Hammerhead Mountains, he spends most of his time in the Emerald City. (From *The Wizard of Oz*.)11, 41, 134, 168, 171, 173, 180, 186-88, 218-19, 221-23, 231-33, 235, 237.
26 **Dee Tortia** – A young lady that Elizabeth meets that gives her incorrect directions to the Emerald City. *Detortion* is a synonym for *distortion* and *detort* is a synonym for *misteach*. (*Dee* like *Dee*; *Tortia* rhymes with *Portia*; *Dee' Tor-tia*.) 123,127-28.
27 **Dielectro** – King of Insulaville. (*Di* like *dye*, *elec* as in *electric*, *o* as in *old*; *Di"e-lec'tro*.) 188.
28 **Dizateroo** – The former Wicked Witch of the South. 150
29 **Douglas Warren** – Elizabeth's father. 122, 209, 211.
30 **Dorothy** – The heroine of the first Oz book who finally emigrated to Oz and is a special friend of Ozma. 5-8, 11-12, 26-28, 38, 40-41, 44, 91, 118-19, 123-24, 126-27, 129, 133-34, 137-39, 160-61, 163-64, 166-67, 183-88, 194-95, 200, 202-07, 209, 218-20, 222-23, 228, 239-40, 249-57.
31 **Elizabeth Warren** – An 11-year-old girl from a home in the Santa Clara Valley of California. Her nickname is Zeebee. She goes to Franklin D.

Who's Who

Roosevelt Grade School. 1-44, 79-85, 87-98, 100, 116-29, 159-65, 169, 181-84, 186, 188-89, 194-96, 201, 203.

32 **Fanny** – Eldest child of Nornan family, a girl. 27.
33 **Flora** – Mother in Nornan family. 27.
34 **Gerab** – Eldest son & second child of Nornan family. (*G* as in *get*, *e* as in *get*, *a* as in *at*; *Ger'ab*.) 27.
35 **Gillikins** – People who live in the Gillikin Country in the north of Oz. (From *The Land of Oz*.) 32, 66, 199, 201, 244, 249.
36 **Gingema** – The Wicked Witch that was destroyed when Dorothy's house landed on her. (From *The Wizard of Oz*.) 132-34, 137-38, 146, 153, 157, 249.
37 **Gralf** – Director of Manufacturing for the Nomes. (Rhymes with *Ralph*] 41-42, 44.
38 **Grinderdael** – Looks like a Groenendael (Belgian Sheep-dog), but his insides are all for grinding – grinds to a powder anything he puts his jaws around. Live Wires fear him. 20-24, 44, 81-82, 85-89, 91-98.
39 **Guardian of the Gate** – A man who guards one of the four gates giving entrance to the Emerald City. 169-70, 181.
40 **Guph** – General who led Ruggedo's attempt to conquer Oz. (From *The Emerald City of Oz*.) 216.
41 **H. M.** – See Professor H. M. Wogglebug, T. E.
42 **Hawa** – A Somali street orphan girl. 51-52.
43 **Hilda** – Giant Blue Eagle that plays basketball for the Munchkin Blues. 244.
44 **Hip-po-gy-raf** – A huge beast with leathery skin and

The Spelling Bee of Oz

a long retractable neck. (*Hip* like *hip*, *o* as in *old*, *g* as in *giant*, *y* as in *by*, *a* as in *at*; *Hip"-po-gy'-raf.*) (From *The Tin Woodman of Oz*.) 133.

45   **Hooper** – The hoop snake that takes his tail in his mouth and rolls across the land. 114-15.

46   **Hop-a-bop** – The rabbit that talks with Elizabeth outside the Emerald City. 118-19.

47   **House Parents** – Job that Ahmed and Mumino would accept at the orphanage and school that Amal wants to build. 255.

48   **Hoztorian** – See Terwilliger.

49   **Invisible Children** – Children, sometimes called "Lost Children," caught in a cursed area where any children that walk within it are made invisible and cannot get out of the area until someone pulls them out. 74-78, 100-14, 129, 159, 169, 186, 192-98, 206, 210, 219-21, 238-41, 243.

50   **Jamal** – Boy who is the leader of the Somali street orphans. 47-48, 50-51, 251-52.

51   **Jellia Jamb** – Ozma's personal maid, more friend than maid, since Ozma has little need for anyone to help her change clothes and brush her hair. Mostly she is head of the housekeeping staff in the Palace. (First introduced in *The Wizard of Oz*, but no name given to her until *The Land of Oz*.) 116, 166-67, 169, 193-94, 203, 210, 241, 254.

52   **Kalidah** – A fierce animal with a body like a bear, head like a tiger and long sharp claws. (*A* as in *at*, *i* as in *it*, *ah* like *ah*; *Kal'li-dah.*) (From *The Wizard of Oz*.) 133.

Who's Who

53 **Kaliko** – Formerly Chief Steward, then King of the Nomes, and now put back on throne by Ozma. (From *Tik-Tok of Oz*.) 85, 216-17, 230-37.
54 **Kara** – Elizabeth's best friend in California. 27.
55 **King of the Gillikins** – One of the regional kings that Ozma introduced to Amal. (From *The Giant Horse of Oz*.) 249.
56 **King of the Live Wires** – See Transformer.
57 **King of the Munchkins** – One of the regional kings that Ozma introduced to Amal. (From *The Giant Horse of Oz*.) 249.
58 **King of the Nomes** – See Korph or Roquat/Ruggedo.
59 **King of the Rock Elves** – See Raimen.
60 **Kings of Oz** - There have been several, but this entry is just for the term in general. 191.
61 **Kladaborn** – The first person to start using the castle of the Wicked Witch of the South's castle as a retirement home. (*A* as in *at*, *a* as in *another*, *born* like *born*.) 153.
62 **Knunk** – A somewhat smaller, thin Nome that is a messenger. (*K* as in *kitchen*, *nunk* rhymes with *bunk*; *K-nunk'*.) 98-99, 164-65, 169-71, 174, 180-81, 211-12, 214-16, 218, 221-26, 229, 236.
63 **Korph** – The current Nome King who has lead a revolt against the namby-pamby ways of Kaliko. (*K* as in *kitchen*, *orph* rhymes with *morph*; *Korph'*.) 2-45, 79-99, 116, 119, 129, 161-64, 169-71, 174, 179-80, 188, 196, 209, 215-17, 219-22, 224-28, 230.
64 **Librarian** – One of the librarians in the library in the Emerald City. 191.

The Spelling Bee of Oz

65 **Live Wires** – Actual live wires that split in two places. The bottom split provides two legs to stand or walk or run upon. Near the top, a three-way split provides arms reaching out from the main body. Each arm, further split at its end to provide tiny fingers – three, four five or more. At the top, a narrow face with mouth, nose, eyes and ears, although no more head above that than what was provided by the top little bit of wire. 12-25, 39, 43, 85, 87, 90, 92-98, 116, 164, 170-73, 175-79, 189.

66 **Lomar** – Father of the Norman family. (*Lo* like *low*, *mar* as in *mark*; *Lo'mar*.) 27.

67 **Lost Children** – See Invisible Children.

68 **Ma** – The Somali word for mother and the only was Amal refers to her mother. 46.

69 **Mayor of Upper Stallingham** – See Cadwallader.

70 **Mombi** – One-time Wicked Witch of the North. 192.

71 **Mona** – A Somali street orphan girl. 47, 250, 252.

72 **Mumino** – Kind wife of scarf dealer. 48, 52, 252, 258.

73 **Munchkins** – The people that live in the blue Munchkin Country of the east of Oz. (From *The Wizard of Oz*.) 28, 249.

74 **Nome King** – See Korph or Roquat/Ruggedo.

75 **Norjil** – The finest artist in Oz. Ozma has him make drawings of the Invisible Children, now simply the Lost Children, that can be taken around to the various parts of Oz to see if anyone recognizes any of them. (*Nor* like *nor*, *jil* like *Jill*; *Nor'jil*.)

Who's Who

200-01.
76 **Nork** – A fast digging Nome. 34
77 **Nornan** – The Munchkin family that Elizabeth and Amal stayed with. See Catloo, Fanny, Flora, Gerab, Lomar and Verm. 27.
78 **Organi** – A Rock Elf that Elizabeth & Korph meet. (*Or* like *or*, *an* like *an*, *i* as in *machine*; *Or-gan'i*.) 83-84, 89-90, 93.
79 **Oz VI** – King of Oz just before the birth of the Spelling Bee and stolen by the Wicked Witches. 131, 192.
80 **Oz VII** – King of Oz, destroyed when the Wicked Witches took over the Kingdom. 132, 192.
81 **Ozian** – A citizen of Oz. (See also under WHAT'S WHAT.) 11.
82 **Ozga** – A fairy cousin of Ozma's, the rose Princess, that married a mortal named Joe Files. 169, 171, 173-78, 180, 187, 189, 201, 204, 206, 209, 218-19, 221, 231.
83 **Ozma** – Ruler of Oz. (From *Land of Oz*.) 7, 10-11, 29-30, 33, 39, 41, 58, 62, 65-66, 86-88, 90, 93, 99, 113, 116, 128, 131, 161-62, 164-67, 169-71, 173-81, 185, 187-95, 196, 198-211, 213-41, 243, 245-25, 259.
84 **Pak** – A young Nome that Korph had go through the Magic Gates leading to the Emerald City. (*Pak* like *pack*.) 33, 161-62.
85 **Pansy** – Chosen as name for wife of Tangell who founded Upper Stallingham, because that was Arlene's mother's name. 242.
86 **Pastoria** – He became the King of Oz when the

The Spelling Bee of Oz

Wicked Witches destroyed his older brother, Oz VII. 132, 169, 192.

87 **Potaroo** – The Nome King's wizard. (From *The Gnome King of Oz*.) 6.

88 **Professor H. M. Wogglebug, T. E.** – He was originally a little bug like any other, but when magnified by a magic lantern, stepped off the screen the size of a human. Having grown up in a classroom, he is highly educated and has been made the head of the Royal Athletic College of Oz. "H. M." stands for "highly magnified" and "T. E." stands for "thoroughly educated." (From *The Land of Oz*.) 196-97, 244.

89 **Quadmunch cat** – See Bouncy.

90 **Quimpy** – An early settler of Stallingham who suggested adding Upper to its name. (*Qui* as in *quit*, *y* as in *candy*; *Guim'py*.) 243.

91 **Raimen** – King of the Rock Elves. (Sounds like *ray men*; *Rai'men*.) 85-86, 88-89, 94.

92 **Rattercobra** – See Sapphire.

93 **Rigmarolers** – Citizens of Rigmarole Town. (From *The Emerald City of Oz*.) 121.

94 **Roquat/Ruggedo** – Former King of the Nomes. 29-30, 174, 217.

95 **Rose Princess** – See Ozga.

96 **Rothene** – A chubby lady that joined the group celebrating the passing of the Wicked Witch Gingema. (*O* as in *old*, *ene* sounds like *lean*; *Ro'thene*.) 145.

97 **Royal Hoztorian** – See Terwilliger.

Who's Who

98 **Ruggedo** – See Roquat.
99 **Sapphire** – A very poisonous snake that has the rattle and the coiling ability of a rattlesnake, and the stretching up and hood of a cobra. 68-72.
100 **Schaumkar** – The Nome shoemaker. (*Aum* as in *Baum*, *kar* like *car*; *Schaum'kar*.) 38-39, 79.
101 **Seven-headed dog** – This vicious animal in the Nome Kingdom is a means of destroying the king's enemies. (From *The Emerald City of Oz*.) 215.
102 **Shaggy Man** – A well-traveled resident of the Palace in the Emerald City who came from America over a century ago. (From *The Road to Oz*.) 195, 221, 239, 241, 256.
103 **Sisters** – Amal had sisters that were killed by the rebels. 46, 247.
104 **Speller** – A nickname for the Spelling Bee (q. v.) used by the Rattercobra. 70-71, 109, 115, 131, 155, 183.
105 **Spelling Bee** – A giant bee that is the master of spells and of spelling. 58-59, 68-72, 74-76, 78, 100-03, 106-10, 112-13, 115, 124, 127-28, 131, 134, 137, 140, 143, 146-48, 151, 153-61, 163-65, 169, 181-83, 185-86, 188-92, 196, 201, 206-09, 218-19, 221, 223, 229, 240, 246-7, 249, 251-53, 255-7.
106 **T. E.** – See Professor H. M. Wogglebug, T. E.
107 **Tangell** – Original settler of Upper Stallingham. (*Tan* like *tan*, *gell* like *gel*; *Tan-gell'*.) 242.
108 **Terwilliger** – Royal Hoztorian of Oz. 243-45.
109 **Tippetarius** – Name that Mombi gave to Ozma when she changed the little baby girl into a boy. Nickname: Tip. (From *The Land of Oz*.) 192.

The Spelling Bee of Oz

110 Transformer – King of the Live Wires. Transforms energy to higher or lower voltages; can open quickly into a large robot, but always has wires wrapped around an iron part of him; transforms people or things into other things. He sits on a throne that is a Generator. 16-21, 86-87, 92-93, 95-98, 164, 173, 175-79.

111 Trot – A 10 year old friend of Ozma's from America now living in Oz. 175.

112 Uthur – One of the Invisible Children that few of them knew was among them because he was too bashful to say much of anything. (*U* as in *rule*, *u* as in *cur*; *U'thur*.) 101, 246.

113 Valentine – Zeebee's cat. 205.

114 Verm – Youngest child, a boy, of Nornan family. (*Verm* sounds like *Vern*.) 27.

115 Wam – One of the greatest wizards Oz ever had. 132

116 Warren – See Douglas and Elizabeth.

117 Wicked Witch of the East – See Gingema.

118 Wicked Witch of the South – See Dizateroo.

119 Wizard – The original builder of the Emerald City, twice arrived there from America by balloon. Originally a humbug wizard, after his second trip Glinda trained him to be a real wizard. (From *The Wizard of Oz*.) 10, 138, 171, 173-74, 180, 191, 218-19, 221, 224, 227, 231, 234, 250.

120 Wogglebug – See Professor H. M. Wogglebug, T. E.

121 Yarna – Chairman of the House at the Wicked Witch of the South's former castle. (*Ar* as in *art*, *a* as in *another*; *Yar'na*.) 152-55.

Who's Who

122 Zeebee – See Elizabeth.

123 Zort –The substitute school bus driver, an agent of the current Nome King, Gorph. 14, 34.

Where's Where

1. **Amira House** – The home and school that gems from Ozma enable Amal to build a home and school for orphans in Mogadishu. 255, 256, 257.
2. **Bakaara ha** – See Suuqa.
3. **Boxes** – The Live Wires live in boxes. 17.
3. **California** – The State that Elizabeth is from. 38, 122, 160, 167, 205.
5. **Castle (1)** – See Tin Castle.
6. **Castle (2)** – Dizateroo had a gray castle in the Quadling Country where, after she was destroyed, lonely elderly people had moved in and formed a community. See House (5).
7. **Castle (3)** – The royal Hoztorian has a tower-castle on the edge between the Munchkin and Gillikin countries. 244.
8. **Cottage** – See House (2).
9. **Earth** – Our home, a parallel universe to that of Oz and home to Amal and Elizabeth. 9, 10, 19, 21, 37, 57, 60,-61, 83, 85, 89, 104, 188-90, 205-07, 244, 250, 253.
10. **Emerald City** – The capitol of Oz and residence of many of the famous Ozians. 30-34, 36, 38, 41, 62, 65-66, 80, 89, 99, 107, 113, 116-17, 119-21, 123, 127-28, 159, 161, 164-66, 169, 179,181, 183, 188, 197, 212, 216, 221, 237, 240, 245, 247, 253.
11. **East Gate** – The eastern gate in the wall surrounding the Emerald City. 169-70.

Where's Where

12 **Farmhouse (1)** – The purple one of the Nornan family that gave overnight hospitality to Elizabeth and the Nome King. 26-27.
13 **Farmhouse (2)** – The Munchkin lady, Rothene, lives in a house at a crossroads near Gingema's old house. 137.
14 **Franklin D. Roosevelt Grade School** – The school in the Santa Clara Valley that Elizabeth goes to. 3, 5, 205-06.
15 **Gate** – Any one of the gates to the Emerald City, but especially, see East Gate. 182.
16 **Gillikin Country** – The northern major country of Oz. (From *The Land of Oz*.) 3, 5, 32, 66, 81, 172, 200.
17 **Gillikin Mountains** – Steep mountains in the eastern Gillikin Country. (From *The Land of Oz*.) 2, 22, 81, 244.
18 **Hammerhead Mountains** – The home of the Hammerheads, somewhat north of Glinda's Palace. (From *The Wizard of Oz*.) 151.
19 **Hive** – See Home (11)
20 **Hoeborn Tower** – The tower-castle home of Terwilliger. 243-44.
21 **Home (1)** – See House (6).
22 **Home (2)** – See Farmhouse (1).
23 **Home (3)** – To the Nomes, their underground caverns are their home. 30.
24 **Home (4)** – The generality of where Elizabeth lives. 35, 79.
25 **Home (5)** – See House (1)

The Spelling Bee of Oz

26 **Home (6)** – The home Amal lived in before it and her family were destroyed. 46

27 **Home (7)** – The generality of where Amal lives. 61-62, 64-66, 100, 128.

28 **Home (8)** – The Winkie Country is the Spelling Bee's home. 66.

29 **Home (9)** – The home territory of the Rock Elves. 83.

30 **Home (10)** – The home territory of the Live Wires. (See also, Boxes.) 93.

31 **Home (11)** – The hive where the Spelling Bee was born. 130-31, 136, 154, 156-58.

32 **Homes (1)** – Needed to temporarily take care of the Lost Children. 107, 113.

33 **Homes (2)** – The real homes of the Invisible Children. 113, 115.

34 **House (1)** – The ruined one in Mogadishu in which Amal slept. 46.

35 **House (2)** – Gingema's old home. 133-34, 137-39, 146-47.

36 **House (3)** – Dorothy's old house in which she arrived in Oz. 133, 137-39, 249.

37 **House (4)** – A Quadling house near which the Spelling Bee asked a woman for directions to the old castle of Dizateroo. 150

38 **House (5)** – The residents of Dizateroo's old castle call it their House. 152-53.

39 **House (6)** – Elizabeth's home is in the Santa Clara Valley. 2-3, 5, 12, 27, 122, 205,

40 **Insulaville** – A town near the Live Wires that is made

Where's Where

up of insulators of all kinds. 94, 164, 170-74, 176-79, 189.

41 **Library** – Next to Ozma's apartment is the public library. 191, 198-99.

42 **Libraries** – After Mogadishu was liberated, libraries were open once more. 251.

43 **Lower Stallingham** – Although there is no such place, the Shaggy Man thought there should be. 241.

44 **Market** – See Suuqa.

45 **Middle Stallingham** – Although there is no such place, the Shaggy Man thought there should be. 241.

46 **Mogadishu** – Home of Amal and ineffective capital of Somalia. 46-47, 57, 59-61, 64-65, 75, 104, 182, 190, 247, 251-52, 255, 257.

47 **Mordon Acres** – A large farm in the SE of the Gillikin Country. 3.

48 **Munchkin Country** – The eastern major country of Oz. (From *The Wizard of Oz*.) 23, 32, 66, 72, 119, 128, 130, 134, 137, 159, 193, 221, 244.

49 **Munchkin Forest** – A deep, dark forest in the Munchkin country. 133.

50 **National Monument of the Munchkins** – Dorothy's old house that landed on and destroyed the Wicked Witch of the East. 249.

51 **Orphanage** – Amal created an orphanage and a school after she returned to Somalia. 255.

52 **Oz** – The magical country where most of this story occurs. The locus of 58 of the books this author

The Spelling Bee of Oz

recognizes as Oz books. (From *The Wizard of Oz*.) After page 2 virtually all of the book occurs in Oz, with the exception of brief parts on pages 210-11 and 250-25 and 257-58.

53   **Ozeria** – The planet upon which Oz is located. Sometime late in 2005, I made the decision to use two similar names, one for the continent and one for the planet. Since "Ozia" fits well with the pattern of Asia, Australia, America Africa, I used it for the continent, and "Ozeria" for the planet. 57-58, 60-61, 84, 99, 130, 165.

54   **Ozia** – The continent upon which Oz is located. See Ozeria. 58.

55   **Palace (1)** – Ozma's Palace in the Center of the Emerald City. (From *The Wizard of Oz*.) 28, 164, 166-71, 182-83, 185-86, 193-95, 197, 212, 218, 221, 238, 257.

56   **Palace (2)** – The Nome King's palace, deep underground. (From *Ozma of Oz*.) 41-43.

57   **Palace (3)** – The palace of the Live Wires. 98.

58   **Palace (4)** – See Winderhime.

59   **Rigmarole Town** – A town in Oz where anyone who talks on endlessly, is assigned, to protect the rest of the citizens from them. Although Elizabeth does not visit there, she runs into a man from there. 121-22.

60   **Royal Athletic College of Oz** – The only college in Oz, founded by the Wogglebug and since, he developed education tablets, little time needs to be devoted to studies, so the students can spend

Where's Where

all their time in athletics. 196, 244.
61 **Santa Clara Valley** – The valley in California where Elizabeth's home is located. 1, 3, 85, 160.
62 **School (1)** – When things were good in Mogadishu, Amal had a school she went to.
63 **School (2)** – Amal created an orphanage and a school after she returned to Mogadishu. 255, 258.
64 **Schools** – After Mogadishu was liberated, schools were open once more. 251.
65 **Somali (Somalia)** – People of and country where Amal lives. 46, 57, 59-61, 68, 128, 189-90, 247, 250-52, 257.
66 **Stallingham** – Original name of Upper Stallingham. 242.
67 **Storehouse** – Throughout Oz there are storehouses where people can find anything they need. This one is in the town of Upper Stallingham. 102-03, 105-06. 111-12.
68 **Suuqa Bakaaraha** – The principle marketplace of Moga-dishu. 47.
69 **Throne Room (1)** – The Nome King's is deep underground. (From *Ozma of Oz*.) 31, 33, 39, 42-45, 79, 83, 98, 180, 216-17, 224, 235.
70 **Throne Room (2)** – The one at the old palace of Winderhime where the wicked witches attacked King Oz VII. 132.
71 **Throne Room (3)** – A large, magnificent room in Ozma's Palace where she dispenses judgment from the Throne and welcomes visitors. (From *The Wizard of Oz*.) 171, 185-87, 194, 199.

The Spelling Bee of Oz

72   **Tin Castle** – The Tin Woodman's castle. 67
73   **Tower-Castle** – See Castle (3).
74   **Upper Stallingham** – The closest town to the Land of Invisible Children where the Spelling Bee led them to find new clothes and a place to stay overnight. (*A* as in *at*, *ling* as in *cling*, *ham* like *ham*; *Stal'ling-ham*.) 112-13, 193, 239-41, 243, 245-46.
75   **Wish Way** – A road in Oz whose sands will grant you a wish. (From *The Lost King*.)
76   **Valley Road** – Home of Elizabeth Warren. 274.
77   **Yellow Brick Road** – The main road going from the Emerald City deep into the Munchkin Country. 22, 24, 116, 137-39, 181, 221.

What's What

1. **Artfulgazmee** – A nonsense word used by the rabbit, Schwartaz. (*Art* like *art*, *ful* like *full*, *az* sounds like *as*, *ee* as in *meek*: *Art-ful-gaz'mee*.) 118.
2. **Berry bushes** – At first this was the only food source that Elizabeth and Binji found. 108.
3. **Blozzy** – A nonsense word used by the rabbit, Schwartaz. (*Ozz* sounds like *Oz*, *y* as in *busy*; *Bloz'zy*.) 118.
4. **Blue trees** – See Trees, blue.
5. **Blues** – See Munchkin Blues.
6. **Book** – See Box (2).
7. **Bottles** - The spelling Bee looked in Gingema's old cottage for bottles, boxes and vials that might have the secret to shrink him back to normal size. 139.
8. **Box (1)** – Contains Communication equipment in the East Gate Guard House. 170.
9. **Box (2)** – The Transformer transformed several Insulators into a wooden box, a flower, a dish, a book, a bush and a kettle. 171, 176. 176.
10. **Boxes (1)** – See Bottles.
11. **Boxes (2)** – There are boxes of clothing and other things stored in the basement of the Palace in the Emerald City. 212-13.
12. **Brush** – See Box (2).
13. **Clothing** – See Boxes.
14. **Computer** – See Phone.

The Spelling Bee of Oz

15 **Cranberry juice** – Elizabeth's favorite juice. 88, 91.
16 **Crown (1)** – The Nome King's is six-pointed and gold. 4, 180, 217, 227, 231, 235.
17 **Crown (2)** – The Transformer was going to change Korph into a crown. 19, 87.
18 **Diamond, yellow** – The Transformer was going to change Elizabeth into a yellow diamond. 19, 87
19 **Dish** – See Box (2).
20 **East Gate** – There are four gates through the walls of the Emerald City and this is one of them. 169-70.
21 **Emerald (1)** – The Transformer was going to change Ozma into a big emerald. 175.
22 **Emerald (2)** – Ozma gave Amal one, along with a ruby, so that she would be able to build an orphan's home and school in Mogadishu. 255, 258.
23 **Flower** – See Box (2)
24 **Gate (1)** – One of the gates to the Emerald City. 182.
25 **Gate (2)** – See East Gate.
26 **Gemstones** – The valuable ruby and emerald Amal takes to Ahmed to trade for money to build their Amira House. 256.
27 **Golden proboscis** – An exaggerated remark by the Spelling Bee. 253.
28 **Guntfliiper** – A nonsense word used by Hop-a-bop. 118.
29 **Halloween** – The holiday being celebrated at her school the day Elizabeth was taken to Oz. 1, 5.
30 **Handheld** – See Phone.

What's What

31 **Jahannam** – The Islamic hell. 55
32 **Kettle** – See Box (2).
33 **Larry Cary is no berry** – Nonsense phrase, a tribute to Bill Holman and his ridiculous, pun-filled cartoon called *Smokey Stover* of the 1930s to '70s which was noted for such phrases. Thank you Mr. Holman! 118.
34 **Lunch-bucket trees** – An Ozian tree that grows lunch buckets, full of delicious, fresh food, both hot and cold. 108, 111.
35 **Message tree** – See Oak tree below, or Message Tree under Magical Magic.
36 **Money** – needing money to buy a place for Amira House, Ozma gave Amal gems to trade for money. 255.
37 **Munchkin Blues** – The famous Munchkin basketball team. 244, 276.
38 **Oak tree** – An old oak tree which the youngsters in Elizabeth's neighborhood call "the message tree," because they leave messages there for each other. 2
39 **Ozian** – Pertaining to Oz.. (Se also under Who's Who) 123, 186, 191.
40 **Quadmunch Cat** – A special breed of cat in Oz that combines the red stripes of a Quadling cat with the blue ones of a Munchkin cat. 27.
41 **Phone** – Elizabeth has a handheld phone she uses for many things — tweeting, computer, Internet, taking pictures, telephoning. 8-9.
42 **Pictures** – See Phone.

The Spelling Bee of Oz

43 **Proboscis** – See Golden proboscis.
44 **Rosebush** – The Transformer was going to change Ozga into a rosebush. 175.
45 **Royal Athletic College of Oz** – The only college in Oz, founded by the Wogglebug and since, he developed education tablets, little time needs to be devoted to studies, so the students can spend all their time in athletics. 196, 244.
46 **Royal Throne of Oz** – See Throne (2).
47 **Ruby** – Ozma gave Amal one, along with an emerald, so that she would be able to build an orphan's home and school in Mogadishu. 256.
48 **Scabbletozer** – A nonsense word used by the rabbit, Schwartaz. (A as in *at*, *le* as in *able*, *oz* like *Oz*, *er* as in *beater*; *Sca'ble-toz-er*) 118.
49 **Sign (1)** – Pointing to Land of the Live Wires. 12.
50 **Sign (2)** – Warning that Live Wires are dangerous. 13-14, 18.
51 **Sign (3)** – Pointing to Rigmarole Town. 122.
52 **Sign (4)** – Designating PIT B, SMELTING, in the Nome Kingdom. 227.
53 **Signs (1)** – Designating the destinations of the various magic Gates. 36.
54 **Signs (2)** – Made by the Shaggy Man, Broman and the sign makers of Upper Stallingham to warn people about the dangers of the Country of the Invisible Children. 193, 198, 219-21, 239-40.
55 **Signs (3)** – Designating the village of Stallingham, later changed to Upper Stallingham. 242-43.
56 **Speedberries** – See under Magical Magic.

What's What

57 **Sumsuty** – A nonsense word used by the rabbit, Schwartaz. (*Sum* like *sum*, *sut* like *suit*, *y* as in *busy*; *Sum-su'ty*.) 118.
58 **Talking Box** – Device providing communication within the Emerald City. They are connected by wires. A crank on the side activates it, several buttons next to the crank are used to select the recipient, and there is a wire out the top that one speaks into. The received voice seems to come out of thin air. 170.
59 **Telephone** – See Phone.
60 **Throne (1)** – The Nome King's throne is a large hollowed out rock covered with precious gems. (From Ozma of Oz.) 37-40, 83, 180, 217, 221, 224-25, 231, 235.
61 **Throne (2)** – The Royal Throne of Oz is a giant carved emerald. (From The Wizard of Oz.) 171, 186-87, 194.
62 **Tree (1)** – See Oak tree.
63 **Tree (2)** – Where the Spelling Bee hid from the Munchkins. 138-39.
64 **Trees, Blue** – If she had known, the presence of blue trees would have told Amal that she was in the Munchkin country of Oz. 55.
65 **Tweeting** – See Phone.
66 **Vials** – See Bottles.
67 **Warning Signs** – See Signs.
68 **Wooden Box** – See Box.

Magical Magic

1. **Magic Belt** – Ozma has a Magic Belt that will take her or anybody or anything else to any place she wishes. 7, 11-12, 38, 62, 65, 116, 164, 174-75, 179, 181, 188-89, 201-03, 207-08, 210, 213-15, 224, 229-30, 237, 239, 241, 246, 249-50.
2. **Magic Door** – The Wizard has a Magic Door that will take one to anyplace chosen. 173.
3. **Magic Gates** (Nomes) – A pair of gates, such that when you step through one at any location, you step out at the other, wherever it may be located. 30-31, 33-34, 36-38, 80, 90, 98-99, 116, 161-62, 169, 215-16, 218-19, 221-24, 235-37.
4. **Magic Picture** – Ozma has a picture that will show her any person, place or thing, anywhere it might be. 39, 93-94, 171, 173, 180, 203-04, 206, 208-10, 217, 221, 238, 245, 250, 252-53, 256.
5. **Magic Telescope** – Potaroo has a magic telescope that will show whatever he looks for at any distance. 6.
6. **Magic Umbrella** – Button-Bright has used a Magic Umbrella that would take him to wherever he wished. 207.
7. **Magic Wand (1)** – Like all fairies, Ozga has a magic wand. 176.
8. **Magic Wand (2)** – Like all fairies, Ozma has a magic wand. 214-15.

Magical Magic

9 **Magic Words** – "To the message tree" were the words that transferred Elizabeth to the Message Tree in Oz. 3-4, 188.

10 **Magical Cape** – The cape that Lurline's fairies provided for Glinda to defeat Dizateroo. 132.

11 **Magical Charm** – The basic magic of Oz that keeps a person from dying unless he or she is completely destroyed. 130.

12 **Magical Implements** – The magic that Dizateroo had, but which was long gone by the time the elderly people took over her empty castle. 154.

13 **Magical Spell** - Any one of the many spells that the Spelling Bee can perform. 146,

14 **Magical Equipment** – The magical potions, charms, recipes, instruments found in Gingema's old cottage. 138-39.

15 **Message Tree** – A tree in the Gillikin country of Oz that types out messages to answer any question asked of it. 2-4, 38.

16 **Pointing Sign** – A sign that waves its pointer in the proper directions and speaks to tell you what is in that direction. 239.

17 **Oona booma kroona, dit!** – magical words to be used in making chicken soup out of anything. (*Oo* as in *moon*, *a* as in *another*, *i* as in *it*; *Oo'na boom'a kroon'a dit".*) 144.

18 **Ramble kabamble, hosh melalao. Fido, fa faddo, fell** and **beetauw** – Magical words that begin the Light Spell. (*Ramble* like *ramble*, *a* as in *another*, *bamble* rhymes with *ramble*, *o* as in *odd*, *e* as in

The Spelling Bee of Oz

end, *a* as in *another*, *a* as in *agent*, *o* as in *old*; *fido* like *Fido*, *fa* like the musical note, *fad* like *fad*, *o* as in *old*, *fell* like *fell*, *and* like *and*, *bee* like *bee*, *auw* sounds like the *o* in *old*; *Ram'ble ka-bam'ble, hosh me-la'la-o. Fi'do fa fad-do,' fell and bee-tauw'.*) 140.

19 **Sign (1)** – See Pointing Sign.

20 **Sign (2)** – Sign that Dorothy could use as a signal that she wanted to return to Oz and which now Elizabeth and Amal know the sign.. 204-05, 248.

21 **Speedberries** – They look like raspberries, but have leaves like a laurel bush and taste more like peaches. They impart great speed to the eater. 117, 119.

22 **Transformer's Magic** – By which he can transform anything into anything else. 16, 19, 86, 173, 176, 178-79.

Made in the USA
San Bernardino, CA
23 September 2016